MW01275594

Artifice and Innocence

Paul Sheppard

Revision 2

Copyright © Paul Sheppard 2018

Chapter 1

Evans-Peake leaned up against a smooth tree trunk, one leg bent at the knee. His dark bottle- green jacket fell open to reveal a formal white shirt and black bow-tie. Passers-by would follow down the line of his black moleskin trousers to the deep red suede shoes, long and sharp. They would glance only quickly at his face hidden behind a pair of Ray-Ban sunglasses and the observant might note a silver cross hanging from one ear. Lean faced, you could see every bone and sinew, the outline of his jaw and how it was loosely attached. Curled black hair was swept back over his ears, covering his collar. Everything about his appearance was precise and had been considered at length. Evans-Peake could be seen most days in the park.

Sometimes he played the saxophone. Not because he was good at it would anyone listen, but because it was unusual. Not every London park has a saxophone player. He would shut his eyes tight and puff his cheeks out as he blew. He couldn't play for long before running out of breath, a few runs up and down, a snatch of anything that could have been something. Then he would stand for a few moments with spinning head before sitting down on a bench. But he always stood up to play. And he knew that you shouldn't puff your cheeks out, but being a saxophone player was more important than playing the saxophone to Evans-Peake. He played to the young mothers pushing babies in buggies, he played to the dreamers sitting alone on benches, and he played to the old people behind the lace curtains who watched with watery eyes.

Once he had brought a picnic in a wicker basket. He sat on the grass awkwardly like a bird with a broken wing, legs folded under. Evans-Peake picked at the food; he didn't eat much these days. His eyes flickered around without turning his head, not like a rabbit nervous of being seen, but frightened of not being noticed.

The regulars in the park might have known his name but not who he was. Something about him caused them to take the hand of their child and hold it tightly. His face was worn but certainly he was not old. Not even middle-aged.

The routine was the same each day, he would arrive at mid-day and leave at two. Evans-Peake thought that if you have a routine time goes much more slowly, and that was important. Often he just sat on a bench in the park with one arm laid out along the back as if it was around an imaginary friend, as indeed it was. Or he would find something to fiddle with perhaps appearing to make notes on a small scrap of paper, but he never read books. He didn't like to think about starting something he might never finish. The sun shone on Evans-Peake that summer and warmed his bones. In truth there was little else.

On the day that I remember, I was surprised to find a new A4 size poster pinned to the noticeboard by the park entrance and to many of the trees. It stated that:

'Evans-Peake will be performing on the bandstand on Sunday 16th June.'

Sparse information I thought and I sat on a bench to see what would happen.

Before long He arrived in a tall black hat wearing a black frock coat over a bright gold waistcoat. He paused to adjust his blue cravat before making his entry through the park gates, out of the shady trees and into the sunshine. As he did so, his sharp pointed ankle boots made a satisfying scrape and click on the path. I watched as he made his way to the bandstand in the centre by a circuitous route. Occasionally he turned and walked backwards for a few steps as if waiting for someone else to catch up. Children were running around playing ball games, old folks sat on benches watching them. It was lunch time and girls from the local shops chatted as they ate their sandwiches or picked at salads in Tupperware boxes.

4

Evans-Peake leant up against the railing around the bandstand and, under his breath, he counted all the people he could see. He brought three brightly coloured balls out from his deep coat pockets and began to throw them up into the air one at a time, then all three at once. Round and round they flowed; red, yellow and blue. Evans-Peake looked into the distance with the fixed gaze of a juggler, his head nodding slightly in time with the rhythm. He kinked his leg and relaxed his back against the bandstand pillar. It was his natural easy confidence that made people turn and look. Faster and faster the balls revolved until suddenly he snatched his hat off his head and caught them.

Evans-Peake's Adam's apple jumped as he swallowed and looked around. He wiped the back of his hand across his mouth. The nucleus of an audience had formed, some of them clapped and little children ran in front of them to see, they looked on expectantly. Evans-Peake bowed deeply. He took the balls from his hat and sent it somersaulting up his arm and onto his head with a flick of his wrist. Then he began to juggle again, this time throwing the occasional ball behind his back and high into the air. The growing crowd were enthralled as he stepped backwards and up the steps onto the bandstand without breaking his rhythm. There was a ripple of applause and a few shouts. He was even able to lift his hat in acknowledgement whilst throwing the balls high. He could wait for the balls to fall into his hands or he could snatch them from above.

Then Evans-Peake began to dance.

A shuffling step, clicking heel and toe on the old bandstand floor. The spectacle had an unreal mesmerising quality; the shop girls stopped eating, forks poised and children fell silent. They watched the coloured balls go round and listened to the clickety-clackety clickety-clackety rhythm of his shoes on the concrete floor, never missing a catch, never missing a beat. Such a sight had never been seen on the bandstand in the park.

When he stopped they waited for more but Evans-Peake climbed down from the band stand steps. He had played his best

5

hand, there was no more. One little boy stood close, looking up squinting against the sun. He stayed there as the others began to turn away. Evans-Peake held the balls out, the child took them one by one and stood cradling them in his arms. They stood and looked at each other for a few seconds, until the boy's mother took his hand and the balls fell. "Don't speak to strangers. Don't have anything to do with strangers. Come along now."

It was some time before Evans-Peake had recovered sufficiently to make his exit from the park. I watched as he strode towards the perimeter, his open coat flapping. Something small dropped to the ground but he didn't seem to notice. I should have shouted but, not wanting to make a fuss, I jumped up and went to see what it was in case it was nothing. Almost lost in the coarse gravel path was a long silver chain with a small locket strung on it. I picked it up and looked for Evans-Peake. I ran half-heartedly down the path to the road but he was nowhere to be seen. People on their way home pushed past me as I stood in the middle of the pavement looking in both directions with the chain dribbling from my clenched hand, held out. The chain wasn't broken. I turned the locket over, it looked old, a swirly pattern was engraved into the silver on one side, the other was a plain polished surface. There was no inscription. Feeling I was snooping, I pushed on the catch with my thumb and it flipped open easily.

What I saw then momentarily obscured every other sight and sound. Adrenalin tingled through my body and I looked around self-consciously as if everyone in the park was watching me as tables were turned. Faded and indistinct, yet unmistakable, set in the locket was a picture of my face. I hadn't been watching Evans-Peake, Evans-Peake had been watching me.

Making for the nearest bench I sat down, tense and distant from my surroundings. I took another look at the picture in case, beyond all possible reason but just hoping that I had been mistaken. That it had simply been a reflection of my face as I looked at the polished silver. I was bothered and bewildered, filled with a panic of confused and unsettling thoughts. What possible reason could

6

there be for a complete stranger to carry a picture of me around in a silver locket, and worse, why at this point in time had he deliberately allowed me to find it. Who should I tell? What should I say? Was I in danger?

During the ten minutes or so it took me to walk back to the office I began my analysis of the situation, starting with the only tractable piece of evidence I had, the picture in the locket. It was black and white but not glossy and I was looking directly at the camera, without expression. I decided not to say anything to my colleagues in the office, there was probably a perfectly understandable explanation and I didn't want an over-reaction. I would puzzle it out when I got home.

The afternoon dragged. Faith, our receptionist, commented that I was very quiet as she put a cup of tea on my desk. "Lost in your own little world Steve?" She wondered.

"It's called thinking, Faith," I replied. "Our clients don't pay us to drink tea all day, they pay us to think. Thanks for the tea by the way," I added with, what I hoped was a cheeky smile. She turned back to her work, shaking her head slowly from side to side at my arrogance. I picked a few box files from a high shelf and rummaged through them but returned to my desk empty handed. Fingers clattered on keyboards, nobody in the open plan office looked up, all absorbed in their work. Shutting the lid of my laptop I announced, "I'm pushing off early, can't concentrate. I'll do a bit later at home". Several muttered, "See ya's," followed me to the door.

Once home I examined the locket under a powerful desk light and using a tiny watchmaker's screwdriver, eased the photo out of its case. There was nothing hidden or engraved behind it, nor was anything written on the back of the photo, this was disappointing. From the quality of the paper I could tell it was news-print. There have been very few occasions when I have had my picture published in a newspaper, I opened my desk drawer and pulled out a suspension file hoping I had kept a cutting of the most recent occasion. It didn't take long to find a few folded pages from the local paper, dated just over six months ago. Separating the pages with licked finger I found the brief article I was looking for headed, 'Obsidian wins SMART award'. Below the headline were head-shots of me and Brian holding an engraved Perspex block, this was the source of the photo in the locket. The caption read 'Dr Stephen Rockett and Dr Brian Calder receiving their SMART award'. The short article described how Obsidian, our small business, had won a substantial grant to develop new intelligent software techniques for 'data mining', a technique for extracting information from large amounts of data. Our invention was described in the simplest of terms, it was a nice little local success story.

The mystery was partly solved, I now knew where the picture had come from but not why it was in the locket. I was spooked, this was not like any behaviour I had come across before, my stomach tightened as I swallowed the panic, struggling to get a grip on my emotions. I told myself I had spent enough time on a lost necklace for one day. There was work to be done and I needed a distraction. Opening my laptop and tried to lose myself in a forest of numbers, with little success.

The following day was a Saturday. Late in the morning I decided to walk to the park armed with a newspaper to have something to do as I waited. I wanted to see if Evans-Peake would approach me. He must surely have dropped the locket purposely, there was no break in the chain. But could he be sure that I had picked it up? It was a bright warm summer's day, the floral borders were full of vivid colours and the trees were thick with leaves which rustled in the light breeze. I sat down on my usual bench close to the bandstand and flicked through the newspaper. I couldn't concentrate on any of the articles and soon turned to the crossword on the last page, reaching into my pocket for a pen, I held it poised, alert for anagrams and double-entendres. But my mind continued to wander, replaying the events of the previous day. I patted my shirt pocket just to make sure that the locket was still there. I had not replaced my picture, that was mine and not his.

A growing sense of unease welled up in my stomach. I wondered why I was getting so involved. It was nothing, just give him back the locket and go. Better still go now, retreat back into the predictable and throw the locket in the nearest bin. If I meet him what will he say, what possible explanation could there be? Whatever the answer I didn't want anything to do with it, I decided to bail out now and make for the exit.

Too late. Looking towards the road I saw Evans-Peake make his stage entrance. I concentrated on the spread newspaper, head down, hoping and praying that he didn't come my way. He disappeared behind a row of trees at the other side of the park. 'Go now, this is your chance,' I thought. I put my pen back in my pocket and folded my newspaper, then just as I was about to stand up I saw Evans-Peake coming directly towards me. I was completely exposed, there was now no way to avoid the confrontation. I fought against the rising irrational fear of strangers. Why was I being so stupid about this? I reminded myself it was all about the picture, that was the point, but how could there be an ordinary innocent reason? The boil had to be lanced. This was the moment, it would be over and cleared up soon.

Evans-Peake walked towards me with head down as if humming a tune to himself, he carefully placed his feet one in front of another like a model on a catwalk giving the appearance of being unsteady. I began to rise to my feet just as he turned and slumped into the bench next to mine. He placed an effeminate embroidered shoulder bag carefully on the bench. Very deliberately he crossed his legs and brushed the dust off his sharply creased grey pin-striped trousers. He didn't make room for me, all of the bench belonged to him and I stood before him like a penitent child. Reaching into my shirt pocket I pulled out the locket and dangled it from my fingers on the liquid silver chain. Evans-Peake extended his hand and I dropped it into his open palm. He said nothing, just slinked it into his waistcoat pocket.

"You dropped it yesterday."

He looked up and removed his sunglasses. I looked into tired grey eyes. Deep lines on his face like the sand in a dried-up river bed. Evans-Peake said nothing.

"There was a picture of me in it."

He nodded slowly but still said nothing. I needed to know.

"Why? Where did you get it from?"

He moved his arm from the back of the bench and turned his face towards me. I sat down. Evans-Peake spoke in short sentences as if reciting a liturgy.

"I got it from the newspaper." His voice was soft but with a gritty edge, lips hardly moving. He spoke slowly and deliberately. "When I read the article, I knew you could help."

"Help. With what?" I thought about the article in the paper.

He didn't reply. This was not someone who entered into chit-chat, no desire to converse in as much as it implied a two-way transaction. I waited, resisting the urge to fill the silence with more questions. Evans-Peake breathed in and out deeply and rubbed his chin with his hand, for the first time he looked unsure of the next step. His eyes fell and he reached into his shoulder bag, pulling out an almost cubic package wrapped in brown paper and tied most carefully with string gathered into a loop at the top. Clearly this encounter was not going to be over as quickly or as easily as I had hoped. There was some substance to it; a package.

He placed the package on the bench between us very carefully, like the first move in a game of chess. Leaving one finger on it while he thought.

"Dr Rockett, I will entrust these to you."

He knew my name. Of course he did, it was in the newspaper article, but still it came as a shock. I was struggling to understand what I should do, surely it must be some sort of mistake. "What have they got to do with me? Isn't there some one else?"

"No Dr. Rockett. There's no-one else who can do it.", he repeated more deliberately, "I really don't think there is anyone else."

Looking into the weary eyes, the questioning face, head tilted slightly to one side, I saw again that he was much younger than I had thought. Hair still dark, skin pale but clear. I was not looking at an old man, this was the face of a younger man, but a man who was deeply stricken, who had had all of his vitality sucked out leaving only vanity.

I picked up the small package and pulled at the loose ends of the knotted string but he put his hand on mine, I felt it shake.

"Open it later." He paused, thoughtfully. "You have a week, that's all I can afford."

I was about to ask more questions but the interview was over. Evans-Peake rose to his feet and, without any pleasantries or a backward glance, he strolled off down the path between the neat floral borders, hands in pockets. My eyes followed him as he left, unhurried but purposeful. Exotic.

*****

Sitting at my desk in the corner of the living room, I carefully unwrapped the little parcel. Inside I found a stack of black, hard backed, Moleskine notebooks, each with its distinctive band of elastic wrapped around keeping it shut. There were no labels on the outside of any of them and, as far as I could see, they were identical. I picked the top notebook off the pile and opened it. The first page was filled with rows of letters and numbers, there were no breaks, just row after row of characters forming a square block on the page. Looking closer I saw that the numbers and letters had not been directly written in the books, they had been printed on thin paper which had then been cut down to size and very carefully pasted onto the page. Flicking through the book it was apparent that each page was similarly filled with row upon row of random characters.

I picked up the next book and flicked though its pages; all the books were similar. In total there were fifteen of them, each one filled with page after page of numbers and letters. I thought about what Evans-Peake had said and wondered why he had chosen me, why was I the only one who could be entrusted with them? Was it perhaps because he knew I would be intrigued. When he saw the article in the paper, had he picked me out as the sort of person who would enjoy a puzzle? Presumably he had seen my photo in the newspaper and then recognised me in the park. If so, then he had been making plans for some time, this was clearly something which was very important to Evans-Peake. Was he looking for a puzzle solver? A cryptographer? Was he hoping I wouldn't be able to resist trying to make sense of the characters.

I took a blank sheet of paper from the printer and sat, pen poised. Where should I start? The code, and I was already thinking of it as a code, was mostly numbers but also contained some letters, all in upper case. A simple substitution code perhaps where each character in the original text was replaced by a different letter or number according to a table supplied in a separate code book. I concentrated on the first page of around a thousand characters trying to see a pattern. The letter 'E' is most common in English so I looked for the most common letter or number in the page and guessed that it corresponded to the letter 'E'. The next most common is the letter 'T' and then 'A', so I substituted these letters into the code based on the frequency of occurrence. After some time I gave up on that approach, it wasn't working, no recognisable words appeared. My initial enthusiasm was leaking away. The odd thing was that there were no gaps in the rows of characters, just one long line, so even if I could decode the letters, how could I break it up into words? Had the coder just removed all of the spaces between words to make it a bit more difficult to interpret?

In the back of my mind was the thought that Evans-Peake might be completely deranged, that there was no message hidden in the code, he was just a weird attention seeker. I had fallen into his trap and would waste hours trying to do the impossible. But then, it had surely been arranged too carefully for that and he had taken the trouble to pick me, someone who just might take on the challenge.

Cupping a mug of tea, I looked out of the window at the terrace of houses across the street. A woman was struggling to collapse a buggy whilst preventing her two toddlers from running into the road. As I watched it occurred to me that I could wait until tomorrow, then go to the park and talk to Evans-Peake again. It was worth a try but somehow I knew he wouldn't go to all this trouble just to give the solution when asked, assuming that he even knew the solution. And why bother to encode a message anyway, what secrets were contained in these plain black books and why should I be their custodian? Presumably Evans-Peake didn't know what they meant either. Or had I just jumped to a conclusion, perhaps it wasn't a code at all. He hadn't said anything about a code, but he did say that he needed my help. He whispered in my sub-conscience, flattering my ego, "There's no-one else who can do it."

I looked around the room and chewed the end of my pen, my mind flitting between random thoughts. A picture of my family taken at my cousin's wedding was propped up on the book case, Mum and Dad looking much younger, a copy of my PhD thesis bound in blue with my name and the year on the spine in gold lettering, a picture of a field full of sunflowers reminding me of a holiday with Lucy in Normandy. None of them were there because they were particularly beautiful, they were there to remind me of good times. Place holders in my memories.

I worked at the code, off and on, during the following week, extending my repertoire to a substitution technique based on pairs of characters. Each session ended with disappointment as I made no progress. Not only had I failed to decode the message, I couldn't even identify the encryption method.

When Evans-Peake had given me the notebooks he said I had one week, and that week was up tomorrow. I had tried and failed, what should I do now? I could meet him in the park and simply hand them back, but I was spooked, I didn't know how he would react and wanted to avoid a public 'scene' at all costs.

I decided to take the easy route and just do nothing, to shut the notebooks away in a drawer and forget about them. I could avoid the park for a while and hopefully the problem would just go away, and for a time I thought I had succeeded.

Chapter 2

September 14th was a Saturday, I woke up late. It was over three months since I had last seen Evans-Peake. Having failed to decipher the code in the notebooks I had stuffed them in a drawer. I knew I should have told somebody about it, but I hadn't. The longer I left it, the harder it became. It was like a troublesome tooth, it settles down for a bit but you know ultimately that it's only going in one direction, a visit to the dentist to get it exorcized.

The sun shone through my thin bedroom curtains and made patterns on the wall opposite. I pulled up the sash windows letting a breeze of warm air into the room, the trees swooshed as waves of wind flew through my tiny garden below. I padded down the stairs in bare feet and a dressing gown to make a cup of tea, picking up the post from the front door mat as I went. Two envelopes and a leaflet offering free pizza delivery left hanging half way through the letter box. I settled on the sofa with a large mug of tea and a plate of toast and marmalade to open the letters, already knowing what would be inside them.

A card from my spinster aunt Beryl with a picture of a vintage car on the front. Inside, a neatly written happy birthday wish and a crisp £20 note. Every year this was a source of embarrassment. I have much more money than she does but how do I tell her that a simple card and a greeting is quite sufficient. I would buy a round of drinks this evening and drink to her health. Ironically, she hasn't ever let a drop of alcohol pass her lips.

The other card was from my parents, dedicated to me and signed by my Mother for both of them. 'A little parcel should arrive in the post.' I rummaged around in the paper recycling box and found a card from the post office wrapped in the pizza flyer, notifying me that they had tried but failed to deliver the parcel. Something to keep me warm in the winter was most likely but mercifully not loosely knitted by my Mother anymore due to the ravages of arthritis.

I stood the cards on the window sill, wondering why I found them so depressing. Was it the cards or was it the passing of another year, outwardly celebrated but inwardly mourned. I was in my early thirties but still not 'settled down' as Mother would say, meaning not married with kids. 'Don't leave it too late Stephen', she would say. In truth, I was probably too settled. Life was comfortable and well ordered, so why make it complicated?

Lucy let herself in through the front door mid-afternoon. Kicking her shoes off in the hallway she barged into the lounge, "Happy Birthday to you, Happy Birthday to you, Happy…," she fizzled out before the high note.

I looked up from my laptop and smiled. "And a very happy birthday to you too Lucy, please forgive me if I don't sing."

She leaned over and kissed me on the cheek and then went to make a drink. "Any interesting prezzies? A super-dooper new train-set perchance? Are you taking me out for a romantic meal?" Lucy liked birthdays and was in an unusually excited mood. I reflected that she sounded a bit posh, people didn't usually say 'super-dooper'. She was bright and articulate in an arty way. "Something from my parents which I have to pick up from the post office since I was away with the fairies when the postman came this morning," I told her.

"Lucky fairies," she put a mug beside me, then rummaged in her bag and extracted a small parcel constructed from a Tesco plastic bag and generous quantities of sticky tape. She tossed it into my lap.

"A lot of effort went into wrapping it up. Please appreciate."

I pulled it apart. Two T-shirts in a natural hemp colour fell out. I held them up, on one was printed 'It's My Boyfriend's Birthday,' and on the other, 'It's My Girlfriend's Birthday'. I sighed theatrically, "Lucy my dear, I can honestly say that this is the worst birthday present you have ever given me."

"Given us," she corrected. "I know they are utterly painful and what's more I'm going to make you wear yours tonight. She sat cross legged on the easy chair opposite me. "So what have you got me, Stephen with a 'ph'"?

"Wait and see, I'll take it with me to the pub." I wagged a finger at her, "Don't be impatient."

*****

The Nag's Head was filling up by 8 o'clock, bar staff darting between taps and cash register. In the dim light I could just make out a low stage at the far end and a few shadowy figures setting up a sound system, most of whom I recognised. "Where is everyone?"

"Faith can't get a baby sitter so she isn't coming, Dil is over there setting up." Brian nodded towards the stage. "I don't know where Kris is and let me introduce Chloe who I am madly and passionately in love with." He gave the girl sitting next to him a playful squeeze and she giggled appropriately. She held out a slender limp hand, "Hello, I hope you don't mind me gate crashing your party. Brian was telling me that you both have birthdays on the same day, isn't it weird. It's like you're twins but not really." She frowned. "Sorry probably everyone says that, but it is weird isn't it?" I smiled at her reassuringly, "Of course it is Chloe, totally and utterly weird. Not only do we share the same birthday, we were born in the same year. However," I held up a finger, "I am four hours older than Lucy which means I am senior and more advanced in every way." I gave Lucy an emotionless smile and she feigned a yawn.

"Brian's quite a lot older than me aren't you Brian." Chloe sat upright emphasising her curvaceous figure.

Brian admired her, "Yes she told me she was sixteen your honour, how was I to know she was only three years old."

18

I raised my eyebrows. Brian changed his girlfriends as frequently as most people had their hair cut. He was the most roundly educated and highly intelligent person I knew, yet he needed to pick up girls who he could impress and patronise and they in turn dazzled him with their conspicuous physical attributes. Chloe seemed to fit the requirements perfectly.

"And Paul and Lizzie?" I put my parcels down on the table. Brian glanced at his watch. "Yes on their way, be here in about ten minutes."

I rubbed my hands together. "Let's all raise a glass to my dear aunt Beryl who sends me twenty quid every year and insists that I use it to get drunk." I held my pint up and clinked it with the others.

Dil jumped down from the little stage, came over and squeezed in next to Chloe, "Where's Kris?" I asked.

He shrugged. "Oh you know how it is sometimes, she wasn't ready and I had to go and set up, so I left without her. She's fine, she'll be here soon. Putting on make-up with her is like painting the Forth Bridge, once you've finished it's time to start again." He grinned in a boyish way.

Lucy piped up in Kris' defence. "That, Dil, is slanderous. Just because she makes an effort to look her best and doesn't turn up in a free promotional T shirt and dirty jeans." She poked him in the chest.

"It's standard wear for an emaciated drug crazed jazz musician. I have to think of my image."

Lucy was dismissive. "The typical profile of a jazz fan is a male, over fifty years old who wears carpet slippers and incontinence pads." Dil knew that you don't take on Lucy in an argument unless you are prepared to lose. He clasped his hands behind his head and closed his eyes.

"Then here's to the Forth Bridge," Brian over-played his Scottish accent, rolling his 'r's excessively. "And may she always be well painted. And may Kris always be well painted for that matter." He jabbed a finger at Dil. "I still say you're a very lucky man Dil, so be careful. You won't find another like her if she kicks you out."

My attention drifted away from the conversation. I love these big dimly lit, London pubs, a long highly polished bar serving half a dozen decent bitters. Students from all over the world working fast, letting a glass fill with beer while they turned to the optics with a tumbler, then reaching into a cardboard box for a packet of peanuts, all the time adding up the price in their heads. I turned to the street door just as it opened glimpsing standing traffic in the street. Paul and Lizzie walked in. They stood in the doorway then caught sight of my waving arm. The door slowly closed behind them and the drift of car fumes was quickly annulled by a smell of stale ale. Brian grabbed another couple of stools and pushed their drinks towards them.

Looking around at the pub clientele my enthusiasm sank a little. For some, this pub was a major player in their lives. In here every day after work and drinking steadily until closing time. I congratulated myself on my little band of colleagues and friends, on my well-adjusted lifestyle and social contacts. But I knew I wasn't so different, surely there must be more to it than this? I resisted following that line of thought.

A banging and a crashing from the far end of the room woke me from my day-dream and announced that Dil had left us. He was now sat behind his drum kit, adjusting the position of each drum and stamping on the pedals. Spot lights were switched on illuminating the jazz quartet. I knew the other members of the band reasonably well. Martin on the keyboard was generally regarded as the leader. 'Spoons' played acoustic guitar, his nickname reputedly because he was an out of work chef, but more likely because his surname was 'Spooner'. The fourth member was a big black American from Alabama called Randall who hunched over an acoustic double bass, thumbing the strings and adjusting the tuning pegs. Collectively they were, 'The Brondesbury Jazz Quartet'.

Lucy nudged the parcels towards me. "Come on now, open your presents like a good boy before they start playing."

I pushed one of them back towards her. "This one's for you." I watched her meticulously loosen the ribbon and pick at the sticky tape to reveal a celebrity chef cookery book with a Mediterranean theme. She flicked through the illustrated pages making suitable murmurings of pleasure. I turned and kissed her on the lips. Lizzie watched intensely, exhaling an 'ah' as we embraced.

I pulled the remaining parcels towards me. "But you've already given me a present," I was feeling relieved that I had talked her out of wearing the birthday T shirts. I pulled the first present apart. A bright yellow cycling vest and a pair of cycling gloves fell out. I admired them and we kissed again. I was genuinely pleased.

The other parcel was the one from my parents which I had collected from the post office. A large padded envelope with my name and address printed in large letters on a sticky label. I ripped the end off and pulled out a black Moleskine notebook.

My heart sank. "It's a notebook", I said rather unnecessarily, holding it up for all to see. "From my parents."

"You can start writing your memoirs, Steve," Paul suggested.

"Or perhaps you're a budding poet," said Lizzie, not knowing. She looked at me, attentive, eyes bright.

It was another note book identical to the others. Clearly not from my parents, their parcel must still be on its way. I couldn't resist the urge to look inside the notebook, I flicked through the pages and as far as I could see, all of them were blank. But surely it was a reminder from Evans-Peake telling me that we had unfinished business. I began to sweat. Lucy touched my hand.

"Are you alright Steve?"

"Yes, fine. It's just a little hot in here." I flapped a laminated 'snacks' menu at my face.

"You look like you've seen a ghost."

I felt like I'd seen a ghost, and it took me by surprise.

Brian lifted a tall thin brightly coloured bag from the floor beside him, he raised the bottle inside enough to let me see the label, a ten-year-old Talisker. He shuffled it around to sit at my feet. "Don't drink it all at once my friend." I pulled it out of the bag and held it up for all to see. Then looking at Brian, I smiled and nodded my thanks. He was the best of friends, words were not necessary.

The Brondesbury Jazz Quartet started to play, interrupting our conversation. I knew what to expect. They were technically good and effortlessly dovetailed three jazz standards before pausing to allow Martin, the keyboard player, to introduce the members of the band. But their proficiency somehow hampered any sparkle, each number sounded similar, there was little innovation or risk. I leant across the table and Brian inclined his head, "They're good but they just need a melody instrument, a trumpet or a sax. Something to add a bit of colour and spontaneity."

Brian nodded in agreement. I sat back and smiled at Lucy, she smiled back and wrinkled her nose. Our thirty-third birthday celebrated together just like when we were children in the church hall, playing musical chairs and gobbling down jelly. Our Mums producing plates of party food, our Dads blowing up balloons, my Dad, the local country vicar, inexplicably still wearing his dog collar. Many years had drifted by since then but in many respects, we were still the same. Blowing the candles on the cake out in one puff after Happy Birthday had been sung. Not expecting to win 'pass the parcel.' A quiet night in the pub with a few friends. Lucy, always at my side.

I felt a gust of cool air as the pub door opened and I turned. Kris stood behind me, petite in tight fitting jeans and a loose powder blue Cashmere jumper, her jet black hair reaching down to the small of her back. Immaculate as ever. The others hadn't noticed her presence. She bent and whispered in my ear. "Steve can you lend me a tenner for the taxi, he's waiting outside, sorry." I reached into my back pocket for my wallet and held out a note. Her eyes flared as the band finished a number, the applause died down and there was a moment of quiet. "Thanks, I'll make sure that," and pointing at Dil, she raised her voice for all to hear. "That BASTARD pays you back."

That was the way it was with Kris I reflected, feast or famine. Compared to me or Lucy, Kris was an emotional roller-coaster. Lucy and I hardly ever argued, but Dil and Kris were at it every week it seemed. They sniped at each other, they postured, they stormed, they raged but their marriage was strong, the knocks and buffeting somehow fuelled it. Whereas with Lucy, one day was pretty much the same as the next, not much light and shade, life was never a drama.

*****

When I woke the next morning, Lucy was already up and making tea. I heard her carefully climb the stairs, mugs clinking in her hand, she appeared in the bedroom doorway, the 'It's My Girlfriend's Birthday' T shirt nearly reaching to her knees. I sat up in bed and stretched my arms above my head. "Breakfast?"

She put one mug down on my bedside table. "No time. Things to do. My place is in a mess and I've still got to prepare for a client meeting tomorrow. Come round later this afternoon, I'll cook something, we can have a night in and watch the telly."

"Fine", I reached for the mug of tea. "I should probably pop in to the office, Brian is going in. We've got a problem with the data backups on the computer server, it should all happen over the weekend but we came in last Monday and it hadn't started. Oh, the joys of running your own business."

"Your choice". She rummaged in a drawer containing a couple of changes of clothes which she kept at my house. "You could have stayed at Dewar. Big pharmaceutical company, solid pension, share options, fitness centre, not that you ever used it. And you didn't have to buy the tea, coffee and toilet rolls."

"Faith does that."

"When she remembers."

"Sometimes you have to grab life's opportunities. Brian and I had been planning to set up Obsidian for a few years. The time felt

23

right. Anyway you know all this, I don't know why I'm repeating it.''

"Exactly, so why are you moaning. I'll see you later, be good."

"I wasn't moaning." I had to raise my voice as she rattled down the stairs. After a couple of minutes I heard the front door slam. Was I moaning? Certainly some of our initial shiny enthusiasm for being entrepreneurs had been chipped away. But moaning? Perhaps I was.

Lucy and I had grown up together in a little village in the homely Chiltern Hills. As children we fell off bicycles, climbed trees and splashed in streams. Then as teenagers we picked our way through sexual awakening and innocent fumblings, just trying to work out who we were, and in my case not being very happy when I found out, for no good reason. Inevitably we reached the end of our schooling and went off in different directions, Lucy to Art college in Brighton and then on to work in Paris curating a minor art collection. Meanwhile, I settled down in Imperial College in Kensington, a Mecca for scientists and engineers. By chance we both ended up living in North London, Lucy now working for an art consultancy, advising wealthy clients what to buy to put on the walls of their homes or offices to make the right statement. I was still at Imperial, living the life of an academic in the maths department. So we got together again and had been an item for five or six years, partly living together but both needing our own space to retreat to. It was a convenience, someone to go to parties or the theatre with. We both needed the warmth of another body but it should have been more than that surely. If I was brutally honest it was just the birthday twin thing that held us together. Everyone said how funny it was that we were born on the same day, 'just like you're twins', so it stuck. We were meant to be together, birthday twins without the genetic link.

Wearing boxer shorts and pulling a T-shirt over my head, I sank into the soft sofa. The matter of the additional notebook given to me on my birthday had been in the back of my mind since I woke. I was sure it hadn't come from my parents, Evans-Peake was

24

still trying to gate-crash my life. With curiosity masking my fear, I pulled off the band of black elastic and flicked through its pages. Unlike the others, every page in this notebook was blank. I turned the last page. Inside the back cover was a small pocket made from stiff paper, I held the notebook upside down and shook it with frustration. A small rectangular scrap of paper dropped out, written on it were four digits: 1712.

Now this was a new puzzle, what could the number mean? 17th of December or 17 minutes past 12. It was too short to be a phone number, a house number perhaps but it would be a long street. Probably it was none of these. The most likely thing was that it was the key to unlocking the code in the other notebooks, but how? Should I search the codes for this sequence of numbers? Would that produce a pattern? There had to be a pattern, that went without saying, everything is part of a pattern from sub-atomic particles to Lego. That was a statement of faith for me.

I still hadn't told anybody about Evans-Peake or the notebooks, not Lucy, not Brian, not even my sister Helen, in whom I confide most things. If I had really wanted nothing to do with it then I would have thrown the notebooks away, but I had a sense that they weren't mine to throw away, I was their custodian. I put the scrap of paper back in the pocket and shut the notebook in the bottom drawer of my desk with all the others. Perhaps if I ignored them, Evans-Peake would just give up and go away. But he knew my address, he had sent the package to my house. There was no escaping him, he could even be watching me now. Troubling thoughts crowded my mind. I was conscious of a need to breathe deeply, I rubbed my forehead and bolted for the back door. Pulling my bike out of the shed and along the side of the house, I headed for the office. Even though it was Sunday I knew Brian would be there and I needed company.

Chapter 3

I left my bike in the stairwell and climbed to our office on the first floor, picking the post off the mat as I went. On the ground floor was a communal kitchen area which we shared with the other business in the building, a graphic design company called 'Pangolin'. They had helped us from time to time with our web site and printed material. It was staffed by three 'fine art' graduates who really wanted to do something deeper and more meaningful, we called them Harpo, Chico and Groucho.

I pushed the door and eased my backpack off my shoulders, dumping the post on Faith's desk. Some junk mail and an ominous looking letter from the bank. I suspected it would be bad news and decided not to open it, we were sailing close to the wind.

Brian was kneeling on the floor pulling the computer server rack apart and the phone was ringing.

"Just ignore it, Steve It's been ringing all morning, god knows why someone is trying to call us on a Sunday. It's probably a cold caller."

I picked it up anyway. "Hello Obsidian."

A male voice answered. "Is Faith there?"

"No, she only works weekdays, can I help?" He hung up. I put the handset back on its cradle carefully and aligned the phone to the edge of Faith's desk.

Brian, red faced, was reaching around to the back of the computer cabinet grunting as he tried to unclip cables and free one of the units. His large well-padded frame didn't lend itself to working in confined spaces.

"The backup job didn't run because it ran out of space on the tape." Brian eased an anodized silver box forward.

"Can we get bigger tapes?"

"No, this is as big as they go."

"So then do we need another strategy, like backing up to the cloud."

"No Steve, you know very well how sensitive our clients are. We would be tied up in security issues for evermore. None of them trust cloud technology, it's just not secure enough and we can't take the risk of someone getting hold of data which they have entrusted to us."

"So keeping all the backup tapes in a biscuit tin under your bed is better?" I thought Brian might snap back but he chuckled.

"Safest place in the world, under my bed. There are things there that nobody knows about."

"Even Chloe?"

"Especially Chloe." Brian stood up and flexed his back, blowing out through puffed cheeks. "What did you think of her then?"

"Well I could see her obvious attractions. Two obvious attractions to be precise."

Brian sniggered. "She's an attractive girl." He raised an eyebrow and spoke in an exaggerated Scottish accent, a Scot imitating a Scot.

"Does she share your liking for sushi, impressionist music and the Lakeland romantic poets?"

"Haven't got that far yet, we're still on the romantic comedy at the cinema followed by a fish and chip supper. All in good time Steve, she'll come round." He patted the slim box of electronics. "Anyway here's the beast. One tape backup unit."

"Why have you pulled it out?"

"Because, my friend, the data on our server should have fitted on to a tape with ease. So it must be faulty."

"Either that or there's more data on our server than we know about."

Brian ignored my comment and continued to fiddle with the tape unit while I logged on to our network from my laptop. We both knew that this was important. Our typical clients were large pharmaceutical companies, and having worked at Dewar's I understood how they operated. Original copies of all experimental methods and results had to be stored in locked down data safes so that there was no possibility of someone leaking or altering the data. These same regulations were a source of sleepless nights for those of us who carried the can at Obsidian, especially when there were problems with the backups. If our clients couldn't trust us to keep their data safe and confidential, then business would dry up overnight. Word gets around.

I watched Brian as he worked away, reflecting on our long friendship. We had met as undergraduates at Imperial, both studying mathematics. I combined it with applied statistics and Brian took the pure maths route. Whilst I struggled at times, Brian sailed through with ease and came out with a first. He was a true polymath. Not only was he interested in maths and the latest theories in sub-atomic physics, he would also be interested in contemporary poetry, Japanese art, or deconstructing Bach fugues. He had stayed on at Imperial as a post-doc, working his way up to Principle Investigator in a couple of years. There was little doubt that he was in line for the next vacant chair, but he became increasingly disillusioned with academic life. He wanted the accolade of commercial success, the freedom to turn his ideas into something that people would buy and use, a shrink-wrapped product with a price tag. Not something half-baked which anyone could download for free from an academic web site which may or may not work.

So Brian and I risked our friendship and set up in business together. Obsidian was born just under two years ago, we rented office space, borrowed some money from the bank to buy some desks and set up a computer network and we were off with great optimism. We were our own bosses, dressing how we liked and working the hours that suited us, generally starting late in the morning and finishing very late in the evening. We were going to make our mark on the world and possibly get rich.

After a year or so we had realised that we needed a third person. Someone who could find new business and take care of marketing. Someone lively and determined. Somebody for whom networking with people was a natural state. That's where Krishna came on board. Kris had been working towards a master's degree at Imperial, Brian was her supervisor. For a number of reasons, he had kept up an occasional e-mail conversation with her, so when she told him she was studying for a marketing diploma, we approached her with an offer. Loud, opinionated and attention seeking, Kris brought much needed colour to Obsidian. When she joined forces with Faith, our extrovert Jamaican-born receptionist, they were more than a match for two grey bookish PhDs.

Brian interrupted my thoughts. "Well I can't see anything wrong with it." He tapped the tape unit with the tip of a screwdriver." I'll hook it up again but leave it out of the rack, then we can keep an eye on it."

I nodded in agreement.

*****

On Monday morning I was on my own in the office when Faith arrived breathless, twenty minutes late. This was not unusual. She immediately launched into a monologue. "Jackson was throwing up all night and I had to drop him off at my Mother's so I didn't get much sleep what with one thing and another, fortunately it's one of the days she doesn't work. She says the Lord moves in mysterious ways, and I said Mum what are you on about, she watches the god channel on the telly when she's cooking, I don't agree with having a telly in the kitchen but that's her business not mine. Anyway she said it just means that it's all in the Good Lord's hands and I said never mind being in the Good Lords hands it was all over his duvet Mother, you should have seen the state he got himself into." Her large frame rocked as she shrieked with laughter, banging her desk with the open palms of her hands and shaking her head.

Talking to Faith was like being machine gunned with words, delivered in a strong Jamaican accent. I feigned attention while thinking that I needed to check the computer back-ups.

"Well, Faith, must get on."

"Yes, sorry to be late anyway, I'll make the hours up."

I knew she wouldn't. She disappeared down to the kitchen to make a coffee. She would find someone to chat to down there and that would be another half hour gone. Perhaps I'll get Kris to have a word with her I thought, knowing it was a cop out.

Brian was on the phone, asking about the backups. "It's fine," I said, "I ejected the tape and I'm about to look at the log, hang on." I quickly scrolled down a long list of files, "All OK as far as I can see, and room to spare on the tape."

Brian said he thought the last tape must have been dodgy, he would take a look at it when he was next in the office.

So that was it, panic over. I wish I felt more positive, the days spread out before me like a shuffled deck of cards. Take another from the top of the pack, let's see what happens.

*****

It rained constantly until Thursday, but then the sun shone. At lunch-time I told Faith I'd be back in an hour and strolled down the road to a little parade of shops, stopping at the newsagent to buy a paper and at the Greek sandwich shop next door for a tuna roll and coffee to take away. At the end of the road was the familiar park, I found an empty bench and swept the fallen leaves off with the back of my hand. It wouldn't be long before the park would be carpeted in drifts of fallen leaves. A park attendant made a futile attempt to gather them up, he raked them into a little pile and then tried to transfer them into his barrow before they blew away again. Things just naturally mix up, they're never happy in neat piles. That's basic undergraduate thermodynamics.

I quickly turned the pages of the newspaper dipping into anything of interest, then I folded it to concentrate on the cryptic crossword at the back, pen poised, sandwich momentarily forgotten. Were it not for the newspaper I would eat my roll and drink the coffee in a couple of minutes, then leave. Sitting doing nothing, or rather thinking about nothing has never been easy for me, I fill my life with noise and activity, the radio, music, reading research papers, novels, comparing the list of ingredients on packets of breakfast cereal as I eat, counting my steps as I walk. All these stimuli combine into a cacophony in my head, each jostling for my attention. Recently I had been finding it increasingly hard to focus on one source. I re-read pages of a novel several times because I had been distracted by a discussion on talk radio, so I would switch the radio to a jazz station but get the weather forecast, without waiting for music I would flick my valve hi-fi amplifier on with the remote control and listen to Billie Holliday complaining about all of her troubles. The only thing that completely absorbs me and cuts through the thought-tinnitus is a puzzle. It could be working out a solution to a statistical problem, solving a crossword clue or even breaking a code written in a stack of black Moleskine notebooks. The puzzle was the thing, enjoy the chase.

I quickly picked off a few of the easier clues and filled them in on the crossword grid. The sound of an ice cream van chiming 'Yankee Doodle' broke through my fixation on three down. I turned to watch. A teenage boy and girl absent from school holding hands, a mother with a flock of toddlers jumping with excitement, arms raised, a dishevelled traveller in baggy clothes with nothing much to do. The little burst of trade dispersed in different directions, the children to the swings and slides and the teenagers to a secluded spot. The traveller walked straight out of the park, carefully placing his feet one in front of another like a model on a catwalk giving the appearance of being unsteady.

Leaving the newspaper on the bench, I ran to the road looking left and right, my sight partially obscured by the ice cream van. An elderly man walking a dog was all I saw. I stood for a few seconds breathing heavily, then feeling foolish and thinking that everyone was watching me I jogged back to by bench and retrieved my newspaper from the bushes. After trying unsuccessfully to turn my attention back to the crossword, I reached into my pockets for my MP3 player. Screwing the earphones into my ears I turned the volume up, creating my own controlled world. I hurried back to the office and to Faith. 'It wasn't him', I told myself. 'It wasn't him.'

And so after three months of peace it had started again. The thing that I had put behind me as just one of those peculiar events, was back. Yet still I hadn't told anyone, but who should I tell and what should I say? I rehearsed the conversation in my imagination:

"Some strange guy is stalking me. No he isn't, it's more like he's watching me, he seems to appear out of nowhere. He gave me some books containing a puzzle, but I can't decode them. I don't know what to do, every time I see him I start to panic. There is something evil about him."

"Is he dangerous?"

"I think he might be."

"Has he ever threatened you?"

"No"

"Has he spoken to you?"

"Yes, once"

"Do you see him often?"

"No, not often."

"Have you ever dreamt about him?"

"Yes I have, once or twice."

"Do you know his name?"

"It's Evans-Peake"

"How do you know his name?"

"How do I know his name? I don't know, I don't know. I must have heard it somewhere. How do I know his name?"

I stopped going to the park. Even if the weather was good, I took my lunch back to the office and ate it at my desk. At first I saw him fleetingly, getting on a bus or turning a corner in the distance. Once I thought I saw him going into the house across the street. I saw him from behind, sticks in loose clothes, turning the

32

key and pushing the door open. The door slammed shut behind him on a spring mechanism before he turned around. He called my name, 'Dr Rockett', he whispered it in my ear, I smelt his breath, he taped me on the shoulder and I turn to see who. He was never close enough to be sure and I didn't want to suffer the indignity of chasing someone who wasn't him. And anyway what would I say? Sometimes I saw him several times in one day. At least in my mind I saw him but I was beginning to doubt myself. Is this how it goes? You can't tell the difference between reality and invention and then you lose your grip on reality and inhabit invention? I tried to throw myself into my work. Numbers were numbers, I knew the rules for numbers and they always behaved themselves. But it wasn't enough.

I had to get things back in perspective. The reality was that I had let some weirdo get under my skin to the extent that I was beginning to doubt my own sanity. I was starting to see him everywhere, but like the will-o'-the wisp he disappears just when you think you have him in your grasp.

"How did I know his name?"

Chapter 4

The evenings were beginning to draw in, I reached for the light switch. Faith had gone home at four-thirty, Brian and I sat at our desks debugging computer programs and puzzling over mathematics. Kris was turning out her desk drawer. "Has anyone seen the delegate list from the Cambridge meeting?" She thought out loud. "I must have left it at home. Dil's coming over, he could bring it but he's probably left by now."

Kris had met Dil in Nepal during an unsettled time in her life. I had heard many stories about it over pints in the Nags Head, Kris liked to talk. She had struggled through an Applied Physics degree, hating every minute and loathing every sub-atomic particle. As soon as she got a chance she went off to discover her roots in Uttar Pradesh, much to the dismay of her ambitious parents. It was the first time she had visited India, the stratification and nuances of Indian society baffled her and the time it took to get things done frustrated her. Her close-knit family in India suffocated her with a cultural blanket, so at the earliest opportunity, Kris left all the Indian aunties and uncles and headed North and East for the mountains of Nepal pitching up, as many travellers do, in Pokhara. Here she met Dil, a Nepali from Reading who had lived in Britain since he was eight years old, his aristocratic parents having fled one of the frequent Nepali uprisings. Dil was carefree and spontaneous, the perfect antidote to Kris' stifling family and the endless rounds of relatives to visit. She was quickly smitten, here at last was somebody who didn't want to tell her what to do.

Pokhara is a place to relax, set in a valley surrounded by green forested hills with the snowy peaks of the Himalayas hanging in the blue sky beyond. The road running along the southern shore of lake Fewa offers any style of restaurant and night life. Krishna and Dil took pleasure in finding the cheapest Nepali food in the dingiest of backstreet shacks, washed down with a shared bottle of local beer. In the cool of the late afternoon they would rent a small boat. Then Dil paddled them out into the middle of the lake and let the boat drift in the breeze.

Dil told Kris he had been travelling with a friend from England called Sam who had abandoned him and returned home. It wasn't until Dil and Kris arrived back in England that she realised that Sam was 'Samantha' and not 'Samuel'. Dil had a way of knowingly allowing you to accept a half truth. The weeks went by, days merging into one and inevitably, even at Nepali prices, their money ran out and they headed for home. Parental pressure dictated that they should marry rather than live together, so after being back in England for less than a year they were united.

I reflected on my own story. What would I say about my life so far? Born into a close middle class religious family, my father was a Vicar. I was undoubtedly much loved, even if that love had not always been overtly expressed. I had been coaxed along by school teachers, church leaders and relatives who, with all good intention, kept me in the middle of the road. 'The straight and narrow way', my Dad would have called it. But where was my passion? I couldn't even be sure that I was passionate about Lucy. How would I make my mark on the world? Already in my thirties, what had I to show for my life so far? In my head I could hear my Dad telling the story of the 'Five Talents', clearly I had been given a lot of talents but had I invested them or had I just buried them in the ground, too scared to take a risk?

The door buzzer woke me from my day-dream. Kris reached over to Faith's desk and pressed the button. We heard jogging steps on the stairs and after a few seconds Dil bounced into the office.

"Hello you sad people, don't you know how late it is? No homes to go to?"

"Yes Dil, we all have homes to go to, but it's paying for them that's the problem. Luckily for you, you can rely on Kris to solve that little problem for you." Brian smiled at Dil to take the sting out of his words. Dil was not supressed in the slightest.

"Hi Dil, I'll just be five minutes," Kris didn't look up from her laptop.

He flopped into Faith's office chair and swivelled from side to side.

"What are you going to see?" I asked.

"Much Ado About Nothing at The Globe," then putting on a phoney Indian accent, "Oh yes we Asians are very much liking your English bard isn't it."

Kris looked up. "Do you want to wait outside the door or are you going to behave yourself?"

Dil continued to swivel in the chair, drumming a rhythm with his palms on the edge of the desk. Suddenly he stopped.

"Ah now, Steve. I need a word with you. As we have discussed on several occasions, we need a trumpeter or a sax player for the Brondesbury Quartet. So we put an ad in the paper and guess what, we got just one sensible reply."

"Must have been a rubbish advert if you only got one response, why didn't you show it to me?" Krishna continued to clatter the laptop keys as she spoke.

"It was, my dear Kris, the perfect advert since it elicited but one response thereby absolving us from the ignominy of have to make a choice apart from the simple yea or nay forsooth."

I looked up. "What's it got to do with me?"

"Our one and only applicant said he knew you."

"That narrows him down to one of about four people then Steve?" Brian was enjoying the banter.

"It's down to three now." I replied. "And his name was?"

"Dave. I'm not sure if we ever asked what his surname was. I would guess he was in his forties. He wore sort of bohemian gear, kaftan and sandals. Looked slightly weird. He played the sax."

My mind went back several months to Evans-Peake playing his saxophone in the park. I remembered his instrument being laid out on top of the coffin surrounded by flowers. But was I just

36

making random connections? There must be hundreds of sax players in London, I told myself, and a good number will be dressed unconventionally. "So Dil, how did you find out that he knew me?"

"It was when we went down to the Nags Head on your birthday, he was apparently over the other side of the bar and he saw you talking to me. And he thought, hang on a tick I know that chap."

"So why didn't he come over and say hello?"

"I don't know, probably didn't want to barge in. You know how shy some people are."

"Right." Krishna shut her laptop with an air of finality and looked up at Dil.

"I'm all yours, let's go."

As Dil opened the door I asked, "Did he get the job?"

"No. He was alright with the punchy harmony licks but rubbish as a soloist, not a free spirit. I'm going to have to learn the mouth organ."

The door banged shut and I sat, trying to keep things in perspective. I jumped up and ran down the stairs after them.

"Dil, do you have an address or phone number for him?"

They stopped at the front door. "No, but he's currently in a band called 'Stick No Posters' and they're playing tonight in the room above that big pub in Barnes. If you get your skates on you can see him in action."

*****

When we arrived at the pub, the function room was about a quarter full. Unpadded plastic chairs had been set out in rows which became more disorderly as their occupants rearranged them into little social groups. The stage was dark, musical instruments and sound system inert. Tiny green lights twinkled on the stacks of amplifiers looking like a miniature city-scape at night. We took seats in the middle of a row near the front and sipped our drinks.

"Not much of a turn out," Lucy observed.

"Dil said they were good," I lied. I could tell from her silence that Dil's opinion carried little weight.

Gradually people began to drift up from the bar below, drinks in hand, chatting in twos and threes.

'Stick no Posters' turned out to be a Ska band. They came on stage, fifteen minutes later than the advertised time, wearing sunglasses and sharp dark suites. At the back, in the shadows I could just make out a horn line up consisting of a trombone, a trumpet and an alto saxophone.

The horns punctuated the first number with short unison bursts, I couldn't see them clearly, shadowed in the inadequate stage lighting. For the start of the second number they moved forward into the spot light. The trombone player leant back as he played, tilting his instrument up and punching the air with the slide. The trumpeter, short and stocky stood between the other two, feet planted firmly apart, puffing his cheeks out when he played and constantly bouncing the trumpet valves with his fingers when he wasn't. The saxophone player was tall and thin. He wore a dark tight fitting suit and a pork pie hat. Behind his sunglasses I could see that this 'Dave', whoever he was, was very definitely black.

I didn't know whether to be happy or sad. It was a big anti-climax, how can I have been so foolish? What a waste of time. I felt that everyone must know and was looking at me as I squirmed in unnecessary embarrassment. The music was loud in my head and getting louder. All the notes merged into one screeching cacophony. I was sweating, feeling claustrophobic and nauseous. My heart thumped and I started to pant, struggling to get enough oxygen into my lungs. The atmosphere was hot and suffocating, I desperately needed to get out into the fresh air.

"Come on let's go," I spoke closely, into Lucy's ear.

"We've only just arrived."

"I know, I'm just not in the mood for this."

She continued to look at the stage. "Well we might as well stay for a little while, they're not that bad."

"You do what you want, I'm going. Sorry."

I slopped my drink as I squeezed past the knees of the people in the row, apologising as I went. Stumbling down the stairs, head spinning, vision narrowed, not caring about spilling my beer now, I burst out through a fire door into the cool autumn air. I sat on a low wall, shaking, taking deep breaths, trying to calm down. I wiped my beer-sticky hands on my shirt. Then I put my head down between my knees, waiting for the dizziness to subside. After a minute or two Lucy appeared and quietly sat down next to me without saying a word. Hands clasped in her lap, straight backed.

"I'm so sorry," I was feeling fragile. "I must have had some sort of panic attack. I just had to get out of there." I sat, close to tears, unable to tell her and not knowing why. "It's just the business getting me down, don't say anything to Brian. I'll sort it out."

My explanation seemed to satisfy her but I couldn't see through to her thoughts. We walked along the river embankment for some way, hand in hand. She talked about her work, the art, the clients, the flattering of egos. We didn't talk about me and I wasn't listening to her, we were only connected by clasped hands. I was on an emotional edge about to fall off, and all over a strange man and a stack of notebooks. I knew I was susceptible to stress, that I was being over-sensitive, but it was no less real for all that. I had always found dealing with numbers easier than dealing with people. But now I was beyond fragile, my head crowded with fears and close to tears. And Lucy didn't see that, she just kept talking about her own little world as we walked down the river-side path, going on and on about people who I didn't know and who I would never be likely to meet. Or if she did see my distress, then she was ignoring it.

And how could she do that? How could she?

*****

Lucy's parents, Laurence and Barbara, still lived where we had grown up, in the heart of the Chiltern Hills, a forty-five minute train ride from London's Marylebone station. Once through the London suburbs, the sprinter train picks up speed and bursts out into green rolling hills and shady Beech woods, liberally sprinkled with tumble-down pubs serving good ale and a ploughman's lunch.

Laurence is an affable chap who had a small but lucrative accountancy practice. He had officially retired but still looked after a few chosen clients, as much for the social contact as anything else, he didn't need the money. I get on well with him, we talk about business and current affairs, safe subjects, nothing personal. Each time I visited them I noticed how active Laurence is when compared to my Father who seemed to have slowed down a bit more every time I saw him. Barbara is an excellent cook and Laurence knows a good bottle of wine. They appreciated the good things in life and I am always more than happy to take advantage of their hospitality.

After the episode at the concert I realised my stress had risen to a new level, my attention span was even worse than usual and I was short tempered with Lucy. I kept telling myself that it was nothing to get worked up about, but I just couldn't help myself. Lucy was matter-of-fact. She told me I needed some down time and prescribed a break from London and a good night's sleep. After that, she assured me, I'd be back on top of things again. But I was fragile and I was frightened. I felt lonely in the midst of people and I wasn't lying when I said that work was stressful, business was not good. At times I seemed to be hallucinating, unable to tell the difference between reality and my imagination. But it wasn't all ephemeral, there was still something concrete. I still had the notebooks, they at least were real, I wasn't going completely mad. But they worried away at me like a dog with a ball.

On Friday afternoon we took our mountain bikes out to Amersham on the train and then we cycled the short distance to South Heath. Lucy's mother opened the front door as soon as she heard us on the gravel drive. She looked good for her sixty-five years, slender legs squeezed into jeans and wearing a bright striped shirt.

40

"This is a nice surprise." She clasped her hands and smiled.

"Dad's in the kitchen agonising over the choice of wine. Go and find him."

I rummaged in my pannier and pulled out a decent bottle of Burgundy. "Here's another one for him to worry about."

"You look tired Steve, Lucy said you had been working too hard." Barbara pouted in sympathy.

"That's the way it is with a small business, feast or famine. It's a bit down at the moment but it'll pick up."

I woke early the following morning following a restless night, hoping to feel better but not really feeling any different. Lying in bed I listened to the silence, no cars, no dogs barking, no doors slamming, just the rhythm of Lucy breathing beside me. I opened the curtains just enough to let some light in. Lucy stirred, turned over and pulled the duvet up around her ears. I yawned, envious of her ability to sleep.

Laurence browsed the newspaper spread out before him on the kitchen table while Barbara busied herself at the Aga, cooking us a fried breakfast. "Something to set you up for the day. But not for Laurence, he's got to watch his cholesterol." She pushed a packet of muesli in his direction. Laurence sighed and poured some into his bowl. "I might be able to find him a sausage if he's a good boy," Barbara kissed the top of his head as she circled the breakfast table, coffee jug in hand.

Lucy and I cycled many miles that day. Along narrow lanes, taking detours along bridle paths whenever we could. Through little Buckinghamshire villages that I remembered so well from my childhood. Chartridge, Lee Common, Wendover, Little Missenden, Bryants Bottom, little had changed in fifteen years since I was a teenager. The trees were beginning to shed their leaves, vivid in reds and yellows, and there was a pleasant breeze which cooled us as we freewheeled down, and puffed up, the steep hillsides. Lucy struggled with some of the climbs and ended up pushing her bike, arriving at the top red faced and breathless, but she didn't give up.

Lucy was steadfast, willing, uncomplaining, dutiful, and above all rational. She processed life as it came without passing judgement.

Stopping at a rustic pub for lunch and pint of ale, we sat quietly, looking around for something to talk about.

"Are you OK?" I asked.

"Yes I'm fine. Isn't it lovely here."

And we were OK, and it was lovely. But something stopped me from fully appreciating it. I felt as if I were alone.

On Sunday morning we lazed around reading the papers. Lucy chatted with her Mum about books they were reading and new curtains. I knew that if I could just talk to her about it, then the burden would be lifted. I would be able to rationalise my fears and see them for what they were. A weirdo had got under my skin, there was no reason to get stressed, I may even be making it up. But Lucy and I weren't on the same track anymore.

If I couldn't talk to Lucy, perhaps I would be able to talk to Brian. Not only was Brian my best friend, he was also the cleverest person I knew. I could tell him about Evans-Peake and the codes in the notebooks. It just takes one other person on your side to relieve the stress, Brian would know what to do. I could trust Brian not to belittle my fears.

We sat on a platform bench at Amersham station waiting for the train back to London. Lucy fiddled with the straps of her ruck sack trying to stuff her padded jacket into it, then she picked at the quicks of her nails and tapped her trainer clad feet on the ground, restless. She stopped and turned to me, her eyes searching my face unsuccessfully.

"Stephen?" I was suddenly aware that I hadn't taken account of her feelings all weekend. Our worlds didn't seem to overlap the way they once had. I didn't say anything, she continued. "I'm not sure where we are going, together. I don't know what's going on in your head, you don't let me in anymore. We were the birthday twins once, and then we were more than that, but now I don't know what we are. I don't know where our relationship is going, love."

When had she last called me 'love'? When had I last shown any real affection to her?

The train arrived and we sat opposite each other in silence, I closed my eyes feigning sleep to avoid conversation. Was it just apathy? Would I lose her because I couldn't be bothered to do anything about it? We arrived at Marylebone station and I suggested that we sat down for a minute or two and had a coffee. We sipped drinks that we didn't really want and I started to say something about still feeling close to her but I couldn't finish the sentence. And that's where our relationship finished, on a red metal bench by the coffee stand in Marylebone Station, Sunday 30th September at six fifteen. Lucy stood up, eyes filling. She threw her cup, still full of coffee, in the rubbish bin and wheeled her bike out of the station. She didn't look back.

I sat there for a bit longer, it was quiet. I watching as a handful of people got off an incoming train and strode purposefully down the platform, hardly missing a beat as they 'touched out' through the ticket barrier with their Oyster cards.

The last of them, by some way, was Evans-Peake. Brown faced, skin creased and stubbled, it was unmistakably him. His eyes were hidden behind small round blue tinted sun glasses. Long greying hair was gathered tightly into a pony tail high up on his head, the way a girl would arrange it. Falling from his left ear was the silver cross on a short chain. His neck was bare. On his right wrist were three or four brightly coloured bangles. Tall and thin, he walked slowly in textile strapped sandals, carefully placing his feet, not shuffling. His elephant-print trousers billowed as he walked, gathered in tightly at the top around his lean waist. He wore a Nepali style plain undyed shirt, loose sleeves without cuffs and three wooden toggles to close up the V-neck. He looked just like a Himalayan trekker, then I reminded myself that real trekkers wear walking boots, down jackets, light weight trousers with numerous zipped pockets and they carry brightly coloured rucksacks. Evans-Peake was not a trekker. Evans-Peake was a performer and I was his audience.

Once through the ticket barrier he was about twenty yards away. I stared at him as he got closer but he made no attempt at eye contact. By now the station concourse was almost empty, I felt as if it was just him and me in an arty film with soaring strings in my head. He got closer and closer, I sat fixated, clutching my cup of coffee with shaking hand, it spilt burning my fingers. I was terrified, but not sure why. Then he was walking past me without missing a step, looking straight ahead. I panned around keeping him in shot. Once again I thought he looked deeply unwell, his face closed as if he were walking into the wind. On his back was a small knapsack made from a coarse woven textile with leather trimming. It looked empty as it bounced up and down.

I knew it was him. What should I do? I followed at a discrete distance as he passed the fast food outlets but I lost sight of him when he walked out into the street. Quickening my pace, I saw him get into a cab. The taxi signalled, waiting for an opportunity to pull out into the traffic, and I caught up. Close enough to bang on its side, close enough to pull open the door, but did neither. A movement, Evans-Peake turned around. For a moment I thought he was about to tell the driver to stop. I saw his face through the back window of the taxi, he took his dark glasses off and I stared into those cold, tired grey eyes. There was now no doubt about his reality, no need to pinch myself, no need to question my sanity any more. An unexpected feeling of relief surged inside me, this was Evans-Peake, incarnate. The taxi started to move off slowly, Evans-Peake rapped on the back window with his knuckles, as if he needed to get my attention. He pointed his finger at me, his lips moving, mouthing words I couldn't hear. Then he held up a sheet of paper with a number scrawled on it. 1712, the same number as on the scrap of paper in the last notebook. But how do I put the pieces of the puzzle together? What has this number got to do with the other notebooks?

Chapter 5

Brian picked up the menu even though he knew it by heart, we ordered pasta and a bottle of the house red. The quiet Italian restaurant had become the usual place for a management meeting, it was good to get out of the office. Not that we were a secretive company, but some things are better discussed in private. I would have preferred to have the meeting in my house or Brian's. There wasn't enough space on the table in the restaurant to spread out papers and we didn't focus on issues in the same way when we were also consuming lunch. However, Brian insisted that it was one of the perks of running a business, to put the occasional 'slap-up nosh' on expenses as customer entertainment. The waiter cradled the wine as she showed us the label and I determined to limit myself to one large glass. Brian would happily drink the rest, he was physically very robust and alcohol appeared to make little difference to his ability to function.

We sat in silence for a few seconds, not knowing where to begin. Brian wasn't always good at facing up to unpleasant facts and would side-step a difficult decision if he could. And there were some difficult issues to be tackled. I picked up my satchel from the floor and put it on my lap, then I pulled out two copies of the latest profit and loss accounts and put them on the table. Delving deeper I found my notebook and a pen. Brian had brought nothing. I pushed one set of papers across the table. "These are from Merry Mick and take us up to the end of the last quarter."

Mick was our accountant, we added the 'merry' ironically because he was usually anything but merry. His personal life was a disaster and he didn't spare the details whenever we met. His children were always wanting financial support for business ventures which even I could see were doomed to disaster. His long suffering wife seemed to be on the verge of leaving him and going back to her Mother. To cap it all, Mick had bought, what must have been, the only house in the London area which had lost value. A succession of problematic neighbours, subsidence and botched alterations soaked up any spare pennies, leaving him in negative equity. However, as an accountant he had given us good advice, so we stuck with him. Others, especially Kris, took a different view, 'If he can't sort his own life out how on earth is he going to sort out your business?' I could see that she had a point.

Brian slowly turned the pages of the report. It was very obvious that we were some way behind our target and that our costs were escalating.

"How did we spend all that money on entertainment?" He muttered.

"It's mostly Kris, taking clients out to lunch, taxis to restaurants, bottles of wine, a round of drinks in the bar after a conference."

"Yes but does she really have to…"

"It's what we pay her to do Brian," I insisted. "We have to punch above our weight, we are just three people, four if you count Faith, and we are competing with the big consultancies. Our customers are some of the biggest companies in the world. She has to flash a little cash from time to time to be in the club."

"Well we have to put a stop to it."

"That would be like turning the tap off. The last thing you want to cut down on is your marketing and sales effort."

Brian puffed his cheeks and blew out. "Capital expenditure?"

"Again we are over budget, mostly the new computer server." Brian didn't respond, he was the one who had insisted that we needed it. "Then if you look at salaries, we gave Kris and Faith just two percent rises this year and you and I are still just taking the minimum out of the business. So there's not much more we can do there."

Our food arrived and we fell into silence as we ate, Brian tracing columns of figures with the tip of his knife.

I wiped my mouth with the napkin. "The plain fact is that we have been living off the SMART award money, without that we would be in deep trouble, but it's running out. We have to get a grip on the finances before it's too late. Our liabilities outweigh our assets. If the bank saw these figures they would pull our loan, no doubt about it, and then we would be sunk."

Brian put down his fork. "What does Merry Mick say?"

"He says we need a meeting to discuss cutting the budget."

"Alright let's go back to entertainment. I'm sorry Steve but you'll have to have a word with Kris. She just can't have a carte blanche to spend what she likes. At the end of the day it's our money she's spending. Or she has to go."

"Are you crazy? No, we absolutely need Kris. Without her we won't have any business." "Then we have to set some guidelines for her."

The atmosphere was gloomy. "The other approach is to maximise our income. It's my consultancy work that keeps us afloat at the moment but that won't last forever. We need to sell more copies of Merlin and we need to start charging our existing customers for support and upgrades."

"They won't pay." Brian placed his hands palm down on the table.

"They will pay if we get Kris to sell it to them. You don't have to worry Brian, just hand the problem over to her, that's what we pay her for."

I felt we were skirting around the real issue. Brian's pet project 'Merlin' took up most of his productive time and was a drain on resources. It was Brian's baby, the big idea, a super-fast database search engine which revealed hidden trends and correlations buried deep in vast quantities of numbers. The idea was sound but the problem was that the product was never quite finished. It was being trialled by Axiom, a medium sized pharmaceutical company and our biggest client. Brian spent much of his time supporting them and responding to their requests for improvements and bug fixes. The ongoing development was getting bogged down and unless we

48

pushed forward and launched the product properly our competitors would catch up.

We ordered coffee and Brian emptied the last of the wine into his glass. "I didn't think running a business was going to be so hard." He smiled without emotion. "It was OK when it was just the two of us but now we have staff to look after and an office to pay for. It's a big monkey on our backs which we can't shake off and we can't quit."

I wasn't enjoying it much either. The generous pensions and fixed working hours enjoyed by the staff of some of our clients looked very attractive. We fell silent as we drank our coffee. I knew that I needed to say more but I kept putting it off.

"How's Chloe?"

Brian grinned and raised an eyebrow. "Chloe's great." He pushed his chair back onto two legs and drummed the table with his fingers. We were both glad to move on from business figures and, once again, postpone decisions. "Can't get enough of each other, sometimes she's like my shadow. Did I tell you her parents are living in Houston? We're thinking of flying out there for Christmas."

I collected up the accounts and slotted them into my bag, looking down to avoid eye contact. "I broke up with Lucy at the weekend." Brian sat back and kept quiet. "It wasn't working out. Probably my fault, I've been a bit stressed out and hard to live with recently. Partly the business I suppose."

"Is that it then? You've been together for years." Brian knew that, in spite of my off-the-cuff comment, it was a big thing.

"We've been drifting apart for some time. A comfortable relationship isn't enough is it. Needs to be something more than that." I thought of the excitable Chloe, hanging passionately on to Brian's every word, her hair streaming as they accelerated away in his MX5 sports car. Brian seemed lost for words. I looked around, the other lunchtime customers had left and the waiter was polishing glasses. I stood up and hung the satchel from my shoulder "But there's something else I want to talk to you about. Let's take a walk down to the park."

As we ambled down the road, I told Brian everything. Once I got started it all tumbled out. I told him about the meeting with Evans-Peake in the park. The notebooks and the codes they contained. How I kept seeing him but not being sure if I might be imagining it, and finally how I was sure I had seen him at the station. Brian listened in silence. Once in the park we found an isolated bench. Brian was deep in thought. I knew I was making a big deal out of nothing, but he hadn't made light of my story and I was grateful for that.

"And nobody else knows?" he said at last.

I shook my head. "Not even Lucy, and don't ask me why I didn't tell her. Perhaps it proves we weren't ever that close."

Brian wrinkled his nose as if smelling something unpleasant. I knew what was going through his mind. He wasn't sure that Evans-Peake was real either. To save him the pain of having to ask the question, I reached into my satchel and pulled out just one black Moleskine notebook, holding it out for him to take, "I'm not going completely mad."

Brian was silent while he flicked through the pages, looking at the grids of numbers and letters. I waited expectantly. He looked at his watch. "Bugger I nearly forgot, conference call in thirty minutes with the guys at Axiom, better run. Sorry Steve this will have to wait." He jumped up and held up the notebook as he jogged off. "I'll hang on to this."

I had a sudden flash of inspiration and shouted after him. "Brian, I think it could be ASCII code by the way."

He stopped and turned around. "Yea, I'd worked that out. Don't worry Steve, we'll sort it out. We've got Merlin."

He jumped over a small flower bed and onto the path. Then jogged past a stooping park-keeper who stood up stretched his back and watched as Brian made for the exit.

I sat on my own for a while. It was as if the dark night had ended and the ghosts had departed. The storm was over. When you

50

are counting people, one plus one adds up to greater than two, together we were more than a match for Evans-Peake and his bloody code books. I looked around the park, it was beginning to look bare. Something caught my eye just by the base of a tree, mostly hidden in the undergrowth. A familiar looking poster sealed in a clear plastic pocket. I ducked under the low branches and grabbed it. Turning it over I saw that it was one of the posters advertising Evans-Peake's juggling performance. I laughed out loud in relief. I had been worrying about his name, how did I know it was Evans-Peake? Had I just made it up? But there it was in bold black letters, *'Evans-Peake will be performing on the bandstand on Sunday 16th June.'*

I decided to give myself the rest of the afternoon off and walked home, elated and free. However my emotional high would be short lived, the wind was about to change direction once more.

An Optional Computer Lesson

Computers really only handle numbers, so when you need to store some text you have to convert each character to a number. To do this you use the ASCII code, this is a table which gives a two number code for every character you might want to use i.e. letters (lower and upper case), numbers and punctuation marks. For example, the letter 'A' is coded as 41, 'z' is coded as 7A and a space is coded as 20. Normally you don't see any of this when you use a computer to do some word processing, it all happens in the background.

There is a slight additional complication. Our decimal counting system is based on 10 numbers, 0 to 9. Computers use a hexadecimal counting system which is based on 16 numbers so it uses 0 to 9 and also the letters A to F to represent the numbers between 10 and 15. So if you look at ASCII encoded text you will see only the characters 0 to 9 and A to F and you will not see any spaces since the 'space' character itself has a code.

End of lesson

This was our world, familiar and orderly. Now surely it would be a simple matter to translate the messages in the notebooks. I downloaded the ASCII table and picked a random row from the one of the notebooks. It translated to:

Nko%k@prHx7yy

I picked another page and row at random and got similar gobbledegook, a mixture of letters, numbers and characters but no discernible words or patterns. I was sure the assumption that it was ASCII code was correct because each page contained only numbers 0 to 9 and letters A to F, but now it seemed that the text had been double encrypted. I had made solid progress but there was more work to do.

Brian called later that evening. "How did you get on?" I asked trying not to sound too enthusiastic.

"I haven't looked at the code yet Steve, we have a bigger problem." I could tell from his quiet deliberate voice that this was serious. "The conference call was with the head of IT and the head of conformance at Axiom and they are very unhappy with us." Axiom probably accounted for a third of our business. Brian had been developing Merlin with them in mind, if they were unhappy then we would need to address their concerns urgently.

"What's the problem?" In my mind I was already thumbing through various issues we might have glossed over in the past, but nothing too serious.

"Someone's breached our computer network fire-wall, our internal databases are compromised. In short, someone has accessed the Obsidian servers and could have made copies of a load of confidential files."

This was serious, Axiom had provided us with confidential data from their drug safety trials in order to test Merlin. If they had been accessed by someone else, then it was a clear breach of contract.

"Even if was true, how would Axiom know that?" I reasoned, "Surely they don't monitor our server. They couldn't do that, right? Brian, what's going on?"

I heard Brian take a deep breath. "Steve, they know because someone sent them some of their own confidential data in an e-mail. Since we are the only people outside of their organisation who have a copy of this data they say it must have originated with us."

"And that's what they are saying, that it came from Obsidian?"

"That's what they are saying."

"Well perhaps they're wrong. We need more information than that. Come on Brian, there are any number of ways some maverick inside Axiom could have done that. They're just panicking and trying to pin the blame on someone else."

"Well perhaps you're right, let's hope so. I've spent the last four hours looking for a way that someone could get around our firewall. I've run all of the industry tests and it passes every one with flying colours. If there is a problem then I can't find it. In a way, I wish we could find a leak in our IT security because the alternative is going to be much more difficult to handle."

"How do you mean?" I still hadn't accepted that we were to blame.

"If the leak did come from us, and if our IT security is as effective as it appears to be, then the alternative is that one of us deliberately copied some strictly confidential data from our server and sent it to our most important customer in order to discredit Obsidian. So that's you, me or Kris. We are the only ones whose log-in credentials allow us to access the data."

"Not Faith."

"No, definitely not Faith, just the three of us." I heard the soft seductive voice of Chloe cooing in the background. Brian also appeared to hear the Siren call, he lightened his voice. "So anyway don't lose any sleep over it yet, we'll take another look tomorrow."

I wandered into the kitchen to make some coffee. Had we missed something? Had we been too naive, thinking we could pretend we were bigger than we were and work within the demands of big multinational companies? They had well trained IT specialists, and security specialists. They would have the best

54

people on their side, and we just had Brian, and to a lesser extent me. A couple of reasonably bright academics who were muddling through it all. But Brian said he couldn't find anything wrong I reminded myself, that at least was encouraging.

I heard a chime from my phone, I had missed a call while talking to Brian. It was Helen, my one and only sister. As usual she was succinct and to the point. 'Hi Steve, I'm coming to London tomorrow to see a friend. Alright if I make use of your spare bedroom? If you don't call me back, I'll assume it's OK. See you tomorrow, bye'.

I put the phone down. My emotional high following the meeting in the park with Brian hadn't lasted long. I shivered involuntarily. First Evans-Peake, then Lucy and now Axiom.

Chapter 6

I doubt there is anyone in the world more transparently honest than my sister Helen. When she tries to tell even a half-truth, it backfires on her because she hasn't thought it through and so she gets caught out. If Helen was really coming to London to visit a friend, wouldn't she stay with that friend, even if it meant sleeping on the floor? Clearly she had been sent on a mission. I pieced the chain of events together. Lucy calls her parents to say she got back home safely at the weekend and mentions that we had broken up, then probably bursts into tears. Lucy's Mum, Barbara, calls my Mother on some pretext. Did she have the phone number of a long lost mutual friend, or something like that, and by the way had she heard that Lucy and I had broken up after all this time. 'Such a shame, I mean how long have they known each other?' My Mother then phones Helen and explains that she doesn't want to interfere with my love life, however we had been together for such a long time and perhaps Helen might be able to get to the bottom of it. Helen, being a born team player says, 'Right you are Mother I'll see what I can do.'

Our parents were nearly in their forties before I was born, then Helen came along four years later. We grew up in an austere, cold vicarage, always being told to be quiet because one or the other of them was having a nap, or 'forty-winks' as they called it. At meal times table manners were paramount, television was rationed to one hour each evening and reading books or playing board games was applauded so long as the parents were not required to join in. Anything that kept us occupied and out of their way was to be encouraged, running around making lots of noise or an untidy mess was not tolerated under any circumstances. On rare occasions we were allowed to invite a friend to tea, the event had to be well planned in advance, parameters and boundaries defined. Inevitably it was awkward, particularly so when my Father insisted on saying grace at some length before any meal, no matter how small.

Consequently, Helen and I had always been close in spite of the difference in our ages. When we each left home for university we drifted apart, free to make our own lives and encircle our own boundaries. But as our parents had grown older we began to talk to each other again out of concern for them. Should Mum still be driving? Was Dad getting more forgetful? Should we be discussing sheltered accommodation?

I took the phone over to my desk and plugged it into the charger, it would be very good to see Helen. For just a moment I felt the wind in my sails. Here was new found freedom, having broken up with Lucy. I had told Brian about the notebooks and he had been supportive. I had a sister, I had friends, I had work. 'Hang on to those thoughts', I told myself, but I could see a new darkness assembling just at the edge of my vision, Obsidian would probably fold up in the next few weeks. Either we would run out of money or we would be crushed by forces much bigger than we could muster. And then what would I do? Everything we had worked for would be lost. A bead of sweat ran over my cheek, it could have been a tear. I switched on my hi-fi amp and turned the volume up loud, Billie Holiday's tragic voice filled the room:

Good morning, heartache, here we go again
Good morning, heartache, you're the one who knew me when,
Might as well get used to you hangin' around,
Good morning, heartache, sit down.

*****

Helen heard me push my bike into the shed and opened the back door. We hugged. "Sorry sis, crisis in the office, I'm a bit late. You found the hidden key then."

"Isn't there always a crisis in your office?"

"Yes, well this one really is a crisis, but hopefully we are on our way to getting to the bottom of it. If not, it will probably be the death of Obsidian." I dumped my bag on the work surface and filled the kettle. "Anyway you're looking good. How's your friend then?" I saw a moment of confusion pass across her face until she remembered her excuse for visiting.

"Oh must have been some mix up, she wasn't in."

"Really", I spoke with exaggerated surprise. "You came all this way, from the other side of Oxford to London, and your friend wasn't in? Well that is a shame. What a good job that I also live in London and so your journey wasn't entirely wasted."

Helen gave in easily. "OK Stevie, enough. I was never any good at lying. I'm on a mission from Mother."

"And would your mission perchance be anything to do with me and Lucy having broken up?"

"Well you've been together for so long. Admittedly it's been off and on over the years, but it's still a surprise. Barbara says Lucy is pretty upset and you know how Mother gets all worked up about these things. Visions of Grandchildren receding into the distance. Is this really the end?"

I shrugged, "Right now it is the end. Cup of tea?" I didn't want to get into all the emotional stuff just yet.

Helen paged through the local paper whilst I made tea and searched the cupboards for a biscuit. "What do you want to do about eating?" She held up a pizza delivery flyer. "And anyway Stephen with a 'ph', I do have another reason for visiting you as a matter of fact. I have my own little mission as well as Mother's. What do you know about Dil?"

"Dil as in Krishna's Dil? Well let me see. He was born in Nepal but he's lived here since he was ten or eleven I think. He speaks Nepali fluently, but that's about it culture wise. He studied at Reading University whilst living at home and after that I think he worked briefly for a spin-out company. Can't remember what they were called or what they did." Helen sipped her tea and listened attentively. "How did he meet Kris?"

"He went off to find his roots in Nepal, trekking in the Himalayas and living in tea houses up in the mountains. It was his first time away from home, usual story, he goes a bit wild and pretty soon runs out of money. So along comes Krishna trying to shake off her claustrophobic Indian family. Kris has always had her head screwed on and what's more, she had a credit card. She picks Dil up and shakes the dust off him. They team up and do a bit more travelling together and, in a rather old fashioned way, I suppose they fall in love. Then the big Asian family wedding when they get back home, happy ever after, roll the credits. Kris occasionally blows up at Dil and tells him he's a 'bloody Yeti' because he is so disorganised and doesn't plan anything beyond the next ten minutes. But basically they're solid, one of those relationships that thrives on a bit of provocation."

What's Dil doing now?" When she said 'doing' I knew she meant 'how does he make a living?'.

"He's playing drums in a jazz band and probably not making much money at it. I think he occasionally gets some work as a van driver. But essentially he lives off of Kris."

"Does he want a poorly paid part-time job? And when I say poorly paid I actually mean not paid, by the way." Helen continued to flick through the paper.

I blew out through flapping lips. "Hard to tell, he'll usually have a go at anything but he never finds anything that suits him beyond a few months. I wouldn't give him a job. He's bright enough and has a great personality, but he just can't settle. You can't rely on him. That's about it." I picked up my cup of tea and sipped it.

Helen had worked for a charity based in Oxford for the past couple of years. It was quite a big organisation with programmes in several countries and a network of expatriate field workers. The central cause of the charity was education, they provided local schools with teaching materials and training for teachers. Lately they had gone further and set up schools from scratch which they then managed. Helen was based at their head office. She badgered the projects for reports, tidied up the prose, added some poignant photos and passed them back to the sponsors ensuring that the donations continued to flow. Interesting stories were spun out to fill the magazine and provide material for the all-important web site. The job suited her well, she was articulate, well organised and she believed in the cause. Helen had never been motivated by money.

"We have a new initiative to do with migrant workers. Peasant farmers migrate to big towns to find work, often ending up on the streets collecting plastic bags and bottles to sell for recycling. Their children hang around on the streets getting into trouble or being encouraged by their parents to beg. Our plan is to set up schools to specifically cater for these children. We will collect them off the streets, give them a basic education and a nourishing meal at the middle of the day. Unless they learn to read and write they are condemned to repeat the lives of their parents. But if they can be taught literacy and numeracy and we hope some English, then they just might get a muddy bare foot on the bottom rung of the ladder." Helen spoke with intensity, she sat forward. "If you talk to the people who have made it out of poverty they will usually point to education as the thing that made a difference. I think it's a sound idea."

"And where does Dil come in."

"We are going to start in Kathmandu, the capital of Nepal."

I was sceptical about all things to do with Dil. "I can't see what he can contribute."

"I need to set up a network. I need people who know something about Nepal. We have a few people on the ground out there, mostly Nepalis. I need someone here who can understand the language, and help with some translation or at least check translations. For example, Dil might be able to help us with getting permission from the Nepali Education Board to set up our schools. I haven't got it all worked out yet but right now he's the only Nepali I know and I've got to start somewhere."

She sat back in her chair and folded her arms.

"OK" I said cautiously. "What do you want me to do."
60

Helen shrugged, "Well perhaps we could invite him round tonight for a takeaway and a chat. Unless you feel like cooking?"

"A takeaway will be fine", I said without hesitation. "But not pizza", I balled the pizza flyer and threw it in the general direction of the bin. "There's a new Thai restaurant which does takeaways that I want to try, I picked up a menu when I was passing. I'll give Dil and Kris a call to see if they are free tonight."

Helen relocated, sinking into the sofa in the front room. I joined her hoping she might have been distracted from her primary mission.

"Anyway enough of that Steve. I want to know all about what's been going on between you and Lucy."

*****

I opened the front door. Kris and Dil were huddled under the small porch to escape the drizzle. As usual Kris was dressed immaculately, Dil had also made an effort, wearing a loose white shirt under a waterproof jacket and black brush denim trousers. He was immediately at ease, kissing Helen on both cheeks and accepted my offer of a beer.

Guessing that we would all be hungry I passed the takeaway menu around. Without looking at it I went for my usual Thai green curry which everyone else described as being boring. I opened a couple of bottles of wine. Kris and Dil occupied the sofa, she sitting sideways with her legs in his lap. After a while conversation died down, everyone knowing there was an agenda but nobody knowing where or when to start. For some obscure reason Helen remembered back to the comments I had made about the future of Obsidian when she had arrived. "Well here's to good old Obsidian and may she survive the latest crisis, whatever it is." I looked at Helen and very slightly shook my head but it was too late, Kris had smelt something. "Crisis Steve? I know things aren't great but I didn't think it had reached crisis point." She smiled sweetly but I could tell that her short fuse was burning fast. "It's nothing, dismissively, "Well, it's not nothing, but it's not the end of the world. There's an issue with some of the Axiom data, Brian is on to it."

"Well I'm trying to get more business out of them, so if there is anything, let me know because I don't want to walk into a hornet's nest when I contact them next week."

"Don't worry Kris, we'll talk about it tomorrow. Honestly it will be fine. We don't want to spend the evening talking business." I was glad to hear the doorbell ring and I jumped up to get the takeaway.

When we had finished eating I stacked up the empty silver foil tubs and put them straight in the bin outside the back door, thinking that my thrifty mother would have washed them out and used them to pack things in the freezer. Helen and Dil moved to the comfy chairs. Helen sat forward, explaining, and Dil listening, relaxed, hands clasped behind his head with a great smile on his round face. This is always the way it goes, I thought, he seduces everyone at the beginning but after three months it's a very different story.

Kris followed me into the kitchen as I shovelled several piled spoons of Columbian coffee into the cafetiere. She leant against the fridge, arms folded, watching me. "So what's up then? What's all this talk of crisis which Helen seems to know about and I'm just hearing for the first time."

"Helen doesn't know anything Kris. I just told her that there was a crisis because I was late home and she had been waiting, that's all."

"So there isn't a problem?"

I slammed the door of the fridge and turned to face her. "Yes, there is a problem but it's not a crisis, and yes we do need to discuss it tomorrow. In a nutshell, some of the data from Sigma project at Axiom has leaked out and they are trying to pin the blame on us."

Kris jumped on it. "And that isn't a crisis? Shit, you know what this will mean if it's true Steve. Why haven't you told me?"

we only just heard about it a few hours ago. Brian has been checking security on our servers ever since."

"And?"

"And it's all fine. It's probably not us at all." I tried to smile reassuringly.

"And before you say it, yes I am probably a very poor communicator and I should have said something."

I gave Kris four mugs and we took the coffee through to join Helen and Dil. Kris, sank back into the sofa massaging her temples with her fingers, lips tightly shut.

Chapter 7

The following day, Wednesday, Brian, Kris and I were in the office early. We sat around the table in our small meeting room, separated from the main office by a glass partition. Brian had printed out several copies of the e-mails he had exchanged with various people at Axiom. I rubbed my forehead with the palm of my hand as I read them. Axiom had the upper hand and we were on the defensive. I reminded myself that we had to keep calm and work through the issues methodically. We shouldn't snap back before we knew all the facts. The data had not been intentionally compromised and we were not negligent, we had to keep that in the back of our minds. I could see that Kris was up for a confrontation, she sat bolt upright with folded arms on the table. Brian slouched in his chair flicking through the pages of his notebook. I thought I had better set the scene.

"For Kris' benefit, this is the situation so far. Brian was asked to join in a teleconference with some of the key Axiom people yesterday afternoon, namely James Grey their IT security bod, Simon Bron their compliance officer and Edith."

"Edith Summers", Kris jumped in. "She's the group leader and a key figure as far as I am concerned. I'm having lunch with her later in the week. At least I was until this all blew up."

I continued, "As far as we know, they are the only ones on the Axiom side who know about it so we don't think it's gone too high up in their organisation yet. We need to contain the problem before they start to wheel in their big guns."

"I still don't know what the problem is", Kris looked at Brian accusingly and tapped her pen on the table top.

Brian swallowed a mouthful of coffee and wiped the back of his hand across his mouth. "As you both know, 'Sigma' is the project name for Axiom's new block-buster drug, which they believe will halt the progress of Parkinson's disease, if not reverse it. At present they are still running toxicology tests on animals, which they outsource incidentally, but soon it will reach the clinical trials stage. Once they have that data and assuming it is positive, they will have to get it past the American Food and Drug Administration before they can market it. Sigma looks very promising, it could be the holy grail." Brian looked around as if expecting a question but he was telling us things we already knew. "So what can go wrong?" Brian stood up and began writing some headings on the white board.

The door opened and Faith's head appeared, as if trying to squeeze through the gap. "Sorry, Kris it's Dil. He's on the phone and says he needs to speak to you, only needs ten seconds." She indicated something small with her thumb and forefinger. "I tried to tell him that you were all in a meeting but he says it really is urgent. He says he's tried your mobile but…".

Kris looked up at the ceiling. "Sorry guys, won't be a minute." She followed Faith out and snatched up her desk phone handset. Brian filled up a plastic cup from the water cooler. We watched Kris through the glass partition in silence. She stabbed the air with her pen, she hunched her shoulder's and shook her head, we could just hear her saying, "So why is it my problem?" Clearly Dil wasn't getting much of a look in on the conversation, but I knew that his 'little boy lost' routine would produce results in the end. He would plead from an apparent position of weakness and throw himself on her mercy. As I stood there I thought to myself, 'I love you Kris. I love your energy, I love your anger, I love your unpredictability, I love your passion, your fire. You are just everything that Lucy is not.' Kris slammed the phone down and fished around in her bag. Having found what she was looking for, she gave it to Faith and spoke a few words to her before returning to the meeting room.

"Sorry about that." She sat down at the table.

"Everything alright?" I asked cautiously, knowing that it was not.

"Unbelievable. He's lost his keys. No idea where they are or when he last had them." She smiled, having already begun to calm down. "That boy is such a dreamer at times. We hide a spare key but that's not there either, which probably means that he has lost that one as well. And he's got Martin from the band sat outside on double yellows with a van waiting to pick up his drums. I've given my keys to Faith and he's coming round to pick them up in about ten minutes." She sat up, back straight. Somehow that little diversion had released some of our pent-up steam. Life goes on, people lose keys, companies lose data. We were not discussing the end of the world, we were not even discussing the end of Obsidian.

Brian tapped the white board with a marker pen. "So, what might go wrong with the Sigma project? What might make poor Edith Summers lose sleep? Well it might fail the clinical trials, possibly due to side effects or simply that it works on mice but is not effective on humans. Further down the line, it may fail to get Food and Drug Administration approval," he wrote FDA on the board. "All the relevant primary experimental data from all of the testing; animal trials, clinical trials and so on, which incidentally includes the data we have, has to be evaluated and kept securely in a data safe, so that nobody can alter it. This is the primary evidence that the drug works and doesn't have dreadful side effects. If you fail to get FDA approval then you're not going to be able to sell the drug. And finally," Brian drew a line around the final point, "the competition may get access to Axiom's experimental data and be able to take a short cut and come out with a similar drug before or soon after Axiom launch theirs. In theory Axiom have it all tied down with patents, but a competitor can easy make a small modification to the formulation to get around the patent and it becomes a free for all. They will prefer to keep everything secret. And that, in their minds, is where we come in and where we may have let them down."

Brian sat down and I took over. "As I hope we all know, we have a non-disclosure agreement with Axiom which allows them to give us access to their data on the strict basis that we don't give it to anyone else or divulge its contents to a third party, all standard stuff that makes the lawyers rich. There's a signed paper copy of it in the box file behind Faith's desk and an electronic copy on the server."

Kris was anxious to chip in. "And someone has e-mailed Axiom's data to someone in their own organisation and they are thinking, where the hell has that come from. So why do they think it is coming from us? And what are we doing about it?"

Brian responded. "Last night I moved all of their data off of the main company server to our old server that's sitting on the floor by my desk, the one we replaced a couple of months ago. Unlike our main server, the old server is not connected to the outside world, there is no way anyone can get to it unless they physically break into this office and even then they would have to know the password."

"And what about backups," I asked.

"Yes, the data is also on the backup tapes which you can find in the famous box of tapes under my bed. But once again they would have to break into my flat and have the foresight to look under my bed. Of course moving the data doesn't fix the problem because the horse has already bolted, but at least we know the leaky tap is turned off for the time being, if indeed the problem is with us, which we are not accepting."

"So the problem is either someone in Axiom or one of us." I concluded.

"Yes, that's what they are saying, and they think that their internal security is so tight that the finger points at us. It's the normal knee-jerk reaction, everyone trying to protect their own back. But they are much bigger than us so when they jerk a knee, we get a good kicking."

I could see that Kris was much more relaxed now that she knew as much as we did. She leant back, chewing her pen. "Well just a minute, didn't you say earlier that they had contracted out the toxicology tests? Probably to that animal testing lab in Slough." She spread her hands, "so they must also have some of the data, after all they will be creating lots of data from the animal tests."

Brian was sceptical, "They wouldn't have access to the data we have but I agree it's worth asking the question."

Kris reinforced her point. "In theory they may not have had access but if they had access at some limited level then they are already on the inside. Surely they must be on the list of potential leaks."

Brian nodded in agreement and scribbled a note. I picked up the e-mail printouts and paged through them. "Well the obvious question is, where is the e-mail that was sent with the data attached? If we have that, then we will know who sent it. I can't find it here."

"No they won't send me that e-mail until they have done some more internal investigation." Brian held up the printouts. "These are the e-mails I have exchanged with them recently, trying to assure them that we are taking it seriously."

Kris jumped in again. "Then what's all the fuss about? Either they show us the evidence or they shut up about it. Meeting over. I suggest we wait until we have some facts to go on." She very deliberately pushed her chair back from the table.

"Hold on, just before we finish," I said, "I want to clarify something that you said to me yesterday, Brian. If the leak has come from inside Obsidian, then it has to have come from one of us three, right? Or I suppose it could be someone who has broken into our server and is masquerading as one of us."

"Breaking in would be very hard to do. We have our own little data-safe, it's a special locked down folder on the server. Access is strictly restricted to us three."

"And who can change that?", I asked.

"I would normally do that, and in case I get run over by the apocryphal bus you can also Steve, but not Kris." Brian looked around for approval.

68

We all stood up, I gathered the empty coffee mugs to take them down to the kitchen. As we filed out of the room Brian said, "I'm going to talk to their IT security chap, James Grey, later on today. I can give them temporary access to our network if necessary and they can take a look at our IT security, see if they can find any holes. I'll keep you both posted."

Kris waved in his general direction. "Thanks Brian, I'm off to Oxford. Let's hope the M40 is kind to me." She delved inside her bag, then in the little zipped compartment on the outside. She felt her pockets. Then looking up at Faith, hand over her wide open mouth, "Car keys. Has Dil taken my keys yet? I left the car key on the ring with the house keys, bugger."

Faith shook her head slowly. "The Good Lord giveth and the Good Lord taketh away. But in this case she giveth the house key but not the car key. Blessed be the name of the Lord." She opened her desk drawer and held up a solitary key. "So now you owe me a grande latte and double chocolate chip muffin at that new coffee shop on the corner next time we feel like a good old natter."

Kris took the key, "I'll love you forever Faith." Her heels clattered down the stairs and she was gone.

I looked at Brian. "When's the call with Axiom?"

"Oh, around three. Until then it's back to Merlin." Brian sat down at his desk and adjusted the angle of his computer screen.

I plonked myself down in my chair. Was this the beginning of the end for us? Would Obsidian fall prey to Axiom, or would we just screw it all up ourselves by not staying on top of the important stuff like the accounts. I tried to settle my mind but Evans-Peake and the contents of the little stack of black notebooks took up an unwelcome residence. Thinking about the encounter at Marylebone, I was quite sure that he had deliberately tried to contact me again, his gestures through the taxi window seemed to indicate some urgency. But I didn't know what was required of me except that it had something to do with the notebooks. Since telling everything to Brian, other events had taken over, we had bigger fish frying and I didn't expect Brian to give my little problem any time.

One obvious solution would be to run the codes in the notebooks through Merlin. The purpose of Merlin was to find hidden patterns or correlations in data. Letters could just as easily be data as well as numbers, so if there was a meaning to the codes then Merlin ought to be able to find it, or at least point us in the right direction. I needed Brian to help me, Merlin was his baby but I couldn't ask him just now.

It was lunch time, I told Faith I was popping out for an hour or so and rode my bike home. My fridge was almost empty, a sliver of brie, some salami and a couple of cherry tomatoes was all that was still edible. I buttered a soft white roll, piled it all on a plate, and took it through to my desk, grabbing a banana as I went.

I thought back to the image of Evans-Peake, holding up the sheet of paper with 1712 written on it as he left Marylebone station in the taxi. He had mouthed something and pointed at me. 'Do not give up'. There was no 'please' it was an imperative, a command and a jabbing finger. He had continued to stare at me until the taxi was out of sight. Evans-Peake was telling me that he was not satisfied with my progress. He was not happy at all. 'For my sake' had a scent of desperation about it. For some reason the meaning of the codes was very important to him, but he couldn't decipher them. Then one day he is thumbing through the local paper and he sees an article about some clever chaps who have just won an award for solving puzzles and he thinks to himself, that's similar to my problem, I'll use them. So he proceeds to cut my picture out of the article and puts it in a little silver locket and starts the convoluted little game, leading me by the nose.

Was it just fortune that I happened to have my photo in the newspaper when Evans-Peake was looking for someone to solve his puzzle. My Dad would have said it was all part of a divine plan for my life and that the Lord moves in mysterious ways. Or do I make my own fortune?

Lunchtime over, I pedalled slowly back to work. Autumn winds were blowing the leaves across the road. Rounding the corner, I rode alongside the park, the wind now head-on, I changed down a couple of gears and stood on the pedals. My eyes began to water in the wind and I wiped them with the back of my hand. These are strange events, I thought. I'm caught up in something or someone that won't let go of me. Whichever way I turn or dodge he finds me. I had confided in Brian but now he had no time to help me out, I was alone again. I wouldn't tell him about the message on the scrap of paper, it wouldn't be fair to make demands on his time. The Axiom data problem needed his full attention. I thought about Lucy.

I thought about Lucy.

Brian paced up and down in the little meeting room. "I spoke to Simon at Axiom, off the record. I had to push him quite hard for an answer so we must keep it strictly between ourselves, but they are quite sure." Brian took a deep breath and rubbed his cheeks with his hands. I could tell that he had something difficult to say. "They are quite sure that the data was sent from our server and that it came from Kris; *Krishna.Chandrakar@Obsidian.com*." Brian sat down, put the flats of his hands on the table top and shut his lips tightly.

"It can't be Kris," She's as loyal as they come."

"I agree with you", Brian said. "But nevertheless, it is her. At least it definitely came from her e-mail account. Unless of course somebody else had access to it."

I nibbled my thumb nail while I thought. "What should we do? Shut her account down until we've sorted it out?"

Brian shrugged, "I've taken all the Axiom data offline so she can't do any more damage. If we shut her down she is going to want to know why and we don't want her asking questions just now. I suggest we sit on it for a few hours, I'll monitor her e-mails and we can talk about it again tomorrow."

Brian was right, we needed to avoid a hasty reaction. It was in our nature to take time, to consider, to test, to evaluate and sometimes to procrastinate. Dealing with evidence was familiar territory for us but dealing with staff was not our strong suit, and we knew it. "She's coming in tomorrow for a meeting with the graphics guys at Pangolin down below, they're designing a new brochure for us, so she'll be around if we need to talk to her."

We returned to our desks in silence. I carried on with some research on the internet, but struggled to maintain concentration. At the back of my mind a voice was saying, "If you think today was tough, you wait for tomorrow." But then Lucy always criticised me for being a 'glass half empty' type.

Chapter 8

I arrived at the office feeling woolly, my head throbbing. I brewed a strong cup of coffee in the kitchen and took a couple of pain killers. Seated at my desk, waiting for them to kick in, I read a report I had prepared for one of our cosmetic customers on the efficacy of a new hair shampoo formulation. Having read the same page three times, I switched to browsing specialist bike dealers on the internet. I picked up my mug and clumsily banged it against the corner of my computer screen, splashing coffee on my desk, from where it dripped down into my lap. I jumped up, reaching for a box of tissues. "They were due to go in the wash anyway," Faith watched with amusement. "Just don't tell me what the Good Lord has to say about it. I'm not in the mood."

"How would I know what the Good Lord has to say?", she replied. "According to my Mother and the rest of the congregation at the Gospel Hall, I am a back slider, an outcast." Her voice rose to a quivering crescendo. "I have seen the promised land but settled for the fleshpots of iniquity. But it will all be right in the end because they are praying for me. So I'm not worrying about it." She put her hands together and looked up to the ceiling.

"Well at least you don't have a Church of England vicar for a Father. A retired man of the cloth. I think I'm probably a big disappointment to him, on the spiritual side anyway. What happened to unconditional love Faith? Sign me up for the fleshpots anyway, sounds like my kind of place." I dropped the sodden tissues in the wastepaper bin. "Where's Brian?"

"He phoned earlier this morning and said he wouldn't be in until the afternoon. He's helping Chloe move. You can call him on his mobile."

Today of all days. Obsidian was at crisis point and Brian decides to help his girlfriend move. "And Kris?"

"She's in. Gone downstairs to see the Marx Brothers, then I think she's off to see someone in Surrey University."

'The Marx brothers' was our pet name for Pangolin, the graphic designers who occupied the office below. We tended to leave dealings with them to Kris as she was the only one who could fully understand them, everything was 'sweet' or 'sick'. From my point of view, you could never pin them down to the three essentials of a transaction; what are you going to do? How much is it going to cost? And when will it be done by?

I called Brian's mobile phone and got his voice mail. I banged the phone down without leaving a message then picked it up again and tried his home phone number on impulse. The phone rang, normally I hang up after six rings. An unaccented female voice answered on five. "Hello, Brian Calver's phone." For a moment I was perplexed, then it all fell into place.

"Chloe?"

"Yes Chloe Defrey speaking, who's calling?"

"It's Steve, is Brian there?" I wasn't in the mood to chat.

"Steve?"

"Steve Rockett, Brian's business partner, you remember we met at the pub once."

"Oh hi Steve, he's just unloading some stuff from the van. Can I get him to give you a call back in a couple of minutes?"

What choice did I have? I said that would be fine and hung up. Now it made sense, Chloe was moving in with Brian. This was a first, she must have really got under his skin. I caught Faith's eye as I went down to the kitchen for a refill of coffee. She raised a knowing eye-brow. My mobile phone rang ten minutes later. Brian sounded a little breathless, "Sorry Steve, I was just outside with the van."

"Has she got much stuff?"

He laughed. "You mean Chloe? No not too much but I couldn't fit it in my two-seater, it's not designed for moving house. It's mostly clothes and a few knick-knacks. She was renting a furnished place so there's no big stuff to shift. Anyway what's up?"

I wanted to tell him that he really should be in the office today of all days in view of the current crisis, but I didn't want to sound as if I was panicking or that I couldn't handle the situation. "I just wondered if there was any news that's all," I said rather lamely.

"No no, I don't expect to hear from them until the afternoon. They were having an internal meeting this morning. Have you seen Kris?"

"She's downstairs with the Marx brothers and then, according to Faith, she's off to Surrey University."

Brian was clearly wanting to get on, but he sounded surprisingly relaxed. "Look I'll be in this afternoon, we're almost done here but the van's on a double yellow. I'll see you later. Is that OK?" I said that was fine and hung up.

The door to the office was pushed open by a dainty foot clad in sandals with thin sparkly straps. Kris balanced a mug of coffee, her laptop and a sheaf of papers. She glanced in my direction, "Hi Steve." Having put everything down on her desk she went to talk to Faith, pulling up a spare chair. "Expenses," I heard her say with a sigh. Kris was her usual animated self, tapping the receipts, waving a hand dismissively, turning to look Faith in the eye for acknowledgement. Faith patiently took each item one by one, occasionally scribbling a note on the back. I just couldn't believe that Kris, of all people, had betrayed us. What would be her

74

motive? How did she expect to get away with it? But then people who were good at deceit were very plausible.

Merry Mick, our depressed accountant, visited us once a quarter to check up on the books and prepare the formal accounts for auditing. We weren't the most organised company in the world but we did a reasonable job. The accounts were always in order and tax taken care of, we wouldn't knowingly deceive. At least that's what I thought, but clearly there was something going on.

Kris came over to my desk and spread out some sketches for a new brochure. She stood, bent over, pointing, "This is what we have so far from Pangolin downstairs as a general look for all of our promotional literature. I'm going to need you to give me a few paragraphs on the applications of Merlin or some success stories, she indicated a couple of empty rectangles. Under her breath she said, 'I'll never get anything out of Brian." She reached for a chair and sat down. "What's the news?"

"Nothing to report," I lied. "Axiom are having a meeting this morning and Brian is going to talk to them again this afternoon. He's gone off to help Chloe move." I paused, raised my eyebrows and shrugged. "We may know more later."

"You know what I think we should do don't you?" Kris paused and looked straight into my eyes, her make-up perfect and her eyes liquid dark chocolate. "I think we should get in a car this afternoon and drive over there and talk to them face to face. They're only in the Granta Science Park, it's this side of Cambridge, an hour and a half drive max. That's what I would do."

I shook my head. "You can't just turn up."

She interrupted. "Of course you can, and if they're busy, then we wait. They're not going to turn you away Steve, not if this is as important as they say it is. Sometimes you've just got to grow a pair of balls."

"I thought you were going off to Surrey?"

"Then you and Brian should go without me. You're the company directors anyway, in many ways it's better that I stay out of it. Brian should be here now." She pressed her forefinger onto my desk. "Moving Chloe's stuff could surely have waited."

I sighed and nodded my head slowly. I agreed with her in principle but putting it to Brian might not be so easy. I knew I would cop out.

"I'll leave it with you, as you say, I'm off to Surrey to talk to Professor Newell in biological sciences, they've just got a big grant for a research programme, which means they have a pot of money to spend. Wish me luck." She gathered up the art work and piled it on her desk. "Faith have we got any give-away mugs left?"

"I think we do have a couple", Faith swivelled around on her chair and rummaged in a low cupboard. She stretched up again triumphantly holding a presentation box in each hand. "The last two."

Kris managed to cram them into her shoulder bag. "Thanks, would you order up another hundred please." She turned back to her desk checking she hadn't forgotten anything. I thought back to the meeting in the restaurant and I was about to ask if we really do need to order a hundred mugs but I was too slow. She snatched up her car keys. "Bye Steve, give me a call later." I nodded to her departing figure, the door slammed shut and Kris had gone.

Peace descended on the office until Brian arrived at three. "Afternoon one and all."

Faith looked up. "You're sounding pleased with yourself. Has Chloe been moved?"

"Yes, she has Faith. She has been moved in every possible sense of that word. Lots of clothes though, do you know anybody who wants to sell a wardrobe or a chest of drawers?" He didn't wait for an answer.

"How's it going with the lustrous hair project Steve?"

I shrugged trying to sound a bit weary and a bit miffed. I had been working hard to bring in some cash and we were in the middle of the biggest crisis ever to hit Obsidian, yet Brian takes the morning and half the afternoon off. Then he breezes in mid-afternoon, greeting everybody as if all was well in the world. But

76

Brian was not to be subdued, he pulled his laptop and some papers out of his bag and put them on his desk. Then he turned back to Faith.

"Why do women have so many clothes and why do they have so many cosmetics? Shampoos, conditioner, face cream, eye-liner, lip stick, mousses, gels." He counted them off on his fingers.

Faith accepted the challenge. "It's so that we can attract a mate and have beautiful children thereby fulfilling our destiny."

"Are you really that shallow?"

She looked over her spectacles. "It's not us who are shallow Brian. All we have to do it slap on a coat of war paint and before you know where you are, some male sucker comes along like a bee to the honey pot. That's what shallow is. Just in it for the honey."

Brian called across to me. "Found yourself a new honey pot yet Steve?"

I ignored him and clicked my mouse on the 'send' button with a flourish. "Right that will do. Enough of hair products to last me a life time." I stood up and stretched. "Faith, you can now send them the outstanding invoice."

"I'll send it out this afternoon. I guess you know but we haven't invoiced anything yet this month guys and we're nearly half way through." She looked from me to Brian. There were so many issues all of a sudden to deal with, I felt them pulling at my clothing, like children urging me to come this way or that. We needed to get the business under control or we were in danger of not being able to pay our staff. But unless we got to grips with the data loss issue then Obsidian might cease to exist. My personal life wasn't much easier. I was missing the familiar company of Lucy, someone to watch a film on the telly with a Chinese takeaway on our laps in the evening. When I was with her I didn't have to make conversation, just being together was OK. Looming over it all was the threatening figure of Evans-Peake and the notebooks. He demanded my attention and I couldn't shake him off. My usual strategy of burying my head in numbers would not be good enough now. Having confided in Brian and shared my problems, he was distracted by other things, chiefly Chloe it seemed right now. I felt the loneliness, I was on my own once again.

I gave Brian time to open up his laptop and log-on to the server then, raising my eye-brows, I asked him if there was any news from Axiom.

"Yes, I spoke to them earlier. It's all fine, panic over." He looked up and smiled with an air of finality.

I couldn't believe what I was hearing. All that angst, all that worry and capping it all, the suspicion that Kris was trying to sabotage our company. All of that could be dismissed by five little words. "It's all fine, panic over."

"Cup of tea?" Brian raised his usual mug and I nodded.

The kitchen was empty. We sat on bar stools by the counter, waiting for the kettle to boil. Brian splayed his fingers out and placed them flat on the surface. "So, Edith Summers, the group leader, called me just after lunch. She was very apologetic but they have discovered where the problem lies and it's nothing to do with us. Their IT people are still looking into it but they have at least ruled us out. Edith said that Kris had e-mailed a large response to a tender to them recently and they think this is where the confusion lies. But as far as she is concerned Obsidian is off the hook. It's business as usual." Brian pouted his lips. "You never know we may even get a few extra sympathy points when it comes to the tender that Kris is working on."

"Good job we didn't mention it to Kris, we would still be scraping her off the ceiling. Still I suppose it's good news isn't it. As you say, panic over."

Brian fetched the kettle and poured boiling water over our tea-bags. I massaged my tea-bag with the back of a teaspoon. We both knew we weren't quite out of the woods yet. There were things unsaid.

"On the other hand, it could be a damage limitation exercise."

"Exactly," Brian nodded slowly. "Axiom may have decided to just cover it all up and pretend it had never happened. The consequences of having lost data would reflect on them, even if it

78

wasn't their fault. It could affect all of the projects in their pipeline. So they might decide to tighten up their procedures and continue as if nothing had ever happened and hopefully nobody external to Axiom would ever find out."

"So that scenario doesn't let Kris off the hook does it?"

Brian sipped his tea and looked at me over the rim of his mug.

"As you say Stephen with that all important 'ph'. It doesn't let Kris off the hook."

I shut my laptop in a desk drawer as I left the office, determined not to do any work that evening. Coasting slowly down a slight incline with one hand on the handle bars, I enjoyed the satisfying clicking of the free-wheeling gears. As I rounded the corner to ride alongside the park the rear wheel started to bump on the smooth tar-mac. I dismounted and unclipped my helmet, hanging it on the handle bars. I had a puncture repair kit with me but I was close to home and didn't fancy fixing it on the road, knowing I would get grease all over my clothes. I settled down to pushing. In truth the bike was so light it seemed to roll along under its own power. We were like a couple of friends walking side by side.

The park was empty except for the occasional person making a purposeful diagonal short cut across it. I kept my head down fixing my sight on the pavement a short distance in front of my feet, somehow conscious of being vulnerable and encumbered by the bike. Nina Simone's strained and urgent voice sounded in my head.

'I put a spell on you, because you're mine.'

Occasionally I glimpsed the gloomy park through a gap in the trees. Thirty yards to go before I reached the corner. Now twenty, I started to count my steps under my breath. Now fifteen steps to go and then I would reach the entrance at the corner and I could turn away from the park. There was a lull in the traffic, I was alone. Something brightly coloured caught my eye. I stopped and turned, better to know your demons even if they are fictitious. A path stretched in to the interior of the park, ending at the band stand in the centre. Clearly visible on the raised platform was a bright orange mountaineering tent, it's guy ropes stretched out and anchored under bricks. The entrance was zipped up and in the setting evening sun, I could see that there was a faint cosy light inside. A figure moved around, at times blocking the light and casting a shadow on the tent wall. Just outside the entrance was the rucksack that Evans-Peake had been wearing at the station.

I felt confident of my escape route so I stood for a few seconds, shivering in the evening air. The shadow shifted towards the entrance. The zip was being slowly opened by an unseen hand inside the tent and the door flap fell inside the tent, leaving the entrance wide open. I waited for someone to emerge but the shape inside was still, he was also waiting. Waiting for what? Then I realised with a chill that he wasn't going to emerge, this was an invitation to me to go in. The figure shifted towards the entrance, I saw a hand appear and I turned away, pushing my bike across the road to a side road leading away from the park. A bright flash caught the corner of my eye and I stopped to look back. The tent was burning, flames flickered above a cushion of smoke. It burnt too fiercely, even from a distance I could smell petrol, soon there would be nothing left. Dropping my bike, running back I entered the park, there was nobody else around. A few scorched poles lay in a pile, there was nothing else, the rucksack had gone. I imagined a rustle in the trees and a shadow on the grass. I was quite sure that there had been someone in the tent, and I was quite sure that I was being watched now. Steady, be steady, don't rush. Don't let him see you are scared. A car came around the corner, dazzling me with its lights. I picked up my bike and continued up the side road not daring to look around. I arrived home breathless and shaking, finally looking over my shoulder to check I wasn't being followed, half expecting to see someone rounding the corner at the bottom of my road. I locked the bike away in the shed and let myself in the back door. Having locked the back door and drawn the bolts, I went around the house closing the curtains and switching all of the lights on. Would this never end? Would he never give up? I knew the

80

answer, crack the code and then you can have some peace. But to do that I needed Brian.

My hands shook as I busied myself unwrapping a frozen pie and shoving it in the microwave. Gulping a tumbler of wine, I once again checked that all of the doors were locked and the curtains drawn. The phone in my pocket buzzed, a welcomed call, "Hi little sis,"

"How's things Stevie."

I topped up my wine and tried to get my breathing under control. "Up and down to be honest. Work has been a bit stressful, hopefully it's sorted now. I think I told you we had some problems." I paused, uncertain. "Except that now I've started to see things." As soon as I had said it I regretted it.

"What sort of things?"

"Well a tent in the park most recently." I added a short chuckle, trying to say that it wasn't a big deal. But it was.

"And what makes you think the tent wasn't really there?" I had no answer to that, except to say that it was there. "Is this something to do with breaking up with Lucy?"

I felt my throat choking and my eyes began to fill so I continued to stay silent.

"Steve, are you OK?"

"Yes, just stressed that's all." My voice cracked.

"Look Steve I know you don't handle stress well and you sound a bit up-tight but I'm afraid I'm going to have to load something else on to you." Helen paused waiting for me to react. "Dad's had a stroke, he's paralysed down one side. He's in hospital. Mum's beside herself." Her short sentences conveyed urgency. "It's bad Steve, I'm going down this evening. I think you need to come too, sorry."

A strange and inappropriate shiver of elation went through my body. Helen had just played a trump card, this was something more important than Obsidian or Axiom, more crucial than dealing with Kris, more demanding than my relationship with Lucy. Something that would take me away from that park, the code books and

Evans-Peake. Just one thing of overriding importance to think about that let me off the hook with everything else. Someone else would have to carry the load, to make the decisions, to enforce the budget. "Steve's out of the picture for a few days, his Dad's very ill" they would say. And I know I should have felt deep concern for both my parents but just then all I felt was profound and irrational relief.

"Steve are you still there?"

"Is he going to…" I couldn't finish the sentence.

''I don't know, I can't get any sense out of Mum. It's not good. Give me a call when you are on your way, I can pick you up from the station in Dad's car. There's something else I need to talk to you about but it can wait 'til tomorrow."

"If it's about me getting together with Lucy again then…."

Helen interrupted. "No, nothing to do with Lucy."

"Then who?"

"Dil"

"What's he been up to then?"

"Don't worry we can discuss it over the weekend, it's not urgent. I'll see you later."

Chapter 9

Train rides remind me of trips to the seaside when I was four or five and Helen was a baby. I remember the colours, a green wind-break, a blue and yellow beach ball, a red rubber ring with white stars on it, my favourite green striped swimming trunks. I remember jumping up and down in excitement while my mother struggled to pull my T-shirt off over my head, then running across the sand, first loose and easy to trip then hard and wet, the soles of my feet slapping through the shallow puddles. Running into the sea, galloping over the rippling waves up to my knees and back out again, triumphant and brave, not noticing the cold. Mum would occasionally come in for a paddle or would dangle Helens feet in the water to shrieks of excitement. Father settled down in his deck chair in the lee of the wind break, fighting to control his broadsheet newspaper. I don't ever remember him joining in the fun.

After retirement, Dad bought a small touring caravan and spent weeks painting it and generally doing it up, but they never used it because the beds were uncomfortable. It sat beside the house, gradually decaying back to its former disorderly state.

The train gathered speed, escaping the gravitational pull of London's suburbia. I stared out of the window, listening to Billie Holiday on my MP3 player, there was nothing else on the play list.

I thought about all the hours Helen and I had sat on hard bare wood pews listening to sermons, twice every Sunday. Our family was isolated, self-contained, different. I was 'the Vicar's kid', supposed to have higher standards than the rest of the community, standards which took much of the fun out of my childhood. There was no passion for life, just plodding routine and ritual in the hope that the tortoise would one day win, but wouldn't you rather throw everything to the capricious wind and run with the hare? My

Father's tall gaunt figure loomed over my life, looking down on me with an air of disappointment. I had settled for engineering and rejected the church, the upper-second class degree from Imperial College followed by a doctorate came a poor runner up. Mother said he was secretly proud of me and told everyone how well I was doing, but he never told me that, and I had needed to know.

There was nobody sitting opposite me so I slouched down in my seat and stretched my legs out under the table. Closing my eyes, I allowed myself to be rocked to sleep by the motion of the train. The bustle of the guard checking tickets woke me. Looking out of the window I saw the familiar flat Somerset Levels, rich green pastures criss-crossed by brimming drainage ditches.

Helen was waiting on the platform, we hugged, she hung on to me tightly. I heard her swallow and sniff, trying to hold back the tears. She wiped her sleeve across her eyes. Dad's old Peugeot was parked close by. I waited until she had negotiated her way out of the station complex before asking any questions.

"How is Mum doing?"

"Not well. Very weepy and bewildered. Finding it hard to make decisions. She will learn to cope but at the moment she has been knocked sideways, this state is not for ever. People from the church have been nice, phoning up to see if there is anything that they can do and of course remembering him in their prayers."

"That'll fix it then."

"It's their way of showing that they care, if you think it's about making Dad better then you're missing the point. Why must you be so bloody cynical all the time. Christ Steve", she banged the steering wheel with the heel of her hand and pulled over, two wheels bumped up onto the pavement, stalling the engine. Her head fell forward, tears streaming down her face, barely audible words bubbling up her throat. "He may never recognise us again, he may die. What do I do Steve? What do I do." I reached into my pockets for a handkerchief or a tissue. I had nothing to offer."

We walked through seemingly endless corridors following signs to 'All Wards' and then to 'Quantock Ward.' When we arrived Dad was asleep. Mum stayed seated at his side as I stooped to kiss her on the cheek. Helen found a couple more chairs, I sat and took his hand in my own. We were all silent, listening to his laboured breathing, watching his chest rise and fall and his cheeks suck in and out. He looked old and vulnerable. White hair uncombed, bushy eye-browns at rest over closed eyes, his face was translucent skin stretched over sharply contoured bones. I looked across the bed at Mum.

"How was your journey Stephen?" She was trying to be normal.

I dismissed the remark with a shrug. We didn't know what to say to each other. Just as the four of us, who had spent much of our time together when we were children, so now, as we were gathered together again at the other end of a life. Other people carried on around us, footsteps in the corridor, nursing assistants rattling jugs of water, the sound of a distant radio and an unanswered phone.

The curtains were brushed aside by a young nurse. She held his limp wrist for a few seconds, looking into the distance, then she wrote something on the chart hung on the end of the bed. "Hugh? Hugh can you hear me?" She looked for a response. We watched reverently until she gave us all a reassuring smile and moved on.

Mum took a big breath, "Sleep's the best thing for him." She looked around at us, "I don't think I'm ever going to get him back." Tears trickled down her cheeks like condensation on a pane of glass. Helen moved closer and put her arm around her speaking soothing words softly into her ear.

"It's early days Mum. The doctors say he may well make a full recovery. Give it time, he's in the best place." Mum squeezed Helen's hand and we fell into silence again for a few minutes.

I looked at Helen, "I could do with a cup of tea myself."

"I'll come with you," she said.

We found a small waiting area with a drinks machine. I reached into my pockets for change, feeding it into the machine and pressed buttons without thinking. Sitting on hard plastic chairs we nursed cups of hot but otherwise unknown contents. "What do you really think about Dad?" I asked her.

"If he makes it, he's going to need a lot of looking after, it will be a long slow recovery. But I think Mum will be up to it, in fact she may be a lot better once she has got him home. At least then she will be able to do things for him. While he's in here there's nothing she can help with, and that's what she has lived for."

"The women from the church will rally round I suppose."

Helen smiled. "Dropping in with jars of jam and carrot cake. Mrs Badger will start a rota." She swilled the powdery dregs in her cup. "I can stay for a bit if necessary, I mean a week or so. A daughter's role and all that. I know you've got a lot on at work and I've got some holiday I can take."

"Well we can work it out between us," I knew that, when all was said and done, it probably would be Helen who stayed with them.

She shuffled her chair close to mine and rested her head on my shoulder. "Thanks for being here Stephen with a 'ph'."

When we arrived back in the ward we had just missed the consultant. Mum said there wasn't anything new to report. Plenty of sleep was good. She suggested that we all go back home and then come back tomorrow morning.

We drove home in silence, feeling a little down. As we turned in to the familiar drive I noted the little caravan parked at the side of the house, tyres flat, rusting, windows covered with green mildew. They should have used it while they could, I thought to myself. They should have taken off across Europe, eating foreign sausages in Germany and getting lost in impenetrable French one-way systems, crossing the Alps on hair-pinned roads. They should have done it then, it was surely too late now.

*****

I woke early, immediately wondering if Dad was still alive. No phone call in the middle of the night, I assumed that was good news. Mum heard me stir and shouted up.

"Dad's awake, I spoke to the nurse on his ward."

"He'll be running around pinching their bottoms soon," I said.

"He'll what?"

"Nothing Mum, it was a stupid thing to say." I smiled to myself at the absurdity of it.

Late morning saw us once again gathered around Dad's bed. This time he was awake and trying to drink from a glass of water held to his lips but dribbling much of it out of the corner of his mouth. "He's much better this morning," Mum wiped his chin. Then raising her voice, "You're much better than you were Hugh. How are you feeling now?" Dad looked at her bewildered, muttering something which we couldn't understand. There was a look of desperation in his eyes, he made more sounds in the back of his throat and clawed at the bed with his good hand, gripping the sheets, purple veins standing out. We helped him to sit up, propped by pillows he struggled to get his breath. His left arm was draped, lifeless across the bed sheet and the left side of his mouth drooped. He leant his head to one side and Mum drew close to him as he whispered something into her ear before collapsing back against the piled-up pillows.

"What did he say?" We asked.

She turned to us, eyes sparkling with tears. "He said 'Cathleen'". She swallowed hard. "He recognises me." She buried her face in her hands and Helen put her arm around her shoulders as she wept. "Shush, there Mum. It's going to be alright." But when she looked across the bed, directly at me I saw doubt in her eyes.

Mum said she would cook dinner so Helen and I decided to go for a walk before it got dark. We set off down a track across soggy fields without having to discuss the route, both wanting to talk about something other than Dad. I remembered something from our phone call, "What's the story with Dil?" I asked in a 'what's he done this time,' voice. Helen zipped her jacket up. "I don't really know, it's probably nothing. You remember I told you that we were going to start a new school project in Nepal and I thought Dil could help us since he has a Nepali background. Well he seemed to be interested when we had a chat at your place the other evening. I thought I would strike while the iron was hot and I invited him over to our office in Oxford, just to meet a few people."

"Followed by a slap-up lunch at Brown's?" I chipped in, knowing it was one of her favourite restaurants.

"I wish, but not with the current auditors. Grieving widows have given their last penny to help the poor people in Africa and the staff are spending it on lunch? Heaven forbid."

The track narrowed and I dropped behind. We walked Indian file for a bit, picking our way between the muddy clods at the edge of the field and the hedgerow. Helen soldiered on ahead of me. She might once have been called stout or robust. Her hair was kept short in a practical style and she wore clothes designed to contain rather than celebrate the female figure. She forged on against the breeze, swinging her arms vigorously. I caught up as she climbed over a stile.

"And how did it go?"

"Oh fine, Dil's very likeable and I think he genuinely wants to do something for the street kids in Nepal."

"But there's a problem?"

"Not really, just a feeling. He's almost too keen."

We stopped and leant on a gate. The ground fell away and we could see the Quantock Hills in the distance, purple against a grey sky.

"One of the big challenges when working in Nepal is getting stuff in and out of the country, either goods or money. The authorities just make it very difficult. Your stuff gets held up or temporarily lost, and then you have to pay exorbitant import duties which can far exceed the value of the goods. This is also compounded by the fact that very few people have an address in Kathmandu." Helen sniffed and wiped her nose with a tissue. "The usual way around it is to wait until someone from your organisation is coming or going, they can carry whatever it is you want to get in or out in their luggage if it's not too big. But World Reach is quite a big concern so we have been able to set up effectively a PO box and have developed a relationship with a local agent who will go to the depot in person, talk to the right people and liberate our stuff. It's not the first time we have come across these sort of problems."

"Presumably the authorities are worried about drugs and smuggling?"

"Not particularly, we think it's just a combination of incompetence and corruption. Anyway, Dil's ears pricked up when he heard about this. Apparently he has a small business with his cousin in Pokhara, that's where the trekkers head for. Do you know about his business Steve?"

I shook my head. "There's a lot of things I don't know about Dil. What does the business do?"

"They import traditional Nepali clothes into the UK and Dil sells them on to a string of boutiques and shops selling ethnic stuff, the sort of places you find in Camden, you know kaftans and baggy printed trousers." Helen waved her hand dismissively, she shopped for clothes in Marks and Spencer's. "And that is all his business and nothing to do with me, except that he asked if we could help him out by letting him use the World Reach agent we had set up. In other words, import his clothes as if they were part of our fund raising activities. I suppose he thought we might be prepared to do him a favour in exchange for him helping us."

"And you said not on your Nelly."

"I did, or words to that effect, and Dil said he understood our position and that it might easily be misunderstood. That was that and he went off cheerfully with some of our promotional material, promising to spread it around."

"I feel there's a 'but' coming," I said.

"Well I had included one of my colleagues in the meeting, she's the sort of person you would like to be with you when you buy a second-hand car, but a pain to work with. After Dil had left she did some rooting around on the internet. In these days of social media, you can't help leaving a trail. It turns out that the ethnic clothes that Dil is importing are copies of top brand trekking and hiking gear. You know, the sort of stuff that makes you think, 'how can they charge that for a pair of light weight trousers.' Not quite the same as the home-spun ethnical Nepali stuff that Dil had implied."

"So a quick call to trading standards then?"

Helen shook her head. "No, I don't really care if he is smuggling counterfeit clothes. In some ways I welcome it, if it means the Nepalis can benefit from a bit of moonlighting. My main concern is that I don't want World Reach to have any traceable connection with anything or anyone who smells dodgy. Charities have to be squeaky clean. It's a competitive world."

I looked up at silver-grey billowing clouds building up over the hills and pulled the hood of my jacket up. "Well I must say it doesn't altogether surprise me. As I see it, you can either have it out with him, tell him he needs to do a bit of laundry, or you can just quietly drop him without giving any particular reason. I would suggest that quietly dropping him is the best course of action."

Helen dug her hands into her pockets jacket. "Why?"

"Because if you try to confront him he will almost certainly have a convincing argument or excuse, it would all be a misunderstanding, or something like that, I know the way Dil works. Then you're in a fix because, unless you can prove he is guilty, it becomes hard to part company. But since you don't have any contract or agreement with him the easiest thing is just to drop Dil, let it all go quiet. Give your colleague a pat on the back and tell her to sit on it."

I wasn't sure if Helen agreed with me, but the rain began to fall heavily so we put our heads down and tramped back home in silence. I had wanted to tell her about Evans-Peake, I was tired of carrying the load on my own again now that Brian was preoccupied with other things. But somehow I had let the moment pass.

*****

Sunday morning was grey, reminding me of my childhood. The spectre of a boring day, having to dress smartly, go to church and spend the rest of the day reading or playing board games with Helen. I lay in bed looking at the ceiling and listening to the wind blowing through the trees. The daily service played on the radio down in the kitchen, an indistinct echoing voice interspersed by cheery evangelical hymn singing. I rolled out of bed and rummaged in my bag to find some fresh clothes to wear. When I made it downstairs, Helen was just leaving for church.

"Not going Mum?" I asked.

"No, I can't face it. Helen can update everyone on Dad."

I sat down at the kitchen table, poured myself some coffee and watched as Mum busied herself making toast. Her straight grey hair, cut short, emphasised slightly masculine facial features. I noticed how awkwardly and painfully she moved her shoulders and how she had begun to stoop as she moved slowly and carefully around the kitchen, reaching for the back of a chair or a table to steady herself. It was hard to see the long limbed, curly haired, thin faced bride from the wedding photos in her now.

"They mean well."

She nodded and sat down opposite me. "I know they do. I just don't want to listen to stories about 'when I lost my George' and 'when Frank had his first stroke.'"

"Are you going to be alright Mum?" I said not knowing what I would say if she said 'no'.

"Yes I will, and I've told Helen she must go back to Oxford today, and that goes for you as well. You've both got your own lives to lead. I can manage and I've got plenty of people here I can call on."

"I think Dad stands a good chance of making a recovery. He's already making progress."

"It's just that I know it's not ever going to be the same again. I mean we have been slowly going downhill for some time, there's my arthritis and Dad is definitely becoming very forgetful, but we

92

don't feel so different you know. Old age just slowly creeps up on you until something like this happens, and then you know. This brings it home, old age has arrived for good. It's all downhill from here."

"That sounds a bit gloomy, there will be good times to look forward to. Helen might get married." I smiled at her. This had become our family way to express doubt that something would ever happen, like 'pigs might fly'. I knew Mum would love to have some grandchildren to fuss over.

"I don't see that happening. Has she got anyone in mind?"

I shrugged. "I think she's still fond of that curate; they both want to change the world in their own ways. I know she goes out with him to the cinema sometimes but I don't think they are officially a couple. You had better get your prayer mat out Mum." She spread a thin film of butter on her toast. Her swollen knuckles red and raw as she gripped the knife.

"Lucy's Mum called last week. She said Lucy was a bit down since you had broken up. You were like brother and sister when you were little Stephen. What happened?"

"Exactly that. We were like brother and sister and everyone said we would end up as groom and bride, but we never really moved on from brother and sister."

"I think she may ask you to go with her to the opening of a new art gallery. Barbara says she needs someone to go with. If she does, be kind won't you Stephen." She looked at me with tired red-rimmed eyes.

"Of course I will Mum." I took her hand across the table. "But don't start thinking it will put us back together again. I'm sorry, we should have stayed as just friends. I don't know if that's an option now."

We visited Dad again in the afternoon, he was sitting up but still not managing to make himself understood. I noticed how he fiercely gripped Mum's hand all the time as if in a panic. I tried to give him a hug as we left, but it didn't really work. I held his shoulders and put my cheek next to his, feeling awkward. As we left, looking back down the ward from the central nurse's station, I saw him close his eyes while Mum bowed her head to pray.

Helen drove me back to the station. In spite of protests from Mum, she was going to stay the night and return home tomorrow. We hugged and I told her I would come back down in a week or two unless anything happened, the 'anything' being left unspecified. Sitting on the train I felt surprisingly calm and able to think. Life doesn't last for ever, it was time to be more proactive. The fight back would begin and the first item would entail putting to sleep the spectre of the note books, and with them Evans-Peake. I resolved that either I would solve the puzzle this coming week or they went in the bin.

Feeling comfortable with my decision, I stuffed headphones in my ears and settled down to the weekend crossword, pencil poised, Billie Holiday sang in my head.

I've been down so long, down don't worry me.

Chapter 10

I made an agreement with Brian. We would give the codes in the notebooks our best, and last, shot on Wednesday evening. A final heroic effort. If we couldn't break the code, then it was just too difficult for us or it was a hoax, random characters sent to tease us and a complete waste of time. Either way, it ended on Wednesday, regardless of Evans-Peake's protestations. Kris was out visiting prospective customers and Faith went at four-thirty to pick up her kids, leaving Brian and I alone. When I heard the door close downstairs, I got out of my chair and stretched. Brian had his head down, rummaging in his desk drawer. He emerged triumphant, a bottle of claret in one hand and a corkscrew in the other. He poured a generous amount into two mugs.

Brian wore an extra-large T shirt with a silhouette of Bob Marley printed on it under an unzipped red fleece and ragged black jeans, his belly bulged as he slumped in his swivel chair. His fleshy face had a quilted appearance making his features look small, chin stubbled and hair uncombed. Quite what his numerous girlfriends saw in him I failed to discern, perhaps it was his intellect, I found it hard to believe that it was his body. He certainly had an attractive sense of humour and a positive outlook on life, perhaps that's what a girl looks for.

I fished in my ruck-sack and placed the stack of notebooks in front of him with a flourish making sure that they were all exactly aligned forming a cube. "We should invest in some company wine glasses Steve." Brian turned his mug to see an IT Consultancy logo on the side.

I watched as he took a large gulp of wine and swirled it around his cheeks. He raised his eyebrows in approval, picking up the bottle to read the label. We had been best friends for many years, girlfriends had come and gone, other friendships had developed and waned but our relationship was a constant. We were in tune and looked out for each other. I knew deep down that Brian thought this thing with the notebooks was all a waste of time but I also knew he would give it his best shot for my sake. No question.

This is what it had been like when we started Obsidian. When it was just the two of us against the rest of the world and we were revolutionaries. We would focus on the pharmaceutical industry, helping them dig deeper into their experimental results to reveal hidden relationships, and we would save humanity. Nothing less would do. Cancer, Alzheimer's, neurodegenerative diseases, all would fall before our heroic efforts. We enjoyed being own bosses, free from the reins of a big company or a university. Free to take a day off or buy the company some wine glasses whenever we wanted. There were no staff to care for in those days, we were equal partners in a new and vibrant venture.

The last two years had drained us of some of that energy. It was taking longer to develop Merlin and we had to bring in other business to keep us afloat. We had also taken on Faith and Krishna and that meant job descriptions, contracts, payrolls and numerous policies and procedures. Neither Brian or I had been prepared for that, we thought you just offered someone a job, agreed a salary and that was that. Similarly we hadn't anticipated the demands of running a business, having to keep the money coming in month after month to pay our staff and keep the bank and the inland revenue happy. More and more of our own salaries were being ploughed back into the company to keep us afloat.

"It's still fun isn't it" I said, part questioning and part making a statement.

"Is what fun?"

"Obsidian. Struggling to meet our targets and balance the books at the end of every month. Being kicked around by big multinationals. Freedom and the heroic struggle, the little man against all odds. Living in London and going to the pub. But was this ever the dream?" I thought of my parents struggling on in sleepy parishes, week after week, sermon after sermon, driven by a sense of duty. They were on a mission from God. 'Fun' didn't come into it, how shallow I was.

"What would you rather be doing Steve? Who do you aspire to be?" Brian leant back and put his feet on his desk.

I rubbed my chin and sipped my wine. "Well take Dil for example. He doesn't have any pressure, he just plays in the band and muddles along. In spite of his irresponsible attitude, he's got lots of friends and a beautiful wife who adores him…"

"And who pays all the bills." Brian interjected.

"Kris pays the bills but so what as long as she's happy to? I bet he doesn't have problems getting to sleep like I do."

Brian clapped his hands, "That's just who you are Steve, make the best of it. Come on let's get on with these notebooks, the sooner we finish the sooner we get to the Nag's Head and then you can philosophise all you want mate."

We knew that the first step was going to be tedious, we had to digitise all of the coded pages in the notebooks before Merlin could get to work on them. There were fifteen notebooks, each with two hundred pages which would have to be fed into the scanner. We had two scanners and I did a rough calculation in my head, working together we could do it in about two and a half hours. Both the scanners would spit the letters and numbers out as a simple text file. When we had this we could feed it into Merlin, sit back and wait for the results. I suggested that we needn't scan all of the books since they appeared to be so similar, but Brian assured me that the more data we had for Merlin to work on, the better. If this was going to be our one and only shot then we should do it properly, no half measures. Merlin ate that sort of volume of data as a snack.

After three hours, a bottle of wine and several cups of strong coffee we had input all of the data. Now the fun could begin. Brian rubbed his hands together, time to take the dust sheets off Merlin. He started to re-format the data so that it could be fed into Merlin. "It's like cooking, you have to peel and cut up your vegetables
98

before chucking them in the pot. Once you've done that the magic can begin; unexpected flavours start to appear." He held up his hands and waggled his fingers as if warming the muscles up. Brian typed furiously using all of his fingers, then held the backspace key down to erase and correct. We all found this approach amusing, if only he would slow down a little he would not make any mistakes and progress would be faster in the long run.

I looked around the open plan office as I waited for him to finish. Kris' and Faith's desk tops were clear, everything having been filed away when they left the office. Faith put her pens in a mug with a funny quotation along the lines of *you don't have to be mad to work here but……* I thought, how many times can you laugh at the same joke? Brian's desk and my desk were at the opposite end of the tidiness continuum. Stacks of papers in clear plastic folders were piled on the desk top and on the floor. So much for the paperless office. Used mugs growing mould were buried beneath the papers with just enough dregs to cause panic when they were upset. Centre stage were our laptop computers plugged into docking stations, screens dusty and traces of pasta sauce jammed between the keys. Over in the corner of the office there was an enclosure on wheels with a rack of computer servers inside, its door kept permanently open to accommodate additional connecting cables which Brian from time to time required.

Brian hit a final key with a flourish and announced that Merlin was now crunching the data. I looked at my watch, it was a few minutes after nine. Anticipating my question he said, "No idea how long it will take. Once it has completed the first iteration, I might be able to give you an estimate." We both knew we could leave it to run and come back tomorrow but that would mean another day and the feeling that it was dragging on. No, we were clear that the boil had to be lanced tonight, no matter how long it took.

The card from the local pizza takeaway was pinned to the noticeboard behind Faith's desk. I picked up the phone and placed an order. "Twenty minutes," I announced.

Brian pushed back his chair, put his heels back on his desk and ran his hands through his long hair. He had the smile of a confident man, at ease with himself. "If Merlin can't find anything in the data, then it doesn't exist. The deeper he has to look the longer it will take, but he will keep going until all possibilities have been explored." Brian would often refer to Merlin as if it were a person that he had created and which might therefore have a mind of its own. In some ways that was our goal, to create a computer program that could think for itself. We had had many inconclusive conversations at university on the subject of 'can computers think for themselves'. Brian kept an eye on his computer screen, watching for problems or errors, much as a father keeps an eye on his child from a distance in the playground. I made a pretence of looking through a stack of papers on my desk, throwing some in the bin.

"Lucy's going to invite me out," I said.

"What makes you think that?"

"Lucy speaks to her mother, her mother speaks to my mother, my mother speaks to me. That's the way it works."

"Could be Chinese whispers then? The original could be that Lucy never ever wants to speak to you again."

"It wouldn't surprise me if she did take that attitude, nobody would blame her. Mother says Lucy has been invited to the opening of a new art exhibition and apparently needs someone to go with on a purely Platonic basis."

Brian smiled. "Where is the gallery and when is it?"

"Mum didn't know but I suspect it's the one featured in the Sunday Times supplement last weekend, the artist is Kengo Moshida."

Brian took his feet off the desk and sat up, "Moshida San? Can she get a couple more tickets? I'm a big fan, even got some of his prints on the wall in my bedroom." Once again Brian's wide ranging interests amazed me, his roots were in science and mathematics, rational thought, but I had no doubt that he would hold his own in a discussion of contemporary Japanese art.

"I'll ask her, she usually can. But, to be honest, I was thinking of inventing another engagement as an excuse for not going."

"No, don't do that. Chloe and I would love to come. We can make a little foursome, perhaps go out to eat afterwards." Brian had it all worked out, so much so that I wondered if Lucy had primed him.

The door buzzer announced the arrival of pizza. I met the delivery man half way down the stairs with the money, we were hungry.

*****

"I think that's the end of the road Steve." Brian took a deep breath and splayed his fingers. It was now past midnight. We had run the data through Merlin with several initial conditions and settings and we were dog tired. It looked as though Evans-Peake had beaten us and beaten Merlin. We could find nothing that made any sense in the codes. We had a few minor successes, some simple patterns did appear, making us think we were on to something but each one turned out to be nothing beyond what you would expect to get from random data. Statistics was our business and we could both see that there were no connections and nothing of any significance here. And we were still arrogant enough to think that if we couldn't crack it then nobody could.

I slid the notebooks, one by one, back into my ruck-sack. Perhaps it was better this way. If we had found something, then what would be our next move? I didn't relish the thought of more contact with Evans-Peake. Brian looked through the last print out shaking his head. "Sorry mate. But I really think there is nothing there. You've been well and truly marched up the proverbial hill and there's nowhere else to go but to turn around and march back down it again and tell everyone waiting at the bottom that the view from the top was crap."

Turning the pedals slowly, I cycled back home along the quiet residential roads. The decision made, I turned into my street and stopped by a builder's skip parked outside a house that was being renovated. Without giving it a second thought I reaching into my ruck-sack, pulled the stack of notebooks out and dumped them into the rubble. They merged in a cloud of dust, un-seen and irretrievable.

That was the end of that story. Time to move on.

Chapter 11

November the fifth was cold and miserable. There had been no encounters with Evans-Peake since I had thrown the notebooks in the skip, several weeks had passed and I had allowed myself to think he was gone forever. My Dad was making a good recovery. He was back home and, although you could still see and hear the effects of the stroke when he spoke, he was mentally alert.

I watched fireworks in the distance, the coloured light diffused by the mist rising from the Thames. Bangs and crackles mixed in with the noise of the traffic. The soft falling rain was illuminated by street lamps making them look like giant shower heads. Waiting at the southern end of Waterloo Bridge I peered out from under the hood of my coat gathered with a draw string around my face, humming along with Nina Simone in my head.

Oh Lord. Please, don't let me be misunderstood.

I could have been anyone, but I knew Lucy would recognise me in an instant, even though I was wrapped in waterproofs. The anticipated request to accompany her to the opening of the gallery had come in the form of a casually worded text message, she wouldn't want to sound desperate. I looked at my watch and began to regret having agreed to meeting her, what possible good could come of it? I reminded myself that it wasn't a date and there would be no reason for either of us to get intense or emotional. I had been to various arty functions with Lucy over the years. I knew the drill and I had the measure of it. I would be the exemplary 'plus one', polite, interested, attentive but never voicing an opinion.

Lucy worked for a consultancy that recommended art for their wealthy clients to hang on the walls of their homes or offices. The art had to reflect the character of the organisation and they would expect it to be a sound investment. An exhibition is the artist's shop window, and an exhibition in a London gallery on the South Bank of the Thames is very prestigious.

I recognised her transparent pink mac across the road as she waited for the traffic lights to change. We kissed each other's cheek as friends do. She was familiar and comforting and I was surprised to find myself genuinely pleased to see her, beyond the call of duty. We headed Eastwards along the South Bank towards the Oxo Tower, not holding hands and unable to talk as we dodged around the herd of people coming in the opposite direction.

Next to the base of the tower is a disused warehouse, or rather a warehouse which had found other uses. The bare brick walls, wrought-iron staircases and ill-fitting floor boards had been carefully preserved. It was the sort of place an artist would refer to as 'an interesting space'. A reception area had been set up on the ground floor, the girl behind the desk carefully drew a line through our names on the list with the aid of a ruler. We hung our dripping coats on a free-standing coat rail, Lucy dried her spectacles with a corner of her scarf held between two fingers. A kimono clad Japanese woman knelt on a patch of carpet playing the koto, its sparse plinky sound promoting an atmosphere of calm and serenity, so much loved by the Japanese.

Brian and Chloe arrived, hand in hand, Brian full of anticipation. My mood lightened when I saw them, something to do with strength in numbers. I resolved to just enjoy the evening and take everything as it came at face value. We picked up a catalogue and a glass of sparkling wine offered by smiling interns and headed up the stairs. There were several dimly lit rooms on each of three floors, all sparsely hung with individually lit works of art. I peered into the first room and saw to my relief, that they were pictures of things I could recognise and understand. I rubbed my hands together. "OK Lucy this looks interesting, let's have the guided tour," squeezing her shoulder out of habit.

The artist, Kengo Moshida, was apparently well known but he rarely exhibited outside his native Japan. In the early days of photography, soon after Japan opened itself up to trade with the

West, photographers had visited Japan with their heavy equipment and long exposures to capture some remarkable images of Japanese life frozen in time. These black and white photographs were then hand coloured in pastel shades creating pictures which were intensely beautiful and full of nostalgia. Kengo used the same technique but with black and white photographs of modern Japan, coloured by his own hand: A crowded sub-way train, people relaxing in hot onzen baths, the gaudy colours of the Ginza, the Shinkansen speeding towards snow-capped mountains, Fuji-San in the distance. Kengo used colour to draw your eye to significant features and the result was modern Japanese life portrayed using an old technique, catch it while you still can, freeze it in time, for tomorrow it will be different.

Brian was in love with all things Japanese. He sat on the bench in the middle of one of the rooms, hands clasped under his chin supported by elbows on spread thighs. Chloe sat next to him legs neatly crossed at the ankle, cooing softly. "Steve," he called me over with a theatrical whisper, "Look Akihabara. Electronic paradise, you can buy technology there that you won't see in Europe for years."

We went our separate ways for a while, wandering from room to room, peering up close and squinting from a distance, looking for meaning beyond simple photography. I felt Lucy pulling gently on my arm, "Come with me." I willingly followed, winding through the crowds. For a moment, I thought she wanted me to leave the gallery with her but she had spotted the artist and wanted some moral support. Seizing the opportunity, she marched up to him with hand held out.

"Lucy Quick, Su-Kim Associates, what a delightful collection Mr Moshida, many congratulations." I stood dutifully at her side like a sentry.

Kengo instinctively bowed as he took her hand. He smiled like a man who was used to smiling. Turning to the elegant woman at his side, dressed in a close fitting navy blue suit, he said, "Can I introduce my wife Mieko". Lucy started to quiz Kengo about his

106

artistic influences and technique. Oriental art wasn't her speciality but she would have prepared well. That was Lucy, organised, research done, names memorised, objectives enumerated. This was still 'my Lucy'? I felt safe when I was with her. I thought back to the blazing tent in the park. Show yourself now, I taunted Evans-Peake, now when I am surrounded by people I know, now when I have friends, when I am not alone, now that I have Lucy.

Out of the corner of my eye I saw Brian and Chloe enter the room, Brian made straight for us. I intercepted him, wanting to give Lucy a chance to continue her conversation uninterrupted. Lucy gave Kengo her business card and then turned around. Brian saw his opportunity and waded in enthusiastically, telling Kengo how much he admired his work and about the prints he had on the wall in his flat. He turned to Chloe, but before he could introduce her, Chloe introduced herself.

"Defrey San hajimemashite, dozo yoroshiku."

She then proceeded to talk to Kengo in apparently fluent Japanese, while the rest of us looked on in silent admiration. This was a side of Chloe I hadn't seen before and, judging by the look on his face, neither had Brian. Unable to compete, Lucy turned to talk to Kengo's wife, asking her if she was enjoying her visit to London and recommending some lesser known art galleries.

I stood a little back as they chatted. Lucy was dressed in a white blouse, black pencil skirt, jacket and flat shoes. Honest and straightforward, very English, articulate, polite and dependable, hair cut short, a little on the plump side. Chloe wore an electric blue close fitting dress with white shoulder bag and high heels. Petite, curvy, attentive, sexy, mysterious, even her name 'Chloe Defrey' sounded exotic. I thought back over my years with Lucy, had we ever been passionate or mysterious? I didn't think that we had. Had we ever taken the 'road less trod'? Probably not.

Kengo, aware that other people were waiting to speak to him, politely brought the conversation to an end. I stood with Lucy watching as the crowd closed in behind them.

"Is he any good?", I asked.

"What do you think?"

"I like it, but then I'm the guy who thought Van Gogh couldn't draw very well when we visited that gallery in Amsterdam."

"Well if you like it, then it's probably the kiss of death", she smiled confidently. "However I also like it and that means he is good because I spent three years at Art College while you were playing with Lego at Imperial College." She sparkled for a moment, the quick put-down enjoyed. Her wit compensating for her slightly drab appearance.

"Can you place it with any of your clients?" I could imagine it in an Arab sheik's pent house or the foyer of a high-tech Japanese engineering company perhaps.

Lucy ran her fingers through her hair. "If it's expensive enough someone will always buy it, and this is expensive enough. All you have to do is sell it before somebody says 'look the Emperor hasn't got any clothes on and he can't paint either.'" She rubbed her hands together and looked around for Brian and Chloe. "Come on, I think our work is done here, let's go and eat. I've had enough art for one day and I'm starving." We followed her down the stairs to the reception area, picked our coats off the rail and pulled the zips up to our chins. Brian knew a little tapas restaurant just along the South bank by the Globe Theatre. The weather hadn't improved, we trudged Indian file along the embankment behind him, anticipating a warm welcome.

The restaurant was nearly empty, we ordered a bottle of Rioja and a selection of dishes from the tapas menu. The waiter was of the 'quiet but efficient' variety, scribbling on his pad as Lucy read from the menu. Brian was the first to ask the question. "So Chloe San, where did all of that come from?"

Chloe feigned surprise, "What. Oh you mean the Japanese?"

"Yes, the little chat with Moshida San in fluent Japanese. The rest of us didn't get a look in."

Chloe flicked her hair out of her eyes. "I just asked him if he was enjoying London and where his home was in Japan. He said he lived in Nagoya and asked me where I learned to speak Japanese. It was just small talk, we didn't mention his art."

"And where did you learn to speak Japanese?"

"I lived in Yokohama when I was a little kid, my Dad's job took us around the world. They decided to chuck me into a local Japanese primary school rather than the English speaking International School so I learnt to speak Japanese pretty quickly. I've forgotten quite a lot but my accent is authentic and I can still get by with general chit-chat."

"Sounded pretty good to me", I said. "I spent five years learning French at school and I can just about remember how to ask the way to the railway station."

Chloe looked across the table at Lucy. "Sorry if I monopolised him, I think he was just glad to speak some Japanese, his English wasn't that good was it."

Lucy as ever, was very accommodating. "No, that was absolutely fine, he's more likely to remember us. It all helps to form a relationship. That's what tonight was all about, it wasn't the art, we all know what that looks like from the catalogues."

Brian raised his eyebrows. "Have you got any other talents up your sleeve that you haven't told me about? Any little secrets we might be interested in? Fluent Mandarin?" The incident had shown up how little they knew about each other. It was normally Brian who had the surprise interests and expertise, but Chloe had well and truly trumped him on this occasion.

We found ourselves talking in a girl pair and a boy pair across the table as we ate. Lucy quizzed Chloe about her time in Japan, they were chalk and cheese but chatted easily together. Brian topped up everyone's glasses and refilled his own then held up the empty bottle for the waiter to see. He picked at the food with his fork moodily. I could tell there was something else on his mind and I waited for the thunder clouds to coalesce. "Axiom have been in touch again about our data security, they want to send some of their compliance people to visit us for an audit next week."

"Is that a problem?"

"Shouldn't be. It's just a bit of an unknown, I'll try to get some sort of checklist out of them before they come, then we can go through it together. They still seem to be worried that someone might have gained access to our internal network posing as one of us." He pushed his plate of food away and rocked his chair back from the table.

"Well that of course is the fundamental weakness with all computer security." I said, "If someone gets hold of your password and logs on, then as far as the computer is concerned, it's you that is logged on and everything is wide open. And I have to say Brian, that you are one of the worst culprits when it comes to password security." I smiled to take the sting out of my words.

Brian reacted sharply, reverting to his native Scottish accent, but not raising his voice, "Are you saying I've given my password away and allowed someone else into the system, because if you are that's bollocks Steve". He refilled his glass of wine, I noticed he was looking flushed. Usually Brian could drink large quantities of alcohol without any side-effects, but this time he was already looking the worse for wear. Perhaps he was tired.

"I'm not saying you've given it away Brian", I jabbed my loaded fork in his direction but still trying to remain light hearted, "I'm simply saying that we all know what it is."

"Tell me then, what is it?" Brian stuck his chin out, he was in a combative mood.

It's ChloeDefrey, capital 'C' and capital 'D' and you will have replaced the 'l' and the 'o' in Chloe with one and zero because you have to have some numbers in the password. Am I right?"

"No wrong", he shook his head.

"Alright then you have only replaced either the 'l' or the 'o' with numbers. Whatever, I could guess it within three tries. The point is that you always use the name of your current girl-friend."

Brian wasn't about to back down, "OK but you can guess it only because you happen to know some details about my personal life."

110

"Come on Brian", I said. "Even Faith has worked it out. I bet Chloe knows what it is."

"No way."

"All she has to do is to look innocently over your shoulder when you log on from home and watch your fingers on the keyboard. Everyone recognises the key pattern of their own name, she would just have to recognise a few keys and she would guess you were typing her name. And by the way just as a hint, there is a great big picture of her as your desktop background."

Brian's eyes were red, his lips pale and tight shut. He flared up, speech slurred. "Let me get this straight, you're accusing me of letting Chloe onto our network in a flagrant breach of our IT policy. Breaking every rule in the book. I've spent hours making sure that our IT is secure and you think that I would just throw that all away?"

I was alarmed that our conversation had turned into a public argument. Lucy and Chloe stopped chatting and looked in our direction. I spoke quietly hoping they would resume their conversation. "No I'm not saying you have done anything deliberately or that Chloe is a risk, but she has already surprised us once this evening hasn't she. Don't get all upset about it." I could feel my heart beating, this was getting out of control and I wanted to calm the situation down and I didn't want a confrontation, but Brian had had enough.

"OK Steve, well to be frank I couldn't care what you think, so let's just leave it at that shall we." He pushed his chair, stood up and walked over to the till holding out a credit card. Lucy looked at me. "It's nothing," I said in a low voice, "he's just had a bit too much to drink."

Brian came back to the table but didn't sit down. "Right, I've paid the bill. Come on Chloe time to go". He walked to the door, grabbed his coat from the rack, waiting while Chloe buttoned up her coat, she looked back at us and wrinkled her nose. Brian called over, "By the way Steve, Obsidian's finished. I just thought you should know. So I couldn't care less if the whole world knows my password. Axiom can send their IT parasites around to audit us any time they like and I'm sure they'll find all sorts of things wrong because that's what they are paid to do."

And then they were gone, leaving the door to swing shut with a crash.

I held my hand up before Lucy had a chance to say anything. "I don't want to talk about it OK?" We waited until they would be far enough ahead and, leaving a generous tip on the table, we left. The waiter held the door open for us, looking into the distance. He said a polite 'good night' as we passed as if nothing out of the ordinary had happened. And for many, this little spat would be nothing out of the ordinary but for us.... For me, it was a big deal, Obsidian was finished.

Lucy and I walked back along the embankment in silence and paused before going our separate ways at Waterloo. I had calmed down, I hoped it hadn't spoiled the evening but knew that it had. I waited, hopeful, attentive. Lucy gave me a quick peck on the cheek and I said, "Keep in touch." She smiled, then she turned and walked away. I watched until she was out of sight, lost in the post-theatre crowd heading for the station and I realised how much I missed her.

It was gone eleven by the time I got home, tired and dehydrated. I pushed the key into the door lock on the front door. It wouldn't turn. I looked under the light from the street lamp to check it was the right key and tried again but no luck. I could have done without a broken lock but it wasn't a major problem. I followed the passage down the side of the house to my small back garden. The weather had cleared up, a full moon lit the bike shed with a silvery outline, the light wind periodically disturbed the trees. I shivered as I felt along the edge of the shed roof for a place where the felting had pulled away from the woodwork. Tucked under was a spare back door key. I turned it in the door and I was in. For no good reason I was slightly unnerved, I switched all of the lights on. My spare front door key was in the drawer of my desk, I went to investigate. I tried the spare key but again it jammed.

Clearly the lock was faulty and there was nothing further to be done now. It was probably worn out.

I made a cup of tea and sat in the kitchen for a while, reflecting on the evening. It was very rare for me to argue with Brian and it had unsettled me. He seemed to have flared up so quickly, perhaps he was also feeling how vulnerable our business was as we tried to stay on our feet while being pushed around by a commercial giant. Axiom was Obsidians bread and butter, if we lost them there would be famine. But to say that Obsidian was finished? Something had got under his skin, there was more to it and the boil would have to be lanced. I filled a glass tumbler with water, turned the lights off and climbed the stairs to a welcoming bed. But that was work for another day.

Chapter 12

The locksmith turned up at mid-day with a cheerful smile announcing that he would soon have me sorted out. It was an old lock and apparently they eventually wear out and jam, the only option was to fit a replacement. After about twenty minutes he presented me with two shiny keys and an invoice. I hid one key in the usual place under the loose felting on the shed roof and put the other on my key ring.

As I arrived at the office I met Faith coming down the stairs, heading for the kitchen. I followed her in.

"Tea?" she held up a mug.

"Thanks Faith, my front door lock broke last night so I had to wait for the locksmith to come round and sort it out."

"You don't have to make your excuses to me for being late Steve, you're the boss", she stood with her hand on the kettle waiting impatiently for it to boil. "If you want to take the morning off then you can just do it, no questions asked." She waved her hand dismissively.

"I wasn't making excuses, I was just telling you that…."

She interrupted. "Never mind, sit down and tell me how it went last night. I heard you went on a date with Lucy to a fancy art gallery. Are you getting back together with her again?"

I sat on a bar stool and assumed a look of pained patience. "Yes, I did go out with Lucy last night and no, it was not a date. She just asked me, as a friend to go with her, that's all."

"Well you may say that's all it was but I remember the first time I went out with Stanley. It was supposed to be just as friends but he still managed to get his hands in my knickers."

"Faith, we were visiting a bloody art gallery, not sitting in the backrow at the cinema. Admittedly the lighting was dim but I can assure you that there was none of that. Comparisons between me and your oversexed ex-husband are not appropriate. Any more and I will have to claim sexual harassment." I looked her in the eye inviting her to respond, enjoying the banter.

She stirred in some sugar and put the mug of tea in front of me. "You wish", she said, hands on hips.

Kris was on the phone and I found Brian crouching on the floor tracing one of a network of cables, running between computers in the rack. He stood up when he saw me and pointed to the meeting room without saying a word. Once in, he carefully closed the door, neither of us sat down.

I opened for the prosecution. "I'm surprised to see you here since, according to you, Obsidian is finished."

"What do you want me to say? Everything is fine? OK I admit I over-reacted about the password thing, but if we lose Axiom we are finished." Brian flopped into a chair. "This is the real world."

"I know about the real world. It's me who gets out there and wins those stats contracts which are about all that keeps us afloat. It's not me who buries his head in computer code for a project which will probably never recoup its development costs."

The strain showed and we lashed out at each other with words and with gestures. Eventually Brian stormed out. I watched him through the glass as he returned to the nest of cables. What would Lucy have done? She would be calm and deliberate, not raising her voice. Fair and firm, not giving in to shouting or tantrums. Taking the moral high ground, expressing how disappointed she was in our behaviour.

As I emerged, Faith had just picked up the ringing phone. She listening for a few seconds then said, "Would you mind if I put you on hold and I'll see if she's available." She pressed the mute button but still covered the mouthpiece with her hand. "Kris, I've got Edith Summers on the line from Axiom, do you want to speak to her?"

Kris sat up and smoothed her hair as if Edith was going to arrive in person.

"Hi Edith, Krishna here. How are you?" She paused to listen, then continued with some small talk. Faith, Brian and I listened reverently to one side of the conversation, this was where Kris earned her money. She had a little biography in her head for all of our key contacts, always something personal to ask them, a hobby, an upcoming wedding, a holiday in the Caribbean. 'People buy from people', was her mantra. Finally, it was time to get down to business. "What can I do for you?" There was a long pause while Edith spoke at the other end of the line. "That should be fine Edith, did you have a date in mind? This Friday? Well as far as I know that would be OK, let me just take a quick look at my diary." Kris looked around at us all with raised eyebrows. Faith was frantically scribbling on a piece of scrap paper, she held it up; 'Merry Mick'.

"Oh sorry Edith no, our accountant is coming in on Friday. I think he'll be here most of the day. How about next week?" She waited.

"Tuesday? Well that's also the day that your IT people are coming for the audit, they arranged it with Brian Calder. So why not, the more the merrier, it'll be good to see you. Can I meet you with a car at King's Cross, save you the rigours of the tube?"

Kris saw she was getting a thumbs-up from every one as she listened. "OK, I didn't know that. Fine well we will see you here around nine-thirty next Tuesday then."

She put the phone down carefully and swivelled away from her desk. "That's interesting. I had always assumed Edith lives close to Cambridge since that's where Axiom are based. But she lives just around the corner in Queen's Park. How come we didn't know that?"

"She probably likes to keep her address under her hat in case she gets targeted by the animal rights people." I said.

Brian was breathing hard, knuckles on the desk, "Why the hell does she want to visit us Kris?"

"She wants to discuss the data security issues. I thought you said that was all over." She looked enquiringly at Brian.

"I thought it was all over too but now they want to send their IT people round to check us out and Edith also wants be in on it. Something is brewing, we don't usually get this amount of attention. Well, all we can do is to listen to what they say and try to make sure everything is ship-shape from our side." He gave me a 'see I told you so' look and left. An uneasy truce.

*****

Friday came around quickly. When I arrived at the office Mick, our accountant, had pulled up a chair and was sitting beside Faith, peering at her computer screen through his varifocals. Mick, a short rotund elfin man, wore a baggy suit making him look generally dishevelled. He looked up as I arrived with an air of mischievousness, as if caught looking at dirty pictures.

"Hi Mick, how is it?"

"Well it's not good." His big grin and raised eyebrows announced that he was the bearer of bad news, this was his way of softening the blow. And there usually was bad news when Mick was around but often it referred to his personal life which he was more than happy to reveal to anyone who would listen. 'My wife's about to walk out, my grown kids are still at home, the dog's costing me a fortune in vet's bills.' There was always something that Mick would stoically have to bear. It was never his fault, some voodoo spirit was firing poison tipped arrows at him to make his life difficult. Mick had been singled out to bear the troubles of the world, and he wasn't entirely happy about it, but if that was his lot, then he would just have to grin and bear it.

In spite of his chaotic personal life, or perhaps because of the challenges it posed, Merry Mick was good at his job and we liked him. We needed someone who wasn't afraid to tell us some hard truths from time to time. It was all too easy to bury ourselves in the all-consuming world of computer programming and mathematics, we loved the intensity of it. You made some changes to a spread sheet or a program, then you ran it and got almost immediate results, no down time. At times it would absorb us until late at night, building software empires in minutes then, just as quickly, tearing them down in favour of a different approach. It was addictive, always one more try beckoned. We were the ultimate solvers of puzzles. In terms of our interest levels, profit and loss accounts didn't even come close.

Brian, Mick and I sat down together in the meeting room. Mick placed a copy of the updated accounts for the quarter in front of each of us. We turned the pages slowly. Several columns of numbers in brackets on the last page indicated a significant short fall. It didn't look good. I was the one who tended to look after the business side of things while Brian concentrated on the development of Merlin, but I wasn't a born businessman and I knew it. The figures were plain enough. I thought back to our board meeting in the Italian Restaurant, we knew back then that things weren't good. I looked up from the figures, "What do we do Mick?" He responded by passing around more sheets of paper showing our invoiced income against target month by month and predicting a short-fall at the end of the financial year.

Mick sat back and folded his arms while we assimilated the figures. "Forget trying to run your own business. Go and get a job in a big company with a decent regular salary and a generous pension scheme is my advice."

We both looked up.

"Your biggest problem is the bank. If they get wind of this then they will call in their loans, and that really will be the end of the line. Even without the bank pulling out, you might need some more investment capital to see you through, so if either of you has a rich Fairy Godmother, my advice is 'don't forget her birthday'." I thought of my Auntie Beryl who sent me a crisp twenty-pound note every birthday. Very little money in my family unfortunately.

Mick continued, "Secondly, you need to get out there and sell Merlin or find another way to get some cash in. Steve's consulting work is not enough to keep you afloat. Not at the rate you are spending money."

Brian and I looked at each other across the table. I knew this was not the approach he would want to hear but there was a danger that Merlin would never be finished, Brian was a perfectionist and there was always something to be attended to before the first official release. It was being beta tested at Axiom and they were still coming up with minor problems but essentially it was running well and proving useful. Our hope was that we could sell it to them at corporate level. We needed to aim higher in their organisation and strike a deal to install it in all of the Axiom research labs. If we could do that, then our revenue would be enough to set the company back on its wheels.

Almost as if he could hear me thinking, Mick said, "You need to stop the development of Merlin, slap a 'Release Version' sticker on it, put it in a box and get out there and sell it."

"And we'll fall flat on our faces when it doesn't work", Brian tapped the table with his pen and spoke quietly. "Then we get a bad reputation and nobody will even want to buy coffee and doughnuts from us."

Mick didn't give up and didn't pull his punches. "Brian, you barely have enough cash to run the payroll this month. You would know that if you took any interest in the accounts. Take any orders you can get is my advice, delay the installation date by which time, with any luck, you'll have ironed out the problems. I think it's your only option."

"OK Mick, thanks for being so blunt", I said. "Is that it?"

"Well at the risk of really depressing you", Mick smiled, almost chuckled. "You also need to get your expenses under control, they are way in excess of what they should be. You are wining and dining people as if you were a big drug company. You can't afford it guys."

Brian jumped in, looking at me. "Well that's down to Kris. I don't want to say I told you so but…."

Mick interrupted. "No, it's not Kris. It's you two. Obsidian is your business, so you set the budgets. Forgive me for saying this but you are typical academics. You bury yourselves in your science and your research and, in effect, Kris and Faith are left running the company. You have to keep tabs on your staff. You have to keep tabs on the finances. That's your job and neither of you are doing it."

Mick picked up his papers and slotted them into his brief case, then stood it on the table. He looked at each of us in turn waiting for any final questions. We sat there like penitent school boys. "Got to be somewhere else this afternoon, so I'll leave you to think about it. Any questions, just call me."

I leant back in my chair. "Mick, there is something else we should tell you about." I glanced across at Brian, he shook his head. "We are in trouble with Axiom."

Mick carefully moved his brief case off the table and back down on the floor. He was back in the meeting. "What kind of trouble?"

"Some of their important drug trial data has leaked and they're blaming Obsidian. We have a copy of some of their sensitive data to run through Merlin for testing purposes and they think we have let it out."

"How far has it gone?"

"Well we thought it had been sorted out, but now there is something else brewing. We don't quite know what's up but they're visiting us next week, including Edith Summers who is the group leader. We're pretty sure we are in the clear, but mud sticks. It's our reputation at stake, to say nothing of a law suit which would take us to the cleaners."

"If you're clean then could they be covering up an internal screw-up?" Mick asked.

"Possibly, but how do we prove it. Any advice?"

"It goes without saying that parting company with Axiom would be…" Mick searched in vain for an adjective and settled for, "unfortunate." He folded his arms on the table, this time he wasn't grinning. "I'll tell you what I would do. I would send Krishna in there. She must know everyone involved. Send her in on some pretext and let her chat to people. If anybody can pick up some

120

whispers, she can." We both dutifully nodded our heads. "Let her worm her way into people's confidences." There was little more to be said. We shook hands and I walked down the stairs with Mick. He turned to look back at the building. "You could probably find somewhere cheaper than this to rent."

"My spare bedroom for example." I said, hoping it was a joke but Mick didn't laugh.

"My gut feeling is that you will do it. You just need to sit down, including Kris, and agree a plan. And then you have to stick to it. Cheerio Steve." I slowly climbed the stairs thinking for the first time that perhaps we should pack up while Obsidian was still just about solvent. But I knew that Brian wouldn't hear of it, he would keep going on his own if necessary.

Brian was still sitting in the meeting room when I entered the office, highlighting some figures in the accounts with a marker pen. He looked up, expressionless. "Got any good news Steve?"

I spread my arms, open hands with palms turned up. "Mick thinks we can make it."

"That's probably the kiss of death then." Brian took a deep breath. "Look Steve, let's put last night behind us, I know I take things to heart more than I should, too much red wine on an empty stomach didn't help." It wasn't much of an apology, I deserved more. Lucy would say that I give way to Brian too easily, but this was now a post-Lucy era, I was on my own. I could decide not to accept his apology and let the tension between us grow. Then what? What would be the point? I had enough to deal with, losing Lucy, Dad's stroke and the ever-present Evans-Peake. A stronger person might make more of an issue of it, was I weak or was I just making the rational decision?

I ran my fingers through my hair, "OK, let's make a start after lunch. We'll get Kris in and look at how we can make some savings. Might as well get on with it. I'll tell her it's urgent and she needs to cancel any appointments for the rest of the day."

Brian nodded. "And I'll look through the expenditure figures and try to work out a plan."

"Just before you go Steve." Brian shut the meeting room door and lowered his voice. "I was rooting through Kris' e-mails yesterday. I'm still trying to find out why Axiom thought Kris had leaked that data last month."

"Perhaps she really did?" I sat down.

Brian shook his head. "I just can't see why she would do it. But what I did discover was that Dil had been using her account. So she has probably told him her password. It seems that I'm not the only one who might have given away personal details."

"What was in the e-mails that Dil sent?"

"Nothing of any great interest. Chatting with friends, arranging a night out with the band, I'll send some of them to you."

"OK, well it's lunchtime." I stood up. "Do you want anything from the shop?" Brian shook his head.

*****

Brian and Kris were already chatting in the meeting room when I joined them after lunch. Brian looked up. "Some good news for once, Steve." He nodded towards Kris.

She folded her arms on the table. "I've been trying to get Axiom to at least pay us for a pilot study. This will keep the money coming in while they evaluate Merlin, it's not fair that we have to carry all of the costs. Edith followed up this morning's phone call with an e-mail to confirm the visit, she also wrote that she had the budget for a pilot study approved. She wants to discuss it when she visits next week. That means that we get some money up front and that they must be pretty happy with Merlin so far."

I could see that she was desperately trying not to look too pleased with herself. "Well done you", I said.

"It's not in the bag yet", she put her open palms together in a gesture of prayer, "But it's looking promising."

I could see that Brian was also looking pleased with himself. "And well done Brian. Perhaps Merlin really does work after all."

"Of course it works Steve, haven't you read our advertising?"

122

I took a deep breath and slid a set of the accounts across the table to Kris. "Perhaps that good news will make this meeting a little easier." I addressed Kris directly. "Merry Mick says we need to make some serious savings on our expenditure otherwise we will go under. I know he can be a bit of a pessimist but we can't ignore his advice. We need to include you in this Kris."

"Should I be looking for another job?" She said, only partly as a joke.

"No, heaven forbid we need you Kris. Mick says he thinks we will pull through and the money from Axiom will help if we get it." I handed out a sheet of paper to each of them.

We went through my plan point by point: Cutting back on advertising, focusing on PR which is free. The biggest bone of contention was hospitality, we needed to limit this to a few sandwiches at lunchtime or some pub grub. Kris needed some persuading but we told her it was just for a limited time, until we got out of the financial hole we were in. We all agreed to stick with the plan and if any unforeseen expenditures surfaced, then we would discuss them on a case by case basis.

The meeting was going well so I decided to stick my neck out. "Kris, what I am about to say is water under the bridge, so no need to get up-tight. It has to do with the data security problems we had last month." I looked questioningly at Brian who assented with a slight nod of his head. "As you know Axiom accused us of leaking their data, then it all went quiet and we haven't heard anything about it for a while. Now we are wondering if there is another problem since they want to come and audit our IT next week. I need to bring you up to speed in case something is said." Kris sat up, attentive. "We managed to find out whose e-mail account the data had been sent from. And perhaps we should have told you about this earlier. To cut a long story short, the leaks came from your e-mail account Kris: Krishna.Chandrakar@Obsidian.com."

Kris fell silent for a few seconds. "Well I hope to God you don't think it was me." She looked at each of us in turn for reassurance. "Do you think it was me?"

"No of course we don't," I said. "That's why we didn't mention it to you. But it appears that someone is pretending to be you or that someone knows your password."

She slowly shook her head. "Who would do that?" For a few seconds the usually supremely confident Krishna was wrong footed.

I took a deep breath, "Might Dil know your password?"

"Dil? No, he's not the slightest bit interested in my work. He may have used my laptop from time to time to get on the internet but he doesn't have access to my work e-mails." Kris began to fight back. "Look tell me the whole story, what do you know?"

"We went through your e-mails."

"Without asking me?" Kris interrupted with raised voice, eyes flaring.

Brian jumped in. "Yes without asking you Kris, they are company property. If you want to send private e-mails then use your private e-mail address." Kris was about to interrupt again, but Brian held his finger up. "And we found some e-mails which appear to have been sent by Dil." He paused to let the point sink in. "Can you be sure he doesn't know your password?"

Kris fell silent and I saw a shadow of doubt move across her face. Clearly she couldn't be absolutely sure. She banged the table with her fist. "Shit".

Chapter 13

Much of the rest of the week was spent tidying up in preparation for Edith's visit. When she saw our office she would realise that Axiom was investing a lot of time and money in a very small and relatively insecure outfit. She would find this unsettling. The best we could do was to present a very professional face; copies of all our policies must be updated, cables meandering across the room must be tidied up, desk surfaces cleared, gangways uncluttered. Faith bought a selection of posh biscuits which we were all forbidden to touch. By Friday lunchtime we had been through everything we could think of. Although none of us said it, we all knew that the visit on Monday could be make or break for Obsidian. Everyone would look to the Empress Edith for the thumbs up or the thumbs down, the masses would cheer whichever way it went, only the gladiators really cared.

The weekend came around quickly, I lazed in bed on Saturday morning listening to the radio. My phone buzzed heralding a text message from Dil. 'Do you fancy a coffee this morning 11:00 at Park Side Café?' This was an unusual request. Lucy and I had met up with Dil and Kris from time to time for an evening together as a foursome, but never just me and Dil. There was usually something going on in the background when Dil was involved. I replied with a simple 'OK'.

At the appointed time there was no sign of Dil so I sat at a table on the pavement just outside the café door regretting not having brought a crossword with me. I tried unsuccessfully, to make anagrams of 'Park Side Café' in my head. Dil appeared from a side road and strolled towards me, hands in his pockets with a relaxed, unhurried stride. He was wearing loose fitting naturally coloured clothes, reminiscent of his Nepali ethnicity. We bought

126

coffee and bacon rolls and took them across the road into the park so that Dil could have a smoke.

"How's the Brondesbury Jazz Quartet doing?" I asked.

"Good. In fact we are now the Brondesbury Jazz Quintet. Madeleine has joined us as a singer. She's got one of those husky, deep French voices, very sexy." Dil spoke with a false French accent.

Dil lit a cigarette and inhaled. "We were jazz purists, but I think now we're heading mainstream. People like songs don't they."

"And they like sexy French singers."

"And sexy French singers," Dil agreed. "We're playing down the Nags Head again tonight, why don't you come along?" He didn't expect an answer.

There was an awkward silence, Dil puffed on his cigarette, untroubled. "It's lots of fun and we get plenty of work, but it doesn't pay very much. Without Kris' salary we'd be in trouble. I'm a kept man. Perhaps we'll get a break and things will look a bit more promising. You never know, it's in the lap of the gods." Dil seemed quite unconcerned, I envied his relaxed attitude. The conversation dropped and I tucked into my bacon roll. Dil sipped his coffee.

My mind went back to the wild goose chase to Barnes when I was sure I was on the track of Evans-Peake. As if he was reading my thoughts, Dil asked, "You remember a while ago we were looking for someone for the band and we tried out a guy who said he knew you. He was a sax player. Then I think you rushed off somewhere with Lucy to see him play. Did you find him?"

I thought back to that traumatic evening when I had panicked and rushed out of the pub in Barnes. "I never really found out," I said. "I went down with a migraine and we left early, so I didn't get a chance to talk to him. But I was in a cycling club for a while and I vaguely recognised him from that." I hoped Dil would accept my lies and drop the subject. It had been an embarrassing episode and not one I wanted to re-live.

The skeletal trees permitted views almost to the other side of the park. I could see the band stand in the centre and a gardener over the other side, slowly heading towards us pushing a wheel barrow with a broom balanced across it. His shuffling gait reminded me of an elderly person with a Zimmer frame, I wondered if he could walk without holding on to a barrow. Dil puffed on his cigarette and said nothing so I began to fish around. "I suppose Kris has told you that it's tricky times at Obsidian."

"Yes she did. That's one of the things I wanted to clear up with you Steve. We had a bit of a ding-dong about it to be honest. Not an unusual event in our household as you probably know. But I don't want to be sleeping on the couch for ever, Kris can be a bit fiery." He grinned at me in a conspiratorial way, as if I would also have had a similar experience. I had not. Lucy and I never argued, perhaps that was our problem? Neither of us could handle conflict so in the end, rather than having a big bust-up and storming off on our separate ways, we just drifted apart.

"Kris says you told her that I used her work e-mail to send private messages." Dil sipped his coffee and looked straight ahead.

I waited for a confession and some form of words which would excuse his behaviour. "I haven't", he said at last. "I don't know what her password is and I haven't ever used her account. Even when she has left it logged on and I could have looked at it, I haven't. Why would I? Most of it is way over my head."

I stirred some sugar into my coffee. "Well there appear to be e-mails sent from you on our mail server. You can understand why this sets alarm bells ringing. It's not what the e-mails might contain, the issue is one of security. How can anyone trust Obsidian with confidential information if unauthorised people are using the system? So if it wasn't you, and I do believe you Dil", I added this even though I didn't entirely believe him, "Then someone has broken into our system and that is very worrying. To be honest I was hoping you would say you had been using her e-mail, because that would have been relatively easy to deal with. Now we really do have a problem."

Dil puffed his cheeks out. "Well anyway, Kris wanted me to tell you or Brian in person because she thinks she is under suspicion. I thought it would be easier to have a chat with you. To be honest I'm a bit overwhelmed by Brian", he chuckled. "When I hear the word 'Merlin' I think of Brian as a wizard with a magic wand, not someone who wrote a clever computer program."

I sipped my coffee. "Well thanks Dil, I appreciate your honesty and I'm sorry if we have thought badly of you. But you can see how it looks from our point of view."

Dil tossed his paper cup into the bin as if that was the end of the issue. "What does Merlin do?"

"Merlin stands for 'Method for Extracting Relationships from Large Information Networks', Brian thought it up. Essentially it finds patterns in large databases, sometimes it's called 'knowledge discovery', sometimes 'data mining'. For example, a supermarket may collect information about what their customers buy and this would tell them something about what products they should promote. But they may not notice that people who bought one brand of baked beans also bought a particular brand of pasta sauce, so knowing that, they might promote them together as a special offer."

I glanced at Dil out of the corner of my eye, he still seemed to be interested.

"In our case, pharmaceutical companies collect vast amounts of data when they are looking for new drugs or testing them. Much of it comes from automated instruments which run twenty-four-seven, churning out numbers. They will usually have a question which they are trying to answer, for example does the drug work? But there might be additional information hidden in the data which they miss because they are not looking for it. Perhaps patient outcome is better if they live in the midlands, so they might then investigate environmental factors.

But there is so much data that the wood gets lost in the trees, there are just too many possibilities for a real person to investigate, so Merlin does that for them. You just chuck in loads of data and it comes up with correlations and clusters. And Merlin is special because we believe it is more accurate and much faster that other methods. It's based on some clever maths that Brian thought out when he was at Imperial College." I rubbed my hands together to warm them up. "End of sales pitch."

"And is it going to be successful?"

"We hope so but it's an all or nothing game. If Axiom buy it, all of their competitors will want it too. Then Brian buys an Aston Martin, I buy a new push bike and we all retire to the Caribbean. On the other hand, if they don't buy it, then it will be much harder to persuade others to invest in it. Word gets around."

"Let's hope they do buy it then, Kris seems pretty pumped up about it." Dil dropped his fag end onto the path and stubbed it out with the heel of his shoe thoughtfully. "I haven't heard from Helen recently." He said it as if it was a throw away remark. "We were going to work on her 'schools' project in Kathmandu but she hasn't contacted me for quite a while. I've tried phoning and e-mailing but she doesn't reply. Is she OK?"

"Yes, she's fine. Our Father had a stroke and she's probably a bit preoccupied with getting him back on his feet. She often visits them to support my Mum. I'm afraid she is a bit more dutiful than me." We both instinctively withdrew our outstretched legs as the gardener trundled his barrow aimlessly past. I wondered why he was working on a Saturday.

We started to amble slowly along the perimeter path, Dil looking at his feet with hands clasped behind his back. "OK Dil, this is probably something which Helen should talk to you about, but I think I know what the issue is. You import clothes from Nepal right?" He didn't say anything. "One of Helen's researchers found your business and thought it was a bit dodgy. She thought you might be importing fake designer trekking clothes and selling them here as the real deal." I spoke as if it was just conjecture but I was sure it was true. "Anyway I think that's what it's about and of course Helen would be very wary of her charity getting involved in anything which wasn't squeaky clean, or which might be misinterpreted."

We walked on in silence. "Are you?"

Dil stopped and turned towards me. "Am I what? Importing fake clothing and passing them off as genuine? No Steve, of course I'm not." I began to think that I had given Helen bad advice when I had suggested she quietly dropped Dil. "I buy genuine handmade clothes from Nepali tailors and sell them here through small shops, most of which are Fair Trade outlets. I ensure that the Nepalis are fairly paid for the clothes and I ensure that there are no nimble-fingered children involved. If you want to take a look at my accounts, you're welcome. And yes, I make a return but so do the Nepalis. Steve, don't take this the wrong way, but if I compare my ethical position to your friends in big pharmaceutical companies, I think I come out of it quite well." Dil paused to let the point sink in before continuing. "Look, what you should do is take a trip down the Kilburn High Road. About half way down, next to the florist is a Fair Trade shop. Go in there and take a look for yourself, you're looking for clothes labelled, 'Adventure Himalaya'. See what you think. You might even want to buy something, it's all good quality. The alternative is to go to one of the cheap sportswear shops and buy a T shirt made in a sweat shop in Sri Lanka."

Trying to detach myself from Helen in a rather cowardly way I said, "Well sorry Dil if I have misunderstood, I'm just repeating what Helen told me. I should have spoken to you about it before jumping to conclusions."

I was hoping Dil would let the matter drop but he continued. "Steve, I think of you as a friend. I'm a bit disappointed that you think I might be doing this."

As far as I was concerned Dil was just an acquaintance who I had met through a work colleague. Clearly he saw me as a friend and that came as a surprise. He lit another cigarette and inhaled, blowing the smoke out through his nostrils, looking at his watch. "Right, got to get off to a rehearsal. We are still breaking Madeleine in."

"Look Dil I really am sorry. I was out of order." I offered my hand as he turned to face me, but he suddenly lunged towards me and clasped me in a hug, thumping my back.

"No problem buddy. See you later at the Nags Head? Kris is coming. I'm glad we've had this little chat."

"Yes. Thanks Dil." It wasn't until I got home that I thought, if Dil's business is all above board, even worthy, then how come he or Kris hadn't ever mentioned it?"

*****

It was nearly nine o'clock when I pushed open the heavy door and entered the familiar Nags Head. It was heaving. Compared to the dimly lit quiet street outside it was like stepping into another, more real world. A world where everything was bright, noisy and shiny. People excusing their ways between bar and table with glasses brim full, bumping into friends and stopping to chat. Sudden loud coarse laughter as a group of lads share a joke. Saturday night in a busy London pub with your mates and a pint of ale, the cares of the week forgotten for a few hours. Drink and be merry, for this world is much better than the one outside.

It took me a while to spot Krishna, Dil and the rest of the band. They were squeezed around a small table in the corner of the bar. Kris happened to look in my direction and I mimed a drink, she held up her empty glass, it would be a white wine spritzer. By the time I had meandered my way to their table, the Brondesbury Jazz Quintet were standing up to go. Amongst them I saw a strikingly tall woman wearing a deep red, full length, backless dress with a plunging neck line. She wore white lacy gloves which almost reached her elbows and a white rose, pinned in her jet black hair which tumbled down her back. Martin, the keyboards player and leader, nodded toward Madeleine who was weaving her way, hands in the air, towards the small stage crowded with instruments and sound gear. "What do you think of our new singer?" I raised my eyebrows approvingly without saying anything. "A French fancy.

132

That's what I call her." He leered at me, licking his lips salaciously. "Wouldn't mind a few French lessons from her. Eh Steve?" He nudged me with his elbow. I could also see that Madeleine would open a few doors for the band if she could sing even half as well as she looked. Dil clapped me on the back. "Good to see you mate." Randall the huge bass player jogged my elbow as he passed. Then in a turmoil of 'mind your backs' and 'coming throughs', they were gone.

I sat down at the table, now just me and Kris. She smiled and we clinked glasses. I was suddenly aware that I had more friends than I thought. I thought of the guys in the band as acquaintances, but they all knew my name and wanted to say hello to me. I was one of them, they were my friends. Not as close as Brian, but friends nevertheless. I couldn't explain why I had never realised it. Perhaps because I always relied on Lucy to make friends for both of us.

Kris drew close, her presence accompanied by a cloud of perfume. "Thanks for clearing up the e-mail thing with Dil this morning," she touched my hand. "He's much happier." The spot lights were switched on, Kris turned toward the stage shouting back over her shoulder. "By the way, the Brondesbury Jazz Quintet has gone electric". It didn't work for Bob Dylan, I thought as I also turned to face the stage. Sure enough, Spoons was putting the strap of an electric guitar over his head and plugging in a jack lead. Randall no longer hunched over a double bass, was tuning up an electric bass and hitting a few funky slap notes, nodding to the other guys as he did so. Dil was seated behind his drum kit grinning from ear to ear. He waved at Kris with a drum stick. There was a vacant microphone at the centre of the stage, standing patiently like a groom at a wedding, but his bride was nowhere to be seen.

Martin looked over his stack of keyboards, establishing a connection with each of the musicians in turn with a raised eyebrow, then he nodded at Dil who clapped his sticks high above his head. "One, two, three, four". They all hit the first explosive note simultaneously and continued with a pulsating rhythm. Dil beating his sticks on the floor tom and crash cymbal, his feet operating the bass drum and the ride cymbal, Randall strode around the stage trailing a long lead, freed from a static double bass. They continued with the driving riff, all heads nodding in time as they settled into the groove. The Brondesbury Jazz Quintet had not only gone electric, they had gone Jazz Funk. After a minute or so, every head in the pub turned as the spectacular Madeleine slowly stepped up onto the low stage, gathering her full length gown in her left hand. She picked the mike off the stand with her right, swivelled on her heels to face the audience, eyes shut tight, then struck a pose with one leg bent at the knee and held up her arm. The band stopped. Madeleine opened her eyes wide and waited, like a school teacher, for absolute silence. Then she growled into the microphone, "C'est si bon." The band joined in and the pub went wild as they continued with an up-beat version of the old Eartha Kit standard. Then they blasted their way through three more up-tempo numbers without a break, after which it was Madeleine, not Martin, who introduced the band. She spoke quickly in a low voice with a thick French accent. It was almost impossible to work out what she was saying but, I thought, when you look like that and can sing like she can, frankly, who cares?

At the end of the set, the pub erupted in applause. Kris was jumping up and down and wolf whistling. The spot lights went out and the band descended. Spoons and Randall went to join a group of their friends over the other side of the bar. Dil and Martin came over to join us. Kris gave Dil a hug and I clapped Martin on the back. "Great stuff", I said. "Really enjoyed it."

"Isn't Madeleine amazing." Martin turned away without waiting for an answer. Kris was still congratulating Dil leaving me momentarily on my own. I scanned the bar looking for that strikingly tall figure in the shimmering red dress, hopeful. But Madeleine had gone, leaving a seared image in my memory.

Chapter 14

On Tuesday morning we were all in the office awaiting Edith. It was an important meeting but we were confident in our abilities. Whatever she threw at us, we thought we could handle it. At nine-thirty the intercom buzzed. Faith pressed the button to open the door and got out of her chair, but Kris was already on her feet and heading down the stairs. We heard her greet Edith warmly as they tramped back up.

Edith was thin faced and angular, with stick-like limbs, her silver-grey hair was cut short, designed to be manageable rather than attractive. She wore blue jeans and a light weight cardigan over a T-shirt and trainers on her feet. I guessed she was in her fifties, the clothes looked too young for her. Anyway, I thought, there is no need for power dressing when you are 'top dog'. Edith was 'top dog' and she knew it. She had many years of experience and several very prestigious publications behind her. Edith tended to do things her way and the management just had to put up with it, nobody would risk criticising her.

She sat herself down at the head of the table in the meeting room, carefully placing her shoulder bag on the floor. Looking down the length of the table, she was faced with the lens of our projector, as if staring down the barrel of a small cannon. Edith spoke first, pulling her thick rimmed spectacles down her nose. She indicated the projector, "I do hope you haven't got any boring power-point presentations. We seem to be obsessed with them at Axiom. You see people working at their desks and you think they're doing some science but no, they're putting presentations together." Edith looked around at us expecting nods of agreement. "I just refuse to do it," she continued. "I send the buggers scurrying off to find a flip chart for me and a couple of marker pens."

I looked at Brian, knowing he had spent hours preparing a presentation. He smiled, "That's fine with us. We'll try not to bore you."

Edith opened her notebook, ran her thumb down its spine to flatten the page. She looked up. "Right let's make a start shall we."

"Are we expecting James Grey from your IT security team to join us?" I said.

Edith shook her head. "No, I told him not to come. Once James goes off into his technobabble I can't understand a word he says, he might as well be speaking bloody Klingon. I've invited Sebastian instead, he's the IT specialist from my group. He hasn't been with us very long but at least I can understand most of what he says, which is ironic since he's Hungarian." She looked at her watch. "He should be here any minute".

Kris pitched in with some chatter to oil the proceedings. "I didn't know you lived just around the corner?" Edith was forced into small talk. "London suits me and I never found enough enthusiasm for Cambridge to move over there, it's full of woolly headed waffley academics. Having said all that, the area I live in now is attracting a spate of burglaries so I might have to reconsider, or install a burglar alarm."

Kris glanced into the main office. "Ah, I imagine this must be Sebastian." Edith looked over her shoulder and waved him in to the meeting room with a sharp gesture. Sebastian spoke with a heavy East European accent and excessive politeness. "Good morning to you all, my name is Sebastian Molnar. I am responsible for Group IT, they call it GIT. It's quite funny, git." His serious face broke into a laugh as he looked around at each of us. Edith remained emotionless but I immediately warmed to him.

Edith peered over her spectacles. "Right, I suggest we divide into two groups. Sebastian, you go with Dr Calder," she nodded towards Brian, "And run through the IT security audit. The rest of us can stay here and talk business." Brian and Sebastian were about to get up. "Before you rush off, let me set the tone." Edith sat back in her chair, put the fingertips of her hands together. "We are not here to pull Obsidian to bits or to find fault, as far as I am concerned this meeting falls under the term, 'due diligence'. We are not here because we don't trust you and we are not expecting perfection. Is that reasonable?" She paused. "OK off you go then and leave the rest of us to talk about where we are going with Merlin." Brian and Sebastian left the meeting room like a couple of kids being given permission to play in the sand pit.

Edith folded her arms on the table. "Right Stephen, where would you like to start?" My mind went blank, I couldn't think how to respond but Kris came to my rescue. "Perhaps we should start with our latest proposal for a pilot study and staged payments." She pushed a few pages towards each of us across the table. As we talked, I occasionally glanced through the glass partition. Brian and Sebastian were sitting together, Brian scribbling diagrams on a pad of paper. He was doing most of the talking and I suspected that they had got side-tracked into discussing the specifics of Merlin rather than our IT security.

Edith was measured and reasonable. Having established her dominant position, she was able to climb down a rung or two and be a bit more human. She assured us that money wasn't the issue at stake. A few thousand pounds or even tens of thousand pounds was small beer when compared with the total cost of their Sigma project. The issue simply was, did Merlin work and could it dig up new information hidden in their deep sea of data.

Lunch was a brief affair. A couple of platters of sandwiches from the local delicatessen augmented with some designer crisps and fruit juice. After about thirty minutes we were ready to continue. Brian took the initiative. "Let me bring you up to date with the results of our data analysis. But first a brief recap for Sebastian's benefit." Sebastian sat up straight, bright eyed and attentive. "Merlin is essentially a package of software for intelligent data mining which we have developed here in Obsidian. It will assimilate all of the data we throw at it, looking for correlations and clusters in 'n-dimensional space', in other words, does one thing depend on another. The difference with Merlin is that it learns as it goes. It builds up a 'likelihood matrix' which weights parameters according to past experience. So the more data you give it, the better it gets. This is the way we humans learn. A real person would soon learn that a link between the outcome of the trial and the subjects age was more likely than a link to their shoe size."

"Unless it's a treatment for athlete's foot", Edith said dryly.

"Indeed, which is why we don't ever discard any data, we just weight it differently, giving it more or less significance." Brian looked around to check everyone was still with him. "So we have been running some of the data from your Sigma project as a pilot study. This helps us to fine tune Merlin and establish that it works on real data.

"And what's in it for Axiom?" Sebastian asked.

"You get to try it before you buy it. So far this has been a mutually convenient informal agreement, but I think that we are about to move into a different phase where you are prepared to fund us for the next stage of tests."

Brian continued to talk about Merlin in response to a volley of very perceptive questions from Sebastian. I began to realise that Sebastian was interested in more than IT. Perhaps that was why Edith had brought him, and not the usual IT guys. After a while I decided that I needed to move the discussion on; Brian could talk for hours about Merlin. I waited for a gap and then I jumped in.

"Brian, have we got any results?" knowing perfectly well that we did.

Brian drained his mug of lukewarm tea. "The good news is that we have lots and lots of results, however most of them are relatively trivial, interesting but not significant. As far as the main outcome of the trials are concerned, everything we have found supports the main conclusions which are very positive about Sigma." He smiled at Edith who barely nodded her head in response.

"The latest sets of results however are proving a bit more interesting. We have found some results which might give us some

139

new information. I don't want to go into too many details yet because it's early days. I am going to run some of the biopsy data sets more closely, then we will tweak the input parameters to look for the effect we think we have detected." Brian merrily continued to explain his findings. I glanced across the table at Edith. She was listening intently, her chin cradled in her hands supported by elbows on the table, lips clamped shut and eyes wide open. She cleared her throat and interrupted Brian.

"Thanks Brian for bringing us up to date, I don't think we need to go into any more details just now. If you do come up with some interesting correlations, will you let me know in person please." Brian was about to insist on continuing but he saw sense and relaxed back in his chair. Edith was now back in the driving seat.

Sebastian said that he had been through all the security issues on his list and that he would prepare a report. There were, however a couple of minor problem areas which needed looking at. Sebastian stood up in a formal way, speaking with a heavily accent. "Firstly, there appear to have been some security breaches of e-mail system. This is not critical situation, not big deal but the fact that unauthorised people have managed to get access to the system is troubling. Particular example is Dil." He looked at Brian for support. I jumped in quickly. "Yes, Dil is Kris' husband and we have discovered that he has occasionally used her laptop because his wasn't working," I lied. "So technically it was a breach of security, but in practise Dil does not present a risk. We've had words with him about it. It won't happen again."

Kris kept quiet, but it was clear from her expression that the matter was not closed. This was a flagrant betrayal.

Sebastian continued. "The other issue is data backup tapes. There was fault about a month ago but it was put down to a faulty tape so I think that's OK as long as it is not repeated. Backup tapes are kept off site so I can't inspect them. I decided to pick one month at random and ask Brian to get tape just to prove it exists."

"How about last May." Edith chipped in.

Sebastian continued. "Yes, that's acceptable. I think Edith you could drop in sometime next week to verify that it exists." He looked in her direction.

We all waited but Edith didn't reply. She pushed her chair back from the table and clasped her hands behind her head, a flicker of a smile ran across her face. "A little bird told me that you kept the backups under your bed, Brian." She paused. "I do hope that isn't the case." Brian looked like a schoolboy who had just been caught smoking behind the bike sheds. "Absolutely correct Edith, I sleep with them every night." He smiled defiantly at her.

The meeting was quickly concluded. Sebastian promised to summarise the results of his audit in an e-mail and Kris would send draft contracts across to Edith. I sat on the edge of Faith's desk waiting for Kris to run back up the stairs. Brian returned to the meeting room with his laptop and began typing. Kris walked straight past me. "Debrief Steve." She stormed into the meeting room, I followed in her wake.

Brian looked up as we entered. "Kris I know you are probably angry, and I can understand that but what else could I say? The alternative was to tell Sebastian that we had unauthorised people breaking into our e-mail system."

"And we do." Kris was almost shouting. "But instead of getting to the bottom of it you choose to tell them that it's my husband."

Brian shook his head. "Come on Kris, it's not such a big deal."

"It is a big deal to Dil. He went out of his way to meet up with you last Saturday, Steve, and you told him that you accepted that he wasn't using our e-mail. Then you just sit here and tell Edith that Dil is to blame. Sorry guys, but that was just wrong." She looked from me to Brian, eyes glistening with tears. Her voice began to break up with emotion. "I may be over reacting but I've taken so much stick from my family over Dil. They think he's a waster, they think he's stupid, they tell me he's work-shy, when is he going to get a proper job which pays some money and when is he going to stop sponging off me? And now you two are happy to use him as the fall guy again? Would you have said the same if it had been Chloe or Lucy?"

There was silence, we knew she was right. Kris took a deep breath and put her hands flat on the table. "OK, I know you think I am going way over the top here, but there is history which you don't know about. You both let me down today, you put the business before people, so if you don't mind I'll work at home for the rest of the day and see you tomorrow." She gathered her papers and left the room. I watched as she slung her bag over her shoulder and waved at Faith on the way out. Brian was lost in thought, doodling on his pad. He tapped his pen on the table and looked up shaking his head slowly.

"How did she know?"

At first I thought he was referring to Kris. "Know what?"

"How did Edith know?"

"About the backup tapes being kept in a biscuit tin under your bed?"

"Yeah."

"Just a lucky guess I suspect."

"No, come on Steve, she knew."

"I don't see how she could have known."

"Something is going on Steve. There have been too many things going wrong. You remember that the backup didn't run last month and we thought the tape must be faulty, so we just put it in the tin under my bed and forgot about it. Well it wasn't faulty and you were right. You said that perhaps we had more data in the server than we thought and we had run out of space on the tape. I took a closer look, there were around two terabytes of files sitting in one of my folders and it had run out of space. I didn't put files there and they are not on the server now."

"What was in the files?"

"Junk as far as I can see, just random numbers. Billions of them."

Could it be that Evans-Peake and his wretched notebooks is somehow mixed up in this? Brian continued. "Then what about the
142

Axiom data that was leaked back to them. Who would do that? The finger points at Dil using Krishna's account but why would he do it? Or was it Krishna? It doesn't make sense. So we scurry around trying to get to the bottom of it, fighting amongst ourselves, and all of a sudden Axiom says it's all fine, panic over. But we never did get to the bottom of it." I was beginning to see his point. "You spoke to Dil over the weekend didn't you. Do you think he is telling the truth when he says he hasn't used Kris' e-mail?"

"I know he has a reputation for charming people but to be honest, I think he is," I said. "He went out of his way to clear things up."

"So then who sent those e-mails which were apparently from him? Was it you, me, Kris or Faith?"

The tone of Brian's voice was rising, he had the bit between his teeth.

"And here's another strange thing. Sebastian didn't have a business card and I didn't get his Axiom e-mail address, but I can guess what it is because they all use the same format. Edith is edith.summers@axiom.com, James Grey's address is james.grey@axiom.com and so on. So I have just sent an e-mail to sebastian.molnar@axiom.com and guess what, it got bounced back from the Axiom mail server. Sebastian doesn't exist in Axiom. What do we conclude from that?"

"That he doesn't work for Axiom?"

Brian thumped the table with his fist. "Exactly, so why did Edith not bring her IT specialist, James Grey or her compliance officer, Simon Bron. Instead she brings someone who doesn't even work for Axiom?"

Brian paused. I had nothing to say but he had more.

"And here's the big one. Why did Edith shut me up when I started talking about our latest results from Merlin?"

"I wasn't aware that…."

Brian leaned towards me over the table, his voice soft and intense. "I was looking directly at her Steve and I saw the expression on her face. She shut me up because she was afraid of something. There is something in that data that she doesn't want us to find." He shut the lid of his laptop and began gathering up his papers.

"Alright let me think about it, perhaps you are on to something, but God knows how we have got ourselves mixed up in it. I suggest we wait until they send their reports across and then discuss it again. Brian nodded and headed back to his desk.

Later that evening Brian called me at home. "Steve, if you want more proof that something is going on, how about this. I have just got all the backup tapes out from under my bed and found that tape twenty is missing."

"Let me guess, that's the one from last May."

"Exactly. It's the one I'm supposed to bring in to show Edith."

Chapter 15

On Friday morning I tramped wearily up the stairs to the office. I dumped my satchel on my desk and flopped into the chair. A sense of irrational despair washed through my head. We will get the report on our IT system, we will be exonerated, Kris would settle down and Merlin would be a success. It all seemed a long way off.

The ever-watchful Faith swivelled her chair. "My, my, someone looks tired this morning." I avoided eye contact. "When Jackson comes home from school looking like that, I know it's no good saying anything. I just sit him down in front of the TV and give him a drink and a biscuit. After half an hour, he's running around again."

I shook my head. "Don't you ever get down Faith? Or is it wall-to-wall Caribbean beer and skittles with you, all day long? And by the way don't tell me to count my blessings, I had enough of that when I was a kid at Sunday school. It really doesn't help to know that I am just like your Jackson and it won't be made better with a chocolate biscuit."

There was no excuse for my corrosive mood and words. It wasn't the end of the world, it was me, overreacting to a situation which most people would take in their stride. Faith absorbed my anger. "Well I don't have a TV to sit you down in front of but there are still some chocolate biscuits left from Monday. I'll go down to the kitchen and make you a mug of strong coffee."

I plugged my laptop in, tapping my fingers and staring vacantly at the screen while it booted up. A series of e-mails pushed their way in at the top of my crowded 'in box', jostling for my attention.

Faith returned with coffee and biscuits. "Too much partying and burning the candle at both ends?"

146

I wished it were partying, if only my life was that exciting. "I think it's just a combination of things, Dad's stroke, breaking up with Lucy, the business and now," I raised my voice, "waiting for Axiom to send that bloody report through?"

Brian spoke up, "I chased Sebastian earlier this morning. He apologised and promised to send it over today.

"Well that's good of you since according to you Obsidian is finished."

"Keep your hair on Steve."

Faith refereed. "There you are Steve, it's on its way, that's one thing off your mind already."

"We don't know what's in it yet, and I don't need to be patronised."

Brian pushed his chair back violently, but before he could stand up the phone rang and Faith went back to her desk to answer it. Merry Mick was on the line, wanting to talk to her about the accounts, another little worry of mine. She listened for a bit, then put her hand over the phone handset and mouthed, "He's more miserable than you Steve."

I imagined what Mick was saying at the other end of the line, his continuing troubles colliding with Faith's West Indian inspired optimism, neither giving an inch. And I was heading for depression unless I sorted myself out. I was double dosing sleeping pills regularly, combined with a bottle of wine most evenings. I continued to stare at my screen, sipping coffee while the after effects wore off.

Mid-afternoon, Brian and I received Sebastian's report from Edith via e-mail. I opened the attachment and started to read. I heard Brian mutter, "Christ Almighty," under his breath. Sebastian listed the issues we had discussed along with several more that we hadn't. It was a catalogue of failings with our security, most of them labelled in red as 'critical'. It made us look like incompetent fools. Brian's voice was getting louder and his inflexion more Scottish as he read. "Was this bugger at the same meeting? This is bloody nonsense."

I skipped through the details of the IT survey, looking for the Merlin pilot study agreement that Kris and I had hammered out with Edith. Brian was now shouting. "Right Steve, I've had enough of this crap. Let's get hold of that little arse Sebastian and find out what he thinks he is playing at. He needs to know that we are not standing for this." He reached for his phone.

"Have you seen that last page?" I asked.

"No, I'm not reading any more of this nonsense." He slammed the hand-set back on its cradle and pushed his chair back. "What's in the last page then? 'And they all lived happily ever after?'"

"They are terminating all agreements with Obsidian with immediate effect." I read. "They want us to delete all copies of their data. It says there has been 'an internal change of emphasis driven by business requirements', whatever the hell that means. They have decided they don't need Merlin or us. No pilot study, no staged payments, no product endorsements. They're offering us five thousand pounds as a good will gesture. Take it or leave it."

Brian was now steaming. "Good will? That's an insult for a start. I'll tell that Edith where she can stick her five thousand quid, and she can have it all in pound coins. See how she likes being shafted. Shit. OK Steve we'll sue the bastards."

Faith was still talking on the phone, she covered the handset and clicked her fingers to get Brian's attention, then put a finger to her lips. Brian continued to bluster in a soft voice, "might as well put the phone down now Faith. It's the end of line for Obsidian." He got out of his chair, snatched some pages off the printer and pointed at the meeting room. We closed the door carefully behind us. I had rarely seen Brian quite so emotional, rejecting Merlin was like rejecting his one and only child. He couldn't see past our current position, the road was completely blocked, nothing to do but put Merlin back in its box, turn around and head back home. All his hopes, his ingenuity, his creativity, not to mention his time had been invested in this one project.

Probably that was our biggest mistake, but we were so close to making it all work. We thought it was in the bag. Brian stood with his back to me, looking out of the window onto the street below, shaking his head, finding it hard to believe that the world outside was continuing as normal. Vans still making deliveries, taxis picking up fares, Mums collecting children.

Without turning he said. "Well Steve, where do we go from here?"

There was a ringing in my head, this was it then. I felt strangely calm, the scary monster had been unmasked and we had to face up to it. Brian, flicking through the pages of the report, unreceptive. "Of course we can't sue them. They can hire ten lawyers to every one of ours. It would bankrupt us if we aren't bankrupted already. The ones with the biggest guns usually win." Brian looked at me for some acknowledgement.

"We don't really know what's going on behind the scenes." I said. "We need to talk to more people at Axiom to get a bigger picture. Why was everything so matey last Tuesday and now we get the cold shoulder? Why go to all this trouble to discredit us rather than just politely terminating our agreement?"

Brian wasn't convinced. "And just how are we going to find out any more now? Looking at the tone of the report I don't expect they will invite us back to their place for a chat and more chocolate biscuits." He looked across the table at me, eye brows raised at my naivete.

"We do what Mick suggested. We send Kris in, she knows other people and other groups at Axiom. I've done some consultancy work for some of them. Let's see what they know and what they are prepared to tell us. It's worth a shot, at least it may give us a chance to tell our side of the story."

"That means we will have to tell Kris everything", Brian said.

"We were going to have to tell her that anyway, she's also put lots of effort into the Merlin project. Better to involve her and make use of her networking skills. She will find things out. Who's going to shut the door in her face? People want to talk to her."

"What do you and I do next then?" Brian tapped the table top. "Go down the Nags Head and sob into our beer while wonder woman gets her sparkly pants on?"

"We do nothing for the time being. We won't reply to Axiom yet, it took them long enough to get the report to us after all. We let them wonder what our next move will be. Remember that we still have their data and we could make things difficult for them if we chose to. They will be expecting us to respond."

"And they can bloody whistle for their precious data," Brian interjected.

"We'll get Kris in here on Monday, tell her the whole story and make a plan. She might even already have an idea about what is going on there. Let's not throw in the towel yet, we still have another round in us."

Brian tapped his fingers on the table and looked up, past me into the distance. "OK Steve, let's keep going. Seconds out, round two. But I'm telling you now, it will just bring on more tears."

I didn't stay long in the office, somehow there didn't seem to be much point. Arriving back home to a cold empty house, I switched the lights on and fired up the central heating. My mind had been clear and analytical in the office, but now it was going around in circles, unable to focus. I filled the house with noise from the hi-fi as a distraction. It was at times like this when I missed Lucy. First she would say soothing words to take away the sting, then she would talk through the situation, telling me to imagine the worst that could happen and then explaining to me that it's not the end of the world.

"So what if Obsidian dies, nobody else does, we all go off and find new jobs," she would say. "Without the office rent and the Merlin development, you can easily support yourself with the consultancy business. You just have to get through the next month or so and then things will be clearer." That's what Lucy would say I told myself. Lucy with her steady job and sensible clothes. Lucy with her two feet firmly on the ground. Lucy with her rich mummy and daddy in bloody Buckinghamshire to bail her out.

I called her mobile. She picked up on the fourth ring. "Hi Steve. How's things?"

I couldn't tell from the tone of her voice whether she was pleased to hear my voice or not. "They have been better," I said.

"Is it your Dad?"

"No, it's work really. It's getting me down a bit. We're being kicked around by a big company, and Brian's pretty upset about it."

"Brian's upset?"

"I suppose we both are really. It could push Obsidian over the edge."

More silence, she wasn't making this easy. "So look. You're probably doing something this evening, but just in case you are free, I was wondering if you might like to go out for a bite to eat. Just for a chat, nothing fancy." I said 'nothing fancy' to make the point that this wasn't a big deal. I wasn't trying to get back together again or anything like that.

I steeled myself for the brush off, defensive words already forming in my head, ready to drop the roller blind and hide my emotions. I expected that she would already have plans and she would suggest that I could call next week if I still wanted to go out. And that was probably no more that I deserved.

"Well, as it happens, I'm not doing anything and it is Friday night after all."

"Shall we go to the usual pizza place then. I'll see you there at eight?"

At seven-thirty the phone rang, it was Brian.

"Steve, I need you to get over here now."

"Where are you?" I asked.

"I'm still in the office. You need to get over here now," he repeated. "Merlin's found something."

The personification of Merlin was typical when Brian was excited. He and Merlin were a team, a proud Dad with his arm around his boy.

"I can't Brian, I'm meeting Lucy in thirty minutes. I was about to walk out of the door."

"Lucy? I thought that was all over."

"It is all over, I just thought we………"

"Well you will just have to rearrange it. Take her for a drink later."

"I can't do that to her."

"Then bring her with you." Brian spoke urgently. "Come on Steve, this is more important than taking your ex-girlfriend out. Blame me if you like. Tell her I've twisted your arm, or do it tomorrow, she won't mind. I'll see you in few minutes." He hung up without allowing me to reply.

I called Lucy's number again; it rang. I was hoping it would go through to voice mail and I could leave a cowardly message. She picked up on the fifth ring. This time she sounded warm, pleased it was me calling. I told her that Brian was still working at the office. That he was panicking, in a bad way, very emotional and I needed to get over there. There's no knowing what he might do, I hinted. I was so sorry but perhaps tomorrow evening?

Lucy was as ever, calm and measured. She said she was busy tomorrow and that I wasn't to worry, there were other things she should be doing anyway. And I wished she wasn't so reasonable. I wished she had shouted at me and slammed the phone down. But that wasn't how Lucy behaved, and therein lay the rift between us. Opposites attract and we were not opposites. I realised I had made the wrong choice, obeying the one who shouted the loudest, but there was no going back now.

Chapter 16

The office stairway was in darkness. I felt for the light switch and multiple fluorescent tubes stuttered into life. I climbed the stairs, angry at my own weakness, this had better be important. Brian was sat at his desk in the gloom, staring at his computer screen, face lit by an articulated desk lamp. There were three empty mugs on his desk and an open packet of biscuits. I switched the room lights on, Brian looked up. "I think I've got them by the short and curlies Steve."

"Who?"

"Axiom. I think I know what is going on."

I wheeled my desk chair around to his desk, he moved to one side to share his screen.

"The latest batch of data we received from Axiom were the results from the Sigma toxicology studies. You remember, Edith shut me up as soon as I started to talk about our latest results."

I thought that 'shut me up' was a bit strong but certainly, she had wanted to move on. More likely that she didn't want a full blow by blow of the analysis. Brian had a tendency to go into too much fine detail.

Brian clicked away with his mouse. "Hold on a minute while I find what I'm looking for and I'll show you what I've got." He looked up. "Thanks for coming in by the way."

I sat back and waited, already beginning to think that surely it could have waited until tomorrow. The trouble was that when Brian got his teeth into something he became completely absorbed in it. Then, as he had proved, he could be very demanding and persuasive. Kris always said he could be good at sales if he wasn't such a 'know it all'. I listened to the sparse traffic splashing by on the wet road outside, the fans in the computer cabinet purred away, a chime indicated that Brian had received a text message, he didn't seem to notice. I fished in my trouser pockets for my phone. Looking at the screen, hoping Lucy might have sent me a message. She hadn't.

I heard steady footsteps coming up the stairs. Who else would be in the building this late on a Friday night? The door was slowly nudged open and Chloe appeared with a mug in each hand.

"Hi Steve. Sorry I would have made you a cup." She put one mug on Brian's desk and we pecked at each other's cheeks. Chloe retreated to Faith's desk, humming a tune under her breath. "Don't mind me, I'm just sitting over here browsing the web." She whispered to me conspiratorially. I admired her slim figure as her back was turned.

Brian filled me in without looking up from his computer. "Chloe didn't particularly want to stay alone in our flat so she came over to keep me company. And, before you ask, I've created a guest account on the server which doesn't give any access to Obsidian data. The password is 'guest'."

"Can't you stop him Steve?" Chloe looked pleadingly at me. "It's Friday night and he's obsessed with work. We're supposed to be going for a drink with Paul and Lizzie." She cooed a big sigh at Brian.

Brian wasn't to be distracted, he adjusted the angle of his computer screen to attract my attention. "These are the results from the Sigma animal toxicology trials. As you can see Merlin converts correlation strength to colours on a map. Where you see red there is a strong link between two or more factors." He looked at me to make sure I was following, then he pointed at the rainbow coloured image with his pen. "Here and here you can clearly see the areas we are interested in. The big red area is the strong link that we expect between mice receiving Sigma and disease recovery, the confidence is greater than ninety-five percent. In other words, there is a less than five percent chance that we are wrong."

I interrupted. "Yes Brian I am well aware what 'confidence limits' are all about. It's Friday night, I've given up a nice cosy dinner with Lucy, so I don't need a lesson in statistics." Chloe's head appeared over her computer screen when she heard my raised voice. I smiled at her and spread my arms. "I'm sure Chloe wouldn't mind heading for the pub before too long." She gave me a thumbs-up.

Brian was cornered. "OK here's the point. Look at the other red areas on the map, this one tells us that there is a difference in response between sexes. Male mice did a little better than females. Interesting and good to know but not critical to the general efficacy of the drug. But take a look at this long red ribbon here. It shows that the rate of still births is significantly higher amongst the cohort of mice who had been given Sigma."

"So what, Sigma is meant to halt the progress of Parkinson's and Parkinson's disease is a disease of old age, it's irrelevant. People who will take Sigma will be too old to be pregnant."

"Early onset Parkinson's can be diagnosed in people in their forties. Since women are increasingly having babies later in life, this is important. It may mean that ultimately the application of Sigma is limited to older people but it will have to be investigated, and that will take time. It's going to put the release date back considerably, years. At the very least they will have to run all of the toxicology stuff again."

"Well that's good news for us isn't it? Presumably now that we have really found something significant, they will want to buy Merlin. It's proved itself in the nick of time."

Brian saw things differently. "It may be a last minute reprieve for Merlin, alternatively they may want to shoot the messenger. Last Tuesday Edith realised we were getting close to discovering a problem with Sigma, something which they already know and something she wants to cover up. They didn't think we would spot the problem, but they underestimated Merlin." Brian slapped his pen down on the desk with an air of triumph, issuing a challenge to me to prove him wrong.

"This all sounds a bit James Bond to me," I said. "Surely a big drug company like Axiom isn't going to get involved in cover-ups.
156

This is exactly why they need Merlin, to dig out issues which need to be tackled. The last thing they want is to get to the point of submitting the drug to the FDA only to find it fails owing to side effects."

Brian nodded. "Yes, but suppose we are not dealing with corporate Axiom but with an insider who has her own reasons for not wanting Sigma to fail. Suppose we are dealing with Edith and perhaps a few others who are operating outside of the system, in their own interests. Perhaps they already know that there is a problem and are trying to cover it up."

I wasn't at all convinced. However, like the scientist that he was, Brian had put forward his hypothesis. Now it was up to me to try to shoot it down. I knew this game.

"OK, first objection. Why didn't they just terminate the agreement with us as soon as they realised Merlin might be a threat? Why go to the trouble of getting Sebastian in to discredit our IT system. And where does this tie in with the other IT issues we've had recently? As you said yesterday, who leaked the data and sent those e-mails, now that we have accepted that it wasn't Dil? And where's that missing backup tape and how come it just happens to be the one they requested?"

Brian swivelled his chair to face me. "Put yourself in Edith's shoes Steve. If they terminate their agreement with us, we might still keep copies of their data sitting on an off-line computer, even if we said we had deleted it. Edith would see us as a threat which would always be hanging over her. Potential whistle blowers. You can't bolt the stable door after the horse has bolted and we can't forget things we know."

"You're saying they can't really terminate the agreement."

"They may legally terminate the agreement but they can't make us 'un-know' what we know, so the better tactic is to discredit us. If they discredit us then it doesn't matter what we claim to have found, they can dismiss us as incompetent cowboys. They even have the documentary evidence to prove it. They carry out an IT security survey, then they write a report which says we were in a complete mess and they terminate our agreement on those grounds. And if in the future the little bird starts to sing, they say it's sour grapes and we are incompetent. Anyone would be foolish to pay any credence to anything that comes from Obsidian. Check mate. And while we are on the subject, what about our Hungarian mate Sebastian? He doesn't even work for Axiom and I suspect we will never hear from him again. I suspect Edith brought him in as a contractor to worm his way into our e-mail system and deliver the coup de grace via his report?"

I scratched my head. "And the missing backup tape is all part of the discrediting process?"

"Well this is where it gets a little scary. If I remember correctly, Edith was the one who suggested we look for backup tape twenty."

"The one from last May", I agreed.

Brian drew closer, glancing in Chloe's direction. "I don't want her to worry, but the only conclusion I can reach is that someone has broken into our flat and stolen the tape, and that Edith must be in on it. Because I'm sure that all the tapes were there. And if I had accidentally lost one, the chances of Edith picking that missing one to ask us to produce are vanishingly small."

I thought for a few moments, still looking into Brian's eyes and wondering if I was ahead of him. "Then I think we both know who that 'someone' who stole the tape is don't we?" Brian glanced over at Chloe then back at me. "No she wouldn't and I'm not discussing that now."

Chloe interrupted with a seductive voice. "What are you two guy's whispering about then?"

"Football."

"Fibber. You don't know the faintest thing about football, Brian. Come on, it's nearly nine-thirty, aren't you two getting thirsty?"

Brian went over to the computer cabinet and pushed a button to eject the backup tape, then he picked up a tape lying on his desk. He held them up, one in each hand. "This one," he waved his left
158

hand. "Is a backup of our server, done this evening. And this one," He waved his right hand, "Is a copy of everything on the old server which includes the Axiom data and results, and which we are not going to delete, in spite of them telling us to." Brian put the tapes in a padded envelope, sealed it and handed it to me.

"This is why I particularly needed you to come to the office Steve. I want you to take them home with you and hide them. Preferably not under your bed."

We had gone as far as we could for one evening. Brian shut the lid on his laptop and slotted it in his bag. Raising his voice, he addressed Chloe. "Cinderella, you shall go to the ball, or at least to the Nag's Head."

"You told Paul and Lizzie we would be there at nine". She shut Faith's computer down and stood up. "Coming Steve?"

I declined. The thought of a couple of hours talking to Brian's friends from the flat below, was not an attractive one. I wasn't in the mood to hear about the latest herbal remedy for every disease known to mankind, invented by some new age wizard who lives under a stone in Kashmir. Or their latest exercise regime which would further emaciate their sinewy, anorexic bodies. I had tried in the past to explain that the risk of being run down by a bus during their daily run far exceeded the benefit derived from it, but it seems that there is no place for a good honest statistician in their post-modern world.

We walked down the stairs switching lights off as we went. At the bottom I turned to Brian. "If for one moment I believe there is any truth in your theory, what's in it for Edith?"

Brian shook his head. "Dunno Steve."

So how farther forward had that little episode got us? Brian had worked out an implausible conspiracy theory and spoiled my evening. Why do I always give in to him? I let him drag me into the office on a wild goose chase which glorifies himself and his precious Merlin. Did he need me there to take the backup tapes away? Of course not.

I walked down the road to the small parade of shops, it was getting late but the pizza take-way was still flooding the pavement outside it with light. It was a short distance but late, so I hailed a passing cab. Having pressed the buzzer for the second floor flat I stepped back and looked up. There was a thin vertical line of light where the curtains didn't quite meet in the middle, I saw her pass it.

The intercom crackled. "It's Stephen," I said, "with a 'ph'." There was silence at the other end. "I've got pizza and a bottle of Chianti." I steeled myself for rejection, I was digging a hole for myself. "It's peperoni, your favourite. The pizza is...". I waited and looked up for a twitch of the curtains. Nothing, I turned to go.

The intercom crackled again. "It's supposed to be bloody Milk Tray chocolates." This was either a sign that Lucy was either furious or that she was, at least, a little amused.

"It's a peace offering. I'm very, very sorry Lucy. Can I come in, I'm starving." She made me wait a further ten seconds then I heard the lock click.

Lucy had a two-bedroom flat in what estate agents call 'a desirable part of North London'. Unlike my house, it was always spotless and tidy. She let the second bedroom to a string of lodgers in order to afford the mortgage repayments. The current tenant, Astrud, spent every weekend with her boyfriend who was a chef in a hotel somewhere on the south coast. This suited Lucy very well.

I demolished half of the pizza straight from the box while Lucy nibbled at one segment. The Chianti was a bit too cold but very drinkable. She turned the television sound down so that we could talk but she didn't turn it off, sometimes glancing at it, as if watching for something. Between mouthfuls, I told her about the problems Obsidian was facing without going into much detail. She had never been very interested in my work. I told her that Brian was very upset and it had been a good thing that I had gone in to calm him down.

"What are you going to do about it?" she asked.

"Send Kris in to dig around. She knows lots of people inside Axiom, so we'll stall until we see what she comes up with."

"The usual tactics then. You and Brian dither and stall while someone else makes the decision for you."

"We're not asking her to make a decision."

"If I was you, I'd be on the phone to the chairman of Axiom first thing on Monday morning."

"It's not that easy to phone up the chairman of a big company, and anyway he's going to side with his staff, not us. We don't have any evidence yet."

"Well it's your company Steve. What do I know."

Easy for you to say, I thought.

Lucy went off into the kitchen and came back with two mugs of coffee. She perched on a cream leather upholstered chair opposite me, her legs drawn up underneath. Slightly overweight, hair dishevelled, bespectacled, cosy slippered. We are not young any more I thought, when did we grow up? When did that happen? My hair was getting thin but inside I felt the same.

We exchanged news items. Lucy's Mother, Barbara, had tripped on a step and broken her hip, so Lucy had been going home to visit her most weekends. I brought Lucy up to date with the change to Dil's band and enthused about their new singer. It was all third person talk, nothing about us and what our relationship looked like now. And that suited me very well. She turned the TV up and we watched a late-night chat show together, not needing to talk. What had changed in our relationship? Not much apparently, or perhaps everything that was important had changed.

I stood up to go, Lucy stayed seated. On the spur of the moment, I reached into my bag and pulled out the padded envelope containing the backup tapes. "Would you mind looking after this for me?" I dropped it into her lap. "It's just some old data tapes. We don't want all of our eggs in one basket."

She looked up at me. "Tapes?"

"Yes, they're just backups from the Obsidian computer server. Open it and take a look if you like, it's nothing sinister. Just stick them in a drawer somewhere and forget about them. It's good practise to keep copies in various places."

Lucy stretched her arms up above her head and yawned. "OK Steve, I'm too tired to debate with you now. I'll stick them on top of the wardrobe in my bedroom, they'll be quite safe. Astrud won't go in there. It will be a little excuse for you to pop round again won't it."

"That's not it, Lucy."

I closed the front door carefully as I left and hailed a taxi. I had wanted to stay with Lucy, to snuggle up with her in bed, to listen to her soft breathing and feel her warmth, but she hadn't even got up to kiss me goodbye. As I sat in the taxi the reality began to dawn on me. Lucy was gone.

Chapter 17

The alarm went off at seven, I lingered in bed thinking and listening to the news on the radio. It was Monday morning, the eighteenth of November. This had to be the day Obsidian started to fight back I told myself, without any enthusiasm. The first priority was to bring Kris up to date. She would be upset that she hadn't been copied in on the report from Axiom, but hopefully she would agree to use her contacts and have a dig around. This would be a good time to call in a few favours in return for the many lunches and dinners they had consumed at Obsidian's expense.

I still wasn't quite sure that I agreed with Brian's analysis of the situation, that Axiom had been playing all sorts of under-hand tricks and were somehow 'out to get us'. But if it was the case, then how should we respond to the school bully, fight or flight? And what did those words mean in this context anyway? This was a watershed moment for Obsidian. What we achieved in the forthcoming week would define all our futures. I knew that nothing would be the same ever again, and I didn't want to face the uncertain future. An irrational sense of dread welled up inside me, the quicker I got out of bed and into the office, the better. But just now I wanted to burrow under a protective blanket of numbers, immerse myself in a familiar world where everyone and everything behaved normally and followed the rules. The voice of Billie Holiday crowded into my head:

Don't know why, there's no sun up in the sky. Stormy weather.

I parted the curtains. She was right about the weather. Gusts of wind splattered icy rain onto the window. I looked down onto a garden of overgrown grass and barely visible outlines of once tended flower beds. Moss was growing on the shed roof, preventing the rain from running down to the gutter. Soon the water would break through and drip onto my precious bikes inside. I pulled my thick dressing gown over my shoulders, tying the cord in a double knot and shuffled my feet into my slippers. Conditioned by habit, I stumbled down the stairs to make a mug of tea. As I opened the door to the sitting room at the foot of the stairs, there was an unfamiliar, slightly smoky smell and I could hear a radio playing soul quietly in the background. The single heavy curtain separating the sitting room from the open plan dining area was pulled across the arch. I hadn't closed the curtain. I never closed the curtain. Cold blue light filtered through the windows, I switched all the room lights on anyway. More puzzled than apprehensive, I pulled the curtain aside with one quick sweep.

Evans-Peake was sitting at the other side of my small dining table facing me. He was motionless, eyes closed, elbows resting on the table, chin supported on clasped hands. His face was framed by long locks of dark hair, tangled in ringlets cascading over his ears and down to his neck. Leathered skin adhered closely to his facial bones; eye sockets, nose, cheek bones, the loose jaw, all clearly defined. He could have been alive or he could have been dead.

All the air left my lungs. I panted short breaths, trying to quell the rising panic. The moment I had always known would come, had arrived. Evans-Peake was in my house. The last defence had been breached and fleeing wasn't an option, there was nowhere to go.

At first he didn't react to my presence. Then his reptilian eyelids fluttered and slowly opened revealing those tired smoke-grey eyes. Evans-Peake spoke quietly, hardly moving his lips, his voice pitched low, the words escaping like exhaled cigarette smoke.

"Dr Rockett."

I was yelling, "Get out! Get out!" but my ears heard no sound. I backed slowly towards the door to the hallway, keeping him fixed in my field of view. Would he pursue me? Could I make it to the front door before he did? My phone was in the bedroom, I could run up the stairs, barricade myself in and call for help. I continued to back away slowly as if placating a wild animal, all the time hoping he would say something to put me at my ease. To tell me that he meant me no harm. But he didn't.

"Dr Rockett." He repeated, pushing something towards the centre of the table, but still within his easy reach. I recognised my keys, I usually left them in the front door lock overnight. The front door was locked and he had the keys. "I'm afraid there's no escape." Such was his command of the situation that I didn't doubt him. I couldn't reach the back door without getting past him. There was no escape. I had no escape.

The only other thing on the table was my kitchen radio, tuned to a London jazz station and playing softly. Between tracks it broadcast an advert for a van hire company with a jolly jingle, a window through to another world. In desperation I found my voice at last. "Get out! Get out now!" I was yelling uncontrollably, my voice shaking with emotion. Pleading more than commanding. "Get out of my house!"

Evans-Peake reached for the radio. The presenter was introducing the next track, Aretha Franklin. He twisted the volume control in a single movement. *R.E.S.P.E.C.T* blasted out. The volume was now wound up far too high, the sound was distorted and metallic, I couldn't hear myself shouting anymore. Evans-Peake waited for a few seconds and then turned the volume back down.

I began to recover from the initial shock, fight took over from flight. I took quick glances around the room, looking for something I could use as a weapon, cursing myself that I had tidied up. There was usually a dirty plate with a knife and fork lying around. The best I could come up with was a pair of scissors in a mug on my desk top, along with pens and pencils. If he got violent, I guessed I would be quicker than him. As far as I could see he didn't have a knife, the only weapon he had was surprise, and that had now expired. Stand your ground and talk him round, I thought. Let him see you are not a threat, that everything can be resolved without having to resort to violence.

166

Evans-Peake cleared his throat. I could hear him breathe, it seemed to require some effort. There was no fight in him, only threat. He took a deep breath. "I want my note books."

He waited but I didn't respond. Suddenly, in a single movement, he stood up sending his chair somersaulting backwards into the kitchen. He was taller than I remembered, his brown, waxed stockman's coat reaching down to the ground. It was beltless and fastened with buttons from his neck to his knees. He raised his voice and repeated the command. "Dr Rockett. Give me my note books back."

When I didn't respond, he picked up the radio in one gloved hand and threw it at me. It glanced off my shoulder and crashed onto the glass top of my coffee table where it lay amongst the broken glass, battered but still playing cheerfully, oblivious to the abuse it had suffered.

I was scared by the sudden violence. "I don't have them."

"I know you don't have them. I've looked. But you know where they are."

Where had he looked? Had he been searching my house while I was asleep? I remained silent, wondering how many steps it would take to get to the scissors.

"Dr Rockett. You do know where they are?"

I tried to act defiant in spite of my fear. "They're gone. We couldn't decode them."

"But they weren't yours. They are mine."

I stared back at him, growing in confidence. Seconds ticked by seeming like minutes.

"Who are you?"

"You know who I am Stephen."

I shook my head, "I know your name."

His voice dropped to a rasping whisper.

"I'm the body in the hearse. I'm your worst nightmare. I am number 1712."

"What does that mean?"

He flew into a rage again. "You know who I am for Christ's sake, I'm 1712. And if you don't know, if you can't work it out, then ask her. She knows."

To my relief, Evans-Peake turned and strode back into the kitchen. He ducked as he left though the back door. I heard his steps as he strode down the passage at the side of the road. Grabbing the keys off the table, I locked and bolted the back door. Then I ran to check the front door. I raced up the stairs two at a time, grabbed my phone from the table beside my bed and pressed speed dial number one. Holding the phone to my ear, my heart beating, I looked out of the spare bedroom window at the front of the house, half expecting him to be standing guard outside, but Evans-Peake was nowhere to be seen.

The call went straight through to Brian's voice mail. I tried my sister Helen. She answered after the second ring.

"Steve. A bit early for you isn't it?"

I was pacing up and down the room breathing heavily. The sound of the door slamming played in my head, his voice echoed around. I didn't know where to start. "Where are you?"

"On the park and ride bus, on my way to the office. To be more precise I am on the top deck and third seat from…"

"Helen." My voice cracked and I took a sharp intake of breath.

She heard me this time. "Steve, what's wrong?"

"Evans-Peake was here. He broke into my house, I don't know how he did it. He threatened me. I think he might come back."

There was silence at the other end for a few seconds.

OK Steve, calm down and tell me who the hell Evans-Peake is?"

Chapter 18

By mid-morning the police had been and gone. I was still sitting on the sofa in my dressing gown looking at the broken glass, not knowing what to do next. My mind was looping the recent events again and again, trying to make sense of what had just happened without much success. Had I been burgled? Had I been threatened? Had I been injured? What had the police said?

A doorbell rang, insistent in the distance, then a knock at a door. I got out of the sofa, pulled the curtains apart a few inches and peered out of the window. Brian's distinctive sports car was parked outside, I opened the front door and he followed me into the sitting room.

"Faith told me you had been burgled." He stood looking at the smashed coffee table. "That's a bit of a mess. Did they take much?" I sank once more into the sofa. "Did you surprise them?", Brian took a brief look around, wandering through into the kitchen. "How did they get in?" He returned to the sitting room and stood in front of me. "Steve, talk to me mate. Are you OK? Have you called the police?" I nodded my head and nudged some of the broken glass into a pile with my slipper clad foot. "They've been and gone. I don't think there's much they can do."

"Right Steve, you go upstairs and get dressed and I'll get this glass cleared up to start with. Have you got a dustpan and brush? He started to root around in the cupboard under the sink in the kitchen without waiting for an answer. When I returned to the sitting room, Brian had cleared most of the mess up. He stood in the middle of the room, hands on hips. "I can't see that they have taken much, even your laptop's still here, probably just after cash or anything valuable they can stuff in a pocket. It's usually kids you know. Little buggers. How did the coffee table get broken?"

170

If only it were kids, I thought to myself. I would gladly hand over my wallet and all its contents to them. "It wasn't kids, it was Evans-Peake." I paused while the words sank in, I was telling it to myself as much as to Brian. "He wants his notebooks back."

"Christ Almighty Steve, he actually broke in? I didn't expect to hear from him again. Did you tell the police about him?"

"I started to tell them about him and the notebooks but it didn't fit into any of their boxes. I probably wasn't very coherent."

"But you threw the notebooks in a skip, didn't you?"

"I didn't tell Evans-Peake that, I just said I didn't have them. Then he threw the radio at me but it hit the coffee table." I looked up at Brian. "It was scary. I suppose he wants to give them to someone else to decode since we failed." I shook my head slowly. "He's not going to let me off the hook is he? He told me to find them, what am I going to do Brian?" Brian picked up the radio to inspect it, its plastic case was cracked.

"When I came down to make a cup of tea, he was sitting at the table, waiting for me. I knew it was him straight away." I fed information to Brian randomly as it occurred to me. "And when he stood up he was far too tall", that sounded ridiculous. "I mean he was taller than when I had seen him before. He had to duck his head when he went out through the back door. He must have been wearing platform shoes or something.

"He was trying to scare you." Brian said. He put his hands on my shoulders and looked me in the eye. "Come on Steve, you're bigger than this. If he succeeds in frightening you, he's won. He's just a sick nutcase who tries to exert power over his victims. The chances are you will never see him again."

"I think he will come back", I said. "He almost said as much."

"We can change all of the locks and make sure he can't get in again. Or you can get an alarm fitted if that makes you feel safer. Either way he's not going to see his precious notebooks again is he. They're probably in a land fill site by now." Brian picked up the brush and sat back on his haunches, he paused thoughtfully and then waved it at me. "But on the other hand…"

I continued his sentence, "But on the other hand we do have all of the data from the notebooks on our server in the office. We digitised it before feeding it into Merlin. Since we still have all of the information, there's still a slim chance that we could decode them and then he might go off and bother someone else."

Brian shook his head. "I don't really fancy opening up that can of worms again. We're not going to get anywhere. We gave it our best shot."

Brian was right, I needed to 'man up' as Lucy would have said. I went to the kitchen and put the kettle on. Brian followed me. "You still haven't told me how he got in? I don't see any sign of a forced entry."

"He knew where I hid my emergency key, it's still in the back door. According to the police it's quite easy to get in if you have enough patience. Most of us hide a spare key somewhere in case we lock ourselves out. The thief gets to know the sort of places people use, it will be somewhere dry, under the mat or in an empty flower pot. You think nobody will find it because there are lots of flower pots, but how long does it take him to look under a dozen pots? He probably found my spare key and he was in."

"But there must be lots of people who don't hide a key." Brian was sceptical.

"Correct, it doesn't work all of the time but he doesn't have to break into every house, if he's patient he will often get a key for one or two of them. It's a bit like a car thief walking down a line of parked cars trying the door handles as he goes, looking for one which is unlocked. It's a percentages thing."

"But in your case he needed to get into this particular house, so how does he push the percentage up in his favour. He can't be sure he will find your key."

"Sometimes the thief deliberately jams the front door lock by squirting some superglue into it, then he hides in the back garden and watches where you go to find the spare key. He might have been watching me." It's so simple, all you need is patience.

"What are the boys and girls in blue going to do about it?"

"They might know him, they're going to look through their databases. Typically he will have a record as a compulsive petty thief. Someone who likes to prowl around looking in your cupboards and drawers and somehow gets a kick out of knowing some of your secrets. He's not in it for the money."

"Then why don't they haul him in and bang him up?" Brian reasoned.

"There's not much point. He gets in using a key, so it's not a forced entry and he doesn't steal much. He's not after your valuables, he just likes to look around your house and poke around in your stuff. It's hardly worth the police following it up. More fool me for hiding a spare key. Some would say I was asking for it."

"Except for the violence?"

"They did say that people like him are rarely violent, they're more scared of you than you are of them. His threatening behaviour is unusual, but in the great scheme of things, chucking a radio at someone isn't a hanging offence. I can tell you this, he wasn't scared one bit."

Brian flopped into a chair. "Sounds like he needs a psychiatrist."

"That's exactly what I would be saying from your position, 'the poor chap needs help'. However since he scared the shit out of me, I'm thinking 'lock the bastard up and throw away the key'." I smiled at my own words, remembering the many times, as a wet socialist, I had argued against locking people up in favour of rehabilitation in the community.

"It's odd that he doesn't nick much." Brian said.

"The police said the intruder would often take something as a sort of souvenir. Usually something of low value, half the time his victims don't even notice it's gone; a photo or an ornament. He's a magpie, somewhere in a grubby flat, there will be a pile of shiny curiosities, things he's stolen over the years."

"Has he taken anything from you?"

"Not as far as I can see, but he may have done." I put my head in my hands and spoke through my splayed fingers. "I've had enough questions from the police and now I'm getting confused. I still don't know who Evans-Peake is. Is he a burglar? Is he a stalker? Is he just a weirdo? Is he dangerous? I just wish he would go away and leave me alone, I didn't ask for any of this."

Brian sank back into a chair thinking. "How's this for a theory. Perhaps Evans-Peake stole those notebooks from someone, it might be the sort of quirky thing he might take as a memento, interesting but of no value. And now, having looked at their contents, he's obsessed with finding out what they mean."

"If he did steal the notebooks from someone, it would be to know who that someone was I suppose. Whoever it was would probably be able to tell us what they mean." As soon as I had said it I realised that I didn't care who they belonged to. What had once been an interesting little puzzle was now a stale piece of chewing gum, all its flavour gone. I just wanted to spit it out and get on with my life.

Brian locked the back door and gave me the key, there was nothing more to be done. The locksmith would come the following morning to change all of the locks. I locked the front door as we left, banging it with my fist to make sure it was secure. Once we were in Brian's car, he continued the conversation. "It seems to me Steve that he's obsessive. Once something gets under his skin he can't let go of it. You're not dealing with a rational person."

"I'm right then. He's not going to let me off the hook."

"I just mean that you can't predict what he will do. But don't worry, once you have new locks he won't be able to get in, as long as you don't hide a key somewhere." Brian patted me on the shoulder, then he turned the car radio up and we remained silent for the few minutes it took to drive to the Obsidian office.

*****

That afternoon we sat in the meeting room with Kris, bringing her up to date with our suspicions about Axiom. I was grateful that Brian did most of the talking. She slowly turned the pages of the

174

report, shaking her head. Brian paused anticipating questions but she remained silent.

"So Kris, we need you to dig around at Axiom, take a few of our other contacts out to lunch. Turn on the charm and see if you can find out what is going on. I know we're probably clutching at straws but that's about all we can do. Can you help us?"

Kris continued to look down at the report in front of her, then she closed it and carefully squared it up with the edge of the table. We waited, expectant.

"It's probably not the best time to tell you this." She looked at each of us in turn, searching for the right words. "I've been head hunted. I was contacted by a recruitment agency a couple of weeks ago. The job they are offering is with a medium sized immunology company spun out from Surrey University. They want me to help them commercialise their new products. It's a good opportunity for me, they've got rich investors and a big marketing budget." She opened the palms of her hands and shook her head from side to side slowly. "Sometimes you have to think about your own career, and this is one of those occasions. I need experience of working in a larger company."

I froze not knowing how to respond. Brian sat bolt upright.

"Have you accepted the job?"

"No, not yet. I met up with them one evening last week and I said I needed a few days to think about it, but I'm planning to accept it." She tapped the Axiom report with her finger. "From what you have just told me it looks like it's time to move on anyway. Sorry guys, I know this has come at the wrong time but…..".

"Oh that's just great news," Brian looked up at the ceiling.

This was the last straw. We may as well shoot the camel now and save ourselves any more back-breaking pain. I tried to be more diplomatic.

"Is there any way you could postpone your decision? Let's give it everything we have got for one month." I looked to Brian for agreement. "By then we should have a clearer picture of where we are and then you can make a decision. If you decide to go, then you will go with our blessing."

Kris sat forward on her chair and folded her arms on the table. "I can't Steve. They need a decision by the end of the week otherwise they're going to offer it to someone else."

"Is it the money?" I asked, hoping.

She shook her head and swallowed hard. "Look, I think my contract says I have to give a month's notice. I will give Obsidian all my energy and efforts for that month. No back pedalling, no winding down. If I can help you dig yourselves out of this hole, then I will. But after that….." She stopped talking, tears glistened in her eyes. Then in a barely audible whisper. "After that, I'm gone." She reached for a couple of tissues and rushed out of the meeting room.

******

Brian drove me home at the end of the afternoon, neither of us felt very motivated to work late. I assured him I would be fine on my own, although inside I didn't feel so confident. The empty house had to be faced. The police had told me that a burglar almost never returns to a house he has burgled so I should be quite safe. But I thought otherwise, Evans-Peake was no ordinary thief.

I walked up the short path to the front door, the curtains were still drawn across the front room window. I couldn't remember if I had left them open or not that morning. A dim light filtered through a small gap in the middle, had I left a light on? I crept down the side passage, the light was on in the kitchen and was shining through the frosted window in the back door. I had probably just left it switched on. I felt in my pocket to check that my usual set of keys and the spare key were still there, there were no more keys so Evans-Peake would have had to break in, but there was no sign of a forced entry. Reaching into the shed, I picked up a garden fork then, gathering all my courage, I turned the handle and tried the door with the tips of my fingers. It wasn't locked. I pushed the door
176

open ready to run back to the road if necessary. As I entered, fork held high, the threatening shadows disappeared like scared cats. My sister Helen, was leaning against the fridge waiting for the kettle to boil. She reached for another mug from the cupboard. "Tea, Stephen with a 'ph'?"

I dropped the fork and hugged her tightly with relief. "What brings you here?"

"I have to visit some of our donors in the city tomorrow to tell them how important they are. You know the sort of thing, how we couldn't survive without them and how they have changed hundreds of lives.

"Unlike you to be so cynical sis."

Helen sighed. "Oh, everybody wants to save the babies but nobody wants to pay the rent on our meagre office in Oxford or buy us a box of paperclips. I have to reassure them that the percentage of donor money which goes on administrative overheads is around about the norm and gently remind them that the UK operation can't survive on thin air."

I relished her chatty normality.

"Then I finish by showing them a few slides of kids dressed in rags begging on the streets of Kathmandu, followed by smiling children dressed in smart uniforms at one of our schools. As they say, a picture paints a thousand words." She paused thoughtfully. "I do sound a bit cynical don't I, perhaps I need to move on." She opened the fridge door and pulled out a bottle of milk.

"Anyway Stevie, you sounded a bit rattled this morning on the phone so I thought, why don't I come and stay the night with my dearly beloved big brother and have a more leisurely start tomorrow morning. So here I am. Sorry I probably should have phoned first." She poured the boiling water on the tea-bags in the mugs and gave them a squeeze with the back of a tea-spoon. "Got any biscuits?"

I found a packet of ginger nuts and offered it to her. "How did you get in?"

"The spare key in the usual place." She picked it up from the work surface and waved it at me.

"No, I have the spare key in my pocket." I fished around in my trousers. It was still there.

Then my heart sank. Evans-Peake hadn't used the hidden key from the shed that morning. He had taken the spare key some time ago, made a copy and then hidden the original back in the usual place. That meant he could have made more copies, so until I get the locks changed he could just come back and let himself in any time he liked. I remembered he had said that he had already looked for the notebooks. He could have been in and out several times while I was at work.

We sat in the easy chairs in the front room. Helen kicked her shoes off. The visit from Evans-Peake had had at least one benefit. Now I knew without doubt that he was very much real and I could tell everyone about him without them thinking I might be making it up, a radio had been thrown and a coffee table had been smashed. People would now have to sit up and listen, starting with Helen. I told her everything starting with the first encounter in the park, then about our efforts to decode the information in the notebooks. I also told her about the problems we were having with Axiom, and without going into too much technical detail, finishing up with Kris' announcement that afternoon. She was leaving.

Helen listened patiently, dunking biscuits in her tea. "I presume you haven't mentioned any of this to Mum or Dad?"

I shook my head. "Only Brian and now you, know the full story."

Helen cupped her mug in her hands. "Are the two situations related? Is there a connection between your stalker, Evans what's-his-name, and the problems with Axiom?" To Helen this was just a throw away comment but to me it began to make sense. Was he part of the plot to discredit us, trying to bring my sanity into question and so to bang another nail into Obsidian's coffin? Was there a link between the notebooks which he is so anxious to get his hands on and Axiom's missing data?"

178

Helen playfully kicked my feet, this was still a game to her.

"Or to put it in terms that you understand, what's the statistical probability of both events happening at the same time? If you ask me Steve, you need to take a step back and look at the bigger picture."

I was surprised that I hadn't considered this possibility before. But surely the co-occurrence was a coincidence, I really couldn't see a big drug company or any of its employees, getting mixed up with a petty thief. I shook my head. "I can't see the link sis', I just can't see it."

Helen shrugged, it wasn't important to her. She changed the subject to our parents. Dad had recovered significantly but it was clear, at least to Helen, that he would never get back to the man he had been mentally and physically, his mental state being the bigger concern. He was even more forgetful and would lose the thread in the middle of a conversation. Mum was coping well with day to day life but getting increasingly frustrated by his mental and emotional state.

"Thanks for visiting them so regularly," I was feeling guilty. "I'm sure it's a big help to Mum. I know I should get down there but......."

"They'd love to see you. A change of scene might help you to step back from your troubles, even if it was only for a couple of days."

As ever with Helen, there was no attachment of blame. Just stoic acceptance of how things were and what her role should be. I took her point, I should take a trip down to Somerset to see them before long.

We cooked up some pasta and sat down in front of the telly, Helen was well up on all the soaps and tried to fill me in on the latest plots. I feigned interest, the truth was that I was so pleased to have some company. I would have watched anything, just to take my mind off of the events of the day. We finished off a bottle of red wine between us and stayed up late chatting. I thought the alcohol and a late night would help me sleep soundly but I tossed and turned, unable to settle, listening for sounds, a key in a lock, a tap on a window, a whisper in my ear. Eventually I reached for the blister pack of sleeping pills and glass of water.

But there was something that Helen had said, lodged in the back of my mind, I just couldn't remember what it was. It was important but I couldn't remember why.

Chapter 19

I was woken by noises from downstairs. Helen was singing along to a song on the radio while she made a cup of tea, miraculously it was still working after Evans-Peake had hurled it across the room. The cheerful normality of the sounds and the presence of someone else in the house was like bright sunshine pouring through the window. It was all going to work out, I had survived the night and Evans-Peake was not waiting for me downstairs. In a few hours all the locks would be changed and that would be the end of it. Helen had got me through the darkest midnight hour and out into the sunlight again. I pulled on my dressing gown and went down to join her. Dressed in loose fitting elephant print pyjamas, she was sitting at the table sipping tea and thumbing through the free local newspaper she had found on the door mat.

"Do you think you need a hobby Steve? Look you could join a yoga class." Helen held up the page in the newspaper.

I scrutinised the accompanying picture. "My body doesn't bend like that. In fact, bodies are not supposed to bend like that."

"Salsa dancing? They're usually desperate for men."

"Nobody to go with."

"You might find someone there. How else are you going to find a new girlfriend?"

"I don't need a new a new girlfriend," I said defensively.

"Yes you do, you'll get lonely. Even though you and Lucy didn't do much, you were company for each other. How about getting Lucy back?"

"That's not going to happen."

"Would you like it to happen Steve?"

That was a question I couldn't answer. I told myself that I didn't want her back, but was that just to avoid facing the truth, that she had slipped through my fingers?

Helen hadn't run out of ideas. "How about joining the Church?"

"Definitely not."

"Daddy will be disappointed with you." She waggled a mocking finger.

"I think he's probably resigned to it by now, he stopped sending me bible study notes through the post several years ago. Anyway I do have a perfectly good hobby, cycling. It keeps me fit and provides endless hours of good wholesome fun."

"Endless fun on your own though. You should join a cycling club. Look there's one here." Helen jabbed at the article with her finger. "They go riding every Sunday morning. That would be ideal. You get too wrapped in your work Steve, you know how obsessive you can be. You need a break from it, and a break from Brian if you ask me." She folded the paper and put it down on the table, turning her attention to the bacon sandwich. Helen had always been a bit wary of Brian.

"We are business partners and we are friends. Of course we spend a lot of time together. He's been very supportive over this Evans-Peake thing."

"Well you know what my thoughts on the subject are." Helen swallowed and waved her sandwich at me defiantly. "You keep Obsidian afloat while Brian tinkers away with his own little project. He dominates you Steve."

We had recycled this conversation many times. "Let's not go around that loop again, but I take your point about cycling , I will don the yellow vest Lucy gave me for my birthday and try out the local bike club."

Helen looked at her watch and went upstairs to get dressed. She returned, hair gathered into a bun and wearing a patterned blouse and a grey jacket and trousers. Professional yet feminine, but she wouldn't win the client over with her looks or even her

183

personality, I pictured Kris by way of a contrast. Helen would know every relevant fact and figure, every regulation and statute, she would have answers to every question, she would be eminently sensible and trustworthy. Helen was the genuine article and that would win the day for World Reach every time.

She turned around full circle, like a child going to a party. "How do I look."

"Totally wonderful," I enthused. "Go in there and knock 'em dead sister." We hugged, she waved, flapping her hand from the wrist like a toddler, "I'll go straight back to Oxford after my meeting. Call me later, lots of love." The front door slammed and she was gone.

I poured a second mug of coffee and settled down with some papers to read while I waited for the locksmith to arrive. For once my mind was clear space, Evans-Peake and the troubles at Obsidian were pushed to the edges of my consciousness. My thoughts returned to the conversation with Helen the previous evening. She had said something while she was talking about her presentation to her client and I needed to recall it. I pictured her sitting opposite me and imagined her talking to me, trying to recreate the conversation. I shut my eyes, listening to cars passing by in the street, the ticking of the kitchen clock, my own controlled breathing.

Without warning the phrase crystalized and I turned it over in my mind. Could this simple thought be the solution to the codes in the notebooks? I had decided to put the codes in the notebooks behind me when I threw them in the skip. But somehow I couldn't put them out of my mind. We still had all of the contents of the notebooks on our computer server. Surely it was worth one more try.

I looked at my watch, Brian would probably be in the office by now. However when he answered the phone I could tell from the background noise that he was still in his car. It wasn't a good line but I managed to ask him to e-mail a few of the digitised pages from one of the notebooks to me. Opening my laptop I started

184

writing a little program. After an hour or so it was ready. We had tried so hard to make sense of the data, even the mighty Merlin couldn't come up with anything. If my hunch was correct, then it explained why Merlin had failed, and why it would never be able to make any sense of it.

I checked my e-mails, Brian had sent me the entire contents of one of the notebooks, two hundred pages. I waited impatiently while the attached file was downloaded. Then I fed the data from the first page, a matrix of seemingly random numbers and characters, into my program and clicked the 'Start' button. The screen began to fill up slowly from top to bottom, line by line. I was immediately elated, clenching both my hands into tight fists I waved them above my head. I watched intensely as an image emerged, hoping that it would be something I would recognise, but I was disappointed. It was surely an image from somewhere, I could see shapes and bands of colour, but I had no idea where it had come from or what it was. First I saw swirling pinks on a white background, then smaller regions of intense reds and blues mixed in with occasional wisps of light sky blue. 'A picture paints a thousand words', I thought back to Helen's comment of the previous evening when she was describing her presentation. That was undeniably the case and Helen's chance remark had unlocked the picture for me, but what did it mean?

When the data from the notebooks was displayed as pixel values in an image it all made sense, that's why the characters were in a square matrix. We had seen the pairs of characters we had jumped to the conclusion that it was ASCII code and had tried to make sense of it as text, but this was a step too far, in reality it was much simpler. The character pairs translated to numbers from 0 to 255 and represented pixel values in an image. All my little program had to do was to read each number and use it to set the brightness and colour of each pixel to form an image. This also explained why Merlin couldn't make sense of it. Merlin could handle numerical data and text, but it had no idea what an image was or how to analyse it. You need a human brain to do that.

I extracted the data from the second page and ran it through my program. Once again the result was clearly a coherent image, similar to the first one. I ran the first ten pages from the notebook through and got ten images, all similar but unique. Perhaps we were going to be able to give Evans-Peake the answer he was looking for. All the images were swirling psychedelic patterns, streaks and blobs of varying sizes in reds, pinks, blues and browns. I had made a major leap forward, but now I faced a new problem. I had absolutely no idea what the pictures represented or what the message behind them might be. But I knew someone who might be able to give me some insight.

I sent Lucy an e-mail with a couple of the images attached. Could they be copies of works of art? Had she seen anything like them, perhaps hung on a wall in an obscure art gallery or in a book on modern art? Lucy's knowledge of art was encyclopaedic and her speciality was modern abstract paintings. As I hit the send button I realised that if they were paintings, the artist would have to be very prolific given that I had three thousand pages.

I pictured Lucy sitting at her desk, a tidy 'in tray' with two or three jobs, typing with all of her fingers, not just two fingers and a thumb like the rest of us, pausing to think and scribbling a note on a pad of paper. Did she think of me? Did she still have a foot in the past like I did, or had she shaken herself free, marching on to a new future, looking for someone else. That thought hit me hard. Lucy with someone else?

The locksmith arrived and set to work with assurances that he would soon have me sorted out. It was the same chap who had come a couple of weeks ago when the front door lock had been jammed. Now I knew who had done that, clearly it was part of Evans-Peake's strategy for getting into my house.

Lucy had replied to my e-mail saying that she didn't recognise the pictures and that they didn't have much merit as works of art as far as she was concerned. She thought they looked a bit like images from outer space. I noticed she still signed herself off with a single

'L' followed by 'xxx'. Below that was the official company signature, Lucy Quick, Art Historian, Su-Kim Associates.

My interest, even obsession with the notebooks had been reignited. It was one more step, I thought to myself, even a giant leap. But I was still at square one as far as understanding the message went.

The locksmith had finished. Not knowing what to do with the spare keys and not wanting to hide one in the garden or shed, I put them in my desk drawer for safe keeping. After checking that the house was secure, I cycled into the Obsidian office arriving late-morning. Faith was on the phone when I pushed through the door, she waved her fingers at me and smiled. I fired up my laptop, Brian looked up from his desk but said nothing. Tingling with excitement I beckoned him over, then I double clicked on the first of the images and it filled the screen.

"Looks like something my five-year-old nephew might have done," Brian said. "What is it and why do I care?"

"There are two answers to that", I left it hanging in the air, wanting to prolong the mystery. "The simple answer is that I don't know what it is. The more interesting answer is that it was created from the data in Evans-Peake's notebooks. You are looking at just one page," I clicked the mouse. "And this is another, and this is a third."

"Well bugger me. Are they all like that?"

"Yes, as far as I know. They are all similar but different. But I need to pick a few more pages at random from the other notebooks."

Brian worked it out very quickly. "So the hexadecimal codes were just pixel values. We were on the wrong track, the data doesn't represent text at all, nothing to do with the ASCII code."

I nodded. "And that is why Merlin couldn't make sense of it. But unfortunately I don't know how to make sense of it either. I thought Lucy might be able to help but she couldn't shed any light on them from an arty point of view. She thought they looked like they came from outer space. Any ideas?"

Brian was typically analytical. "If it was from outer space I would expect the background to be black, but the background on these images is white, or at least bright; not dark." He clapped me on the back. "It's aliens. Evans-Peake has had a visitation from little green men. No better still, Evans-Peake is an alien himself and he is showing us pictures of his home planet. Is there a space ship in your back garden Steve?"

The initial euphoria of my discovery was beginning to wear off, not helped by Brian's mockery. I had been so excited, but I now remembered that we had much bigger fish to fry. This was simply a diversion from the real plot. "What are we doing Brian?" I asked not expecting an answer. "Our business is falling apart, I'm wasting time getting excited over images given to me by a weird stalker."

Brian continued to stare at the image on the screen. "We like a puzzle that's all. You and your crosswords, me with my data mining. At least life's not dull Steve. We are living in interesting times."

"Which, according to the Chinese, is a bad thing." I pointed out.

We worked away in silence until lunchtime. Brian stood up, stretched his arms out and yawned. "Fancy a stroll down to the sandwich shop Steve?" The weather was wintry and even though I was wearing a warm coat, I was glad to get inside the little Greek sandwich shop. We ordered filled rolls and coffee, then sat at a small table in the window.

Brian had spent the weekend walking in the Cotswolds with Chloe. I asked him how it had been, he didn't answer. Looking out of the window, he said. "That's who I wanted to talk to you about". I could guess what was coming. "That evening last Wednesday when we were working late on the notebooks, we were wondering how that backup tape went missing from under my bed and you said, 'I think we both know who took the tape?' I assume you were referring to Chloe." He took a bite of his sandwich to give me a chance to respond but I stayed silent, not wanting to goad him into

188

an argument. Brian carried on. "I can see that she had an opportunity, if she knew about the tapes, which she doesn't. But the suggestion that she is somehow involved in discrediting Obsidian is ludicrous, why would she do it? And before you say it, I know we had that little issue with passwords but I'm quite sure she hasn't been near my laptop."

I felt the need to tread very carefully, all I had were some unfounded suspicions. "I've noticed that she's often around in the background that's all, for example she was around last Wednesday evening when we were working on the notebooks."

Brian butted in, "And using a guest account on the computer as I told you, which doesn't allow her access to any of our data."

"But she was still listening in to what was going on." I tried to sound very cautious. "What do you know about Chloe Defrey?"

Brian was understandably defensive, but I thought he had taken my point. "Well it's not really any of your business is it. However for the record, her father works in the oil industry and has been posted all over the world, currently her parents live in Houston. When she was a kid she lived in Yokohama, hence her knowledge of Japanese, she also lived in Norway, Kuwait and Aberdeen. She studied history at Leeds and wants to get into journalism, she moved down to London but couldn't find a way in, so she's been temping. I was introduced to her by Paul and Lizzie who as you know live in the flat below me, and they knew her from Leeds days. Is that enough for you Steve?" Brian rattled off the information in a disinterested way. I felt awkward, what right did I have to peep into her personal life. Saying nothing, I stirred my coffee sheepishly. I had gone too far.

Brian broke the silence. "Steve this Evans-Peake thing has gone to your head. You're looking for conspiracies which just don't exist. I'm sorry, but the thought that Chloe is working against us is just ridiculous."

"OK", I said. "I don't want to argue with you." I finished my coffee and started to get up. But Brian wasn't finished.

"We probably know who broke in and stole the tape don't we? Couldn't it be Evans-Peake, it's just the sort of thing he would steal."

"Are you aware he has been in your flat?", I asked.

Brian put his hands on his head in a gesture of disbelief. "No of course he hasn't Steve. I think I might just have spotted if I had been burgled. I'm just pointing out how ridiculous your argument is. Perhaps he stole a random tape and Edith just happened to ask us for the one he had stolen. Or, here's a good one, perhaps he knows Edith and stole a tape to order. Take your pick of conspiracy theories." Brian stood up. "You are quite entitled to believe what you like Steve, but I can assure you, Chloe is not involved."

Just after four o'clock Faith walked over to my desk. "Do you mind if I take off a bit early? I've got to see Jackson's class teacher. There have been a few scuffles between some of the boys in the playground and they want to nip it in the bud. I tell him that if he gets mixed up with any of these West Indian gangs I'll give him a good hiding. I don't know where he gets all of this violent behaviour from, I really don't."

I said that was fine, smiling at the image of Faith cuffing Jackson around the ear to curb his violent behaviour. She collected the empty mugs from my desk to take down to the kitchen. As she did so, she caught a glimpse of one of the images on my screen.

"H and E?"

"What did you say?" I asked.

"Haematoxylin and eosin stain."

"Faith, I don't know what you're talking about."

"The picture on your screen, it's from a microscope slide, the sample is stained with haematoxylin and eosin, I think it's lung tissue."

"And how do you know that?"

"I used to see them every day when I worked in the labs at the Royal Free Hospital. Sorry Steve I've got to go now because I'm already late. Look it up on the internet."

Faith put her bag over her shoulder and left, the mugs clinking in her hand as the descended the stairs.

I looked across at Brian. "H and E?", I raised my eyebrows.

"Never heard of it." He replied.

I thought back to my conversation with Helen on the previous evening. She had wondered if there was a link between the notebooks and Axiom. Images from a microscope; microbiology. Perhaps she was right.

Chapter 20

I arrived home, my head buzzing with a swarm of thoughts. The stress levels began to rise and I was having difficulty in concentrating. It didn't help being on my own. I thought about calling Lucy, I thought about calling Brian and going to the pub. I turned the TV up and checked that the front and back doors were locked. Perhaps I would take Friday afternoon off to visit my parents in Somerset for the weekend. I really didn't know what I would do.

As I picked the post off of the mat, my phone vibrated in my pocket. I fished it out, no name on the display and I didn't recognise the number. Being wary of calls from unknown sources, I let it run through to voice mail then listened to the message while waiting for the kettle to boil. The cooing sound of Chloe was like a perfume wafting out from the phone. She wondered if we could meet up for a quick chat and asked me to call her back. I inferred that this meeting did not include Brian. I called her back, she picked up on the first ring.

"Hi Steve, I was wondering if we could meet up. Do you fancy meeting me for a drink in the Fox and Hounds this evening?" She sounded bright and breezy, like it really didn't matter one way or the other.

"Sure, but you'll have to remind me where it is. What's the occasion?" I probably sounded hesitant, not knowing why she wanted to meet me, seemingly without Brian.

She ignored my question. "I'll tell you what, why don't I just come round to your house. It's not far and the walk will do me good, then we can go for a drink if we want to."

"Yes, of course. Is it just you?" She could probably hear the caution in my voice. Why would my best friend's girlfriend want to meet me without him? I couldn't really think of any good reason.

"Brian's gone out with Paul from downstairs." She paused. "It's about Brian's birthday. It's only a few weeks away and I'm planning a little surprise party for him. I might need your help."

That sounded plausible, I told her she could come around any time and we hung up. It was Brian's birthday in a few weeks' time but surely we could have just chatted on the phone if she needed my help with organising a party. Still, there were worse ways to spend an evening than in the company of the curvaceous, cooing Chloe Defrey and I needed company. I was still tidying up when the doorbell rang. Chloe handed me her full-length fur coat and followed me into the sitting room.

"This is nice", she looked around before sitting down. I took the use of the word 'nice' as synonymous with 'mediocre' or 'bland'. The description fitted, I was no 'home maker'.

"It's OK, but it misses Lucy's feminine touch and artistic eye. I've rather reverted to function over form since she left. Quite a few of the prints on the wall belong to her. I suppose I should give them back to her some time."

"Nobody else on the horizon then?"

"Not unless you're offering?" I said this as a light-hearted remark but also wanting to be clear, just in case. Chloe smiled, but didn't answer. It wasn't 'maybe, we'll have to see', it was more like, 'I assume you couldn't possibly mean that'. She turned down my offer of a glass of wine so I walked through into the kitchen to make a pot of coffee, calling back to her whilst I searched for a couple of clean mugs.

"What's Brian up to tonight then? You said he had gone somewhere with Paul."

"Paul is besotted with getting a camper van, it's his latest craze. He and Lizzie are going to roam around the highways and byways without a care in the world like post-modern gypsies. They've already given notice on their flat. The camper will become

194

their one and only cosy little home. I have no idea how they are going to fit all of their stuff into it or what they are going to do to earn a living. Knowing them, they probably haven't thought about it either. They plan to be on their way by Christmas. If I were them I would definitely wait until spring and the warmer weather."

Chloe chatted away easily while I poured the coffee and joined her in the sitting room. She sat back in the easy chair, long legs stretched out, toes pointing inward. She was wearing worn jeans and a thick grey jumper, it looked like one of the ones that Dil imported from Nepal. She unzipped it half way revealing a white T shirt. Even in simple every-day clothes she looked elegant.

Chloe continued. "Last year they were going to get a canal boat, but that all came to nothing. I don't think they realised how expensive a canal boat is and then you also have to pay mooring fees on top of that. It all mounts up. According to Brian they are looking for a 'split windscreen VW camper', of course Brian is suddenly the world's expert on classic camper vans. This is apparently the type of camper van everyone wants. Anyway he went off with Paul earlier to look at a few that are for sale locally, they were like a couple of kids. I just hope Brian doesn't get caught up in the excitement of it all and come back with one himself. You know how enthusiastic he can be."

I nodded, amused that Chloe had already taken on a slightly maternal role. I remembered going to an antiques auction with Brian several years ago. His enthusiasm ran away with him and he came home with all sorts of worthless bric-a-brac. The auctioneer had spotted him immediately and kept looking in his direction whereupon Brian dutifully nodded his head or waved his catalogue. Having to make a snap decision with little evidence was far too much of a risk for me, I wasn't the type for auctions.

Chloe's story so far seemed plausible but I was still a bit wary and wanted to nail down the purpose of her visit.

"What's the plan for a birthday surprise then?"

She looked into her coffee mug, cradled in her hands. There was an uncomfortable silence of several seconds, I fought the impulse to fill the space with a throwaway line. "As you may have guessed, that was just a pretext Steve. I'll probably buy him a T shirt with a picture of a camper van on it for his birthday. That is if we're still together." Chloe looked straight at me without expression, her lips firmly clamped together. I wondered what was to come next. Already I knew that she could use her sexual charms to get her own way but here I thought I saw a different, more determined Chloe who would also defend herself like a cornered cat if she was trapped. This was a girl not at all like the homely Lucy or Helen. They wouldn't stoop to flirting to get their way, it was far too underhand. They were products of a middle-class English upbringing and education; dialogue and dispassionate argument were their weapons of choice. Assertive but not aggressive. Chloe was an altogether different animal, moving from country to country during her childhood, being thrown in at the deep end of the social swimming pool. She would have learnt how to make friends quickly using all of her charm and then how to gently drop them without a backward glance when it was time to move on. Another international school, another group of friends, but ultimately Chloe was on her own, cut adrift in an insecure world. She pitches up in London with no support from her family, her parents in America and her older brother, an activist, saving the rain forests in Indonesia. There was a steely glint in her eye and I realised then that she would inevitably drop Brian when it was time to move on. I wondered if that moment had come. Aretha sang in the background.

But what a fool believes, he sees, no wise man has the power to reason away.

Chloe settled back in her chair, relaxed and in control of the situation. Once again I felt the pressure of the silence, the central heating boiler in the kitchen started up with a swoosh, radiators tingling as they warmed up.

"Are you still temping?"

"Yes, although I'm pretty fed up with it. I'm working for the London Festival Orchestra on the South Bank. It's dull. Sending
196

out special offers for the Christmas concert season to their inner circle of supporters, 'The Friends of the LFO'. Occasionally I have to book flights or accommodation for some pompous conductor who insists on sitting on the left side of the plane or who must have a lavender scented pillow to lay his precious head on." She sounded bitter, not amused. "It doesn't help that I'm not in the slightest bit interested in classical music. Anyway, I can't spend the rest of my life temping. Brian may have told you, my original plan was to get into journalism, but so is everyone else. I thought I would walk into a job at the BBC, I've applied for several jobs there but so far I haven't even been called for interview. Then I tried fashion magazines, but they're even harder to get into, unless you know someone, which I don't. So now I'm trying trade magazines, just to get some experience. You know, 'Bee Keepers Weekly' or …"

"Or the Chimney Sweep's Gazette", I offered.

She looked at me to check I wasn't mocking her. "Well there's hundreds of them anyway, I don't exactly have to scrape the bottom of the barrel, I just reach down and dip my hand into the sludge and come out with a fist full of shit."

Here was the other side of Chloe. She could turn on her not inconsiderable charm, cooing soothing words into Brian's ear, hanging on to his arm as she tripped along in high heels. But this was a more honest Chloe. Someone who had been knocked over a few times and who knew that the only way forward was to pick herself up and not to expect any sympathy.

"Before working for the orchestra I had several temping jobs", she played with her mug, turning it round and round in her hands. "And about six months ago, I worked for a lady called Edith Summers. I think you know her."

I sat up. "Do you mean you worked for Axiom?"

"No. Edith has her own company, which she runs from her house. She has a small microbiology lab set up in the basement. It's not far from here."

I was surprised. "What does that involve?"

"The usual lab stuff, pipettes, glass flasks, a centrifuge. But her main thing is microscopy, she has three fancy microscopes which she uses to score slides."

"When you say 'scoring the slides' what do you mean?"

"A pharmaceutical company needs to run a trial to see if their new drug works and if it has any unpleasant side effects. They get some mice and give them all the disease and they treat half of them. Then they look at how the treated animals get on compared to those who haven't been treated. They look for changes in the animal's internal organs, this involves killing the mouse and taking a biopsy. Except they use the word 'sacrifice' rather than kill." She smiled without emotion.

I knew all of this from the Merlin trials but I didn't want to rush her. Chloe continued with the dispassionate air of an uninspiring school teacher.

"For example, they might cut a liver up into very thin slices, stain it with chemicals to give it some colour and stick it on a glass microscope slide."

My ears pricked up and I interrupted her. "The stain they use, would it be 'H and E' by any chance?"

"Yes, that's a common stain but there are others. I don't know much about that stage because Axiom used to send us already prepared slides to look at."

"Wait a minute, Are you telling me that Edith was processing slides from Axiom, the company she works for?"

"Let me finish." Chloe swallowed hard. "The slides need to be evaluated by a qualified microbiologist or histologist. This is something that the big companies like to out-source. They will have their own experts, but looking at hundreds of slides down a microscope is extremely tedious and they would rather someone else did it. Someone who doesn't get an Axiom pension and membership of the gym. So evaluating or 'scoring' the slides is the service Edith provides, and it pays quite well, judging by the fact that she has just bought a nice restored farmhouse in the Dordogne for her retirement. So that was my job. I spent every day staring down one of her microscopes and listening to music on my MP3 player."

"That can't be right," I said. "Firstly, surely Edith, wearing her Axiom hat, should not be subcontracting work to her own company. Axiom would never sanction that on a 'conflict of interest' basis. And secondly, as far as I am aware, you don't learn much microbiology when studying for a history degree. That was what you studied wasn't it?"

"It's actually not that hard. Edith showed me what to look for and if I was not sure about a slide I just put it to one side for her to look at. Usually you have to assign a score to the slide, from one to five depending on how much of the tissue was stained brown, or you might have to count how many cells you could see. I didn't know what it meant or whether the results were significant, but I could do the scoring quite well. After about half a day with Edith watching me, I was on my own."

"Sounds very boring."

"Not really, I quite enjoyed it. Edith wasn't around much of the time, but there were usually two of three of us in the basement working on the microscopes. It was quite pleasant, we were left to our own devices. We took breaks when we wanted to and helped ourselves to tea and coffee from her kitchen. We got on well, I think I was one of Edith's favourites. She could be a bit fiery at times, often angry with herself. Usually silly things like losing something."

This was all very interesting and might explain some of Edith's behaviour but why was Chloe telling me about it. I fished around.

"Are you still in contact with Edith?"

"Yes, she was talking about training me up to run her little business." Chloe paused and looked at me over the rim of her mug before continuing. "So when she realised I had moved in with Brian and she asked me to steal that tape, I did it."

The bombshell had been dropped. I puffed my cheeks out and let the air escape slowly. "You mean the backup tape from May that Brian lost. You stole it?"

"Strictly speaking I didn't steal it. I moved it. I hid it in my empty suitcase which is on top of the wardrobe. But I've put it back now, it's back in the tin under our bed with the other tapes."

My phone rang. I snatched it off the table and peered at the display. "It's Brian." I looked at Chloe, speaking in a stage whisper even though I hadn't accepted the call. "Does he know you're here?" Chloe shook her head. What did he want? We looked at each other while it rang, undecided and relieved when it went through to voice mail. I put the phone down and told Chloe I would call him back later.

Having got that off her chest, she suddenly became animated, picking up our mugs and taking them through to the kitchen. "I think I could do with that glass of wine now." She opened the fridge and found the bottle.

"Why are you telling me this?" I asked as I poured the wine.

"Because I don't want to hurt Brian, because I didn't realise the consequences of what I had done, because I want to undo the harm, if it's not too late. Brian's pretty cut up about the problems with Obsidian, he doesn't show it but I know he is. I thought it would be easier to talk to you and see if we can sort it out between us. All I have done is move a tape, it shouldn't be such a big deal." She looked at me, not pleading. Defiant. This wasn't the cooing Chloe, this was the battle hardened survivor.

The doorbell rang followed by two or three knocks. I looked at my watch. It had just gone nine, rather late for a caller. I made a surprised face at Chloe and went to open the front door. Brian and Paul were huddled on the door step.

"Hi Steve, we were close by and thought you might like to go for a beer. I called a few minutes ago to see if you were in but we came anyway. And Paul's desperate for a wee." They pushed past me as I held the door open and Brian pointed Paul in the direction of the toilet. As Paul disappeared up the stairs, Brian spoke behind his hand. "I've had enough of camper vans to last me several life times to be honest. You've got to help me out Steve, I'm going mad." Before I had a chance to say anything, he had barged his way into the sitting room and found himself, dumbstruck, face to face with his girlfriend. Chloe drew her legs up underneath herself. "Brian," she cooed. "You've interrupted our little tete-a-tete. We are discussing a birthday surprise for someone." She held up her glass and giggled. "But I think Steve is trying to get me drunk."

Trying to carry on as if this was nothing out of the ordinary, I picked up the bottle. "Plenty left if you want a glass."

Brian waved the bottle away. "Whose birthday?"

Chloe cooed. "Yours, you silly boy. So don't spoil it."

There was an uneasy silence, we waited for Brian to respond. Chloe's surprise birthday party seemed a thin excuse but it was pretty much all we had. I could tell him the truth about Chloe and Edith, but I suspected that Chloe had more to say on the subject. Clearly she was very keen to keep it from Brian and I didn't want to put my foot in it.

Chloe seemed to be completely at ease. She stood up, gave Brian a peck on the cheek, and slipped a reassuring hand into his. "Don't look so worried sweet-heart, let's go for a drink. Steve and I can carry on with our secret plans some other time." She gave me a theatrical wink.

I held my hands up in the air and shrugged. "All her idea mate. I was just going to get you a pair of socks."

Brian's face grew cloudy. "I do believe you're going red Steve. Would you like me to disappear and leave you two alone for a bit longer?"

There was a thumping on the stairs and the gangly, skeletal framed Paul appeared at the door, slightly ducking his head in the door frame. "That's much better. Who's going for a drink then? Steve, I can fill you in on the camper van saga. Let's go to the 'White Lion' since it's getting late, it's just around the corner" He didn't seem to have noticed Chloe.

We filed out of the front door, Brian and Chloe holding hands. Paul lingered back to chat to me as we ambled up the road but I was in no mood for small talk, I kept my head down, hearing but not listening. Where did this leave me and Brian? Surely he was suspicious. Chloe was chatting away, she paused and Brian momentarily looked back at me. The question hung in the air. Now what had Chloe done to us?

My phone chimed, a text from Lucy. Paul was still talking, I patted him on the shoulder and pointed at the phone. "Catch you up".

The message was short. 'Came round this PM to get stuff. Thanks for changing locks, really helpful.' I looked at my watch and called her.

"Steve?"

"The locks…"

"Yes, was it really necessary? Did you think I was going to steal your precious bicycle magazines, or worse still, mix then up so that they weren't in chronological order?"

I snapped back. "Did you have to come when you knew I wasn't in? If you had let me know I would have put them out on the street and you wouldn't need to come in at all."

"How was I going to know you would change the locks?"

"It's what you fucking do when you are burgled Lucy. It's what you do when someone breaks into your house and smashes it up. You change the locks so that he can't come back. And you know the scariest thing? He's not come for my stuff, he's come for me, and the next time he comes he's going to have a knife. So come round any time and I'll just leave the front door wide open if that makes it easier for you and anyone can wander in just as they please." I pressed the red button.

At that moment it seemed that everyone was on the other side, teams were being picked and I was the one not chosen; Brian, Cloe, Edith Summers, Evans-Peake, Kris was leaving and now Lucy. And I just needed one other person on my side, and I realised, in the midst of my anger, or perhaps because of my anger, that the one person I wanted was Lucy.

Chapter 21

The following day, only Faith and I were in the office. So many thoughts were swirling around in my head, the unfinished conversation I had had with Chloe the previous evening, the row I had had with Lucy about the locks. I knew that I needed to divert my attention or I would be sucked down, so I threw myself into a new statistics project which had just got off the ground.

Nina Simone tried to sing in my head.

It's a new dawn, it's a new day, it's a new life and I'm feelin' good.

After a few bars, she gave up.

Faith put a mug of coffee on my desk and placed a biscuit beside it. I looked up wondering what the occasion was. She pulled a chair over and sat down, crossing her legs. As usual she had kicked off her shoes. "Busy Steve?" She stirred her coffee slowly.

"A new project to start and Christmas is coming." I replied briskly, anxious to get on and not get drawn into a long conversation about Faith's domestic affairs.

She grimaced. "Don't talk to me about Christmas yet, it's still November. There's already Christmas decorations in the shops. Do you think we'll still be here at Christmas Steve?"

So that was it. "Obsidian? Of course we will," I said breezily. "I've been meaning to ask you to book that new French restaurant in Hempstead for our Christmas lunch."

"I need to work," she said simply. "I'm a single mother and I need the income, especially at Christmas. If I need to start looking for something else, the sooner I know, the better." Her large heavily made-up eyes darted shyly between me and her lap.

I felt bad. She had seen the state of the accounts and heard Merry Mick's pessimistic comments. She would have seen me, Brian and Krishna disappearing into the meeting room for heated discussions. And now something else was afoot, something to do with the report Axiom had sent. Yet we hadn't taken the trouble to include Faith, to tell her what was going on, when it affected her just as much as it affected everyone else. This wasn't the sort of company we had set out to be; open with our staff and everyone sharing equally in our successes or failures.

I put my pen down and swivelled my chair to face her. "Sorry Faith, you deserve better." She looked straight at me, her jet black, straightened hair hanging down the sides of her face like part-drawn curtains. "As I am sure you know the books aren't balancing at the moment and the SMART award money is almost gone. We need to fix that. We could cut back on our expenses and staff," she didn't react. "Or we try to sell more stuff and bring in more money, in other words, consulting time and copies of Merlin, so that's what we are trying to do. It's risky and we will have to keep a lid on expenses, but even Merry Mick thinks we can do it." I could see that having started the conversation in a bright and breezy manner, Faith was now close to tears. Feeling awkward, I leant towards her and touched her hand. "The first thing to say is we will do everything we can to keep Obsidian alive." Faith sniffed. She nodded.

I couldn't just leave it there. "Having said that, there are some things which are beyond our control. We have perhaps put too many eggs in the Axiom basket and now they are about to break most of those eggs. We think it's very unfair, Brian is particularly wound up about it as you will have noticed, and we are fighting back. Kris is going to visit them this week to see what she can find out from some other contacts." I decided not to tell Faith that Kris was leaving. "If we fail to patch it up with Axiom, we still have some other irons in the fire, Axiom isn't the only fish in the pond. We will continue to try to sell Merlin, there are plenty of other pharmaceutical companies we can approach, and we have consulting projects coming in, such as this new one I'm working on." I waved the specification document.

I hoped I had told her the truth but thought I had better make it absolutely clear. "The bottom line is that nobody can make cast iron guarantees, but we are doing our best to keep Obsidian afloat. I think there is a good chance we can do it and we need you to be part of it." I waited for some follow up questions but Faith simply thanked me and returned to her desk. I wondered what was going through her mind and I hoped I could live up to my words.

Had my performance been adequate? The reality was more complicated. We really didn't know what game Edith Summers and Axiom were playing. It seemed now that Chloe was somehow involved, and possibly Evans-Peake. We had decoded the notebooks but had no idea what their significance was, and whether they linked in to Axiom, but it seemed to be more that a coincidence. On top of that my relationship with Brian was strained, my Father was very ill and I had so far failed to get Lucy back, although when I thought about it, I hadn't tried that hard.

While we had been talking, Edith had sent me and Brian an e-mail saying she would be coming in the next day, Thursday, in the afternoon to inspect the backup tape. A couple of minutes later, Brian e-mailed me saying that he didn't know why she was still going through with it since Axiom were dumping us anyway. He thought they probably just wanted to rub salt into the wound by making us admit that we had lost the tape. I replied telling him I would take care of her and asked him to bring all of the backup tapes into the office and not to worry. Thanks to Chloe, I knew where the missing tape was, perhaps the meeting wouldn't all go Edith's way.

*****

There was a quick double knock on the front door. I parted the curtains and saw Lucy's little Nissan parked across the street. She poked her head into the living room before climbing the stairs.

"Did they take much?"

I shook my head.

She came back down with an armful of clothes and declined my offer of a coffee. "How are you Steve?" She said it without much feeling.

"It's been a tricky few weeks", I said. 'I'm not getting on well with Brian, Chloe is being a bit secretive, Kris is leaving, Obsidian is on the rocks and Faith is worrying that she will lose her job and now someone has broken into my house.' I gave her a false smile.

Lucy paused at the door. "Look Steve, stop being the victim, get to grips with your life and make things happen. It's in your hands. You weren't singled out by the thief, they are just opportunists."

How wrong can you be? I thought. I rummaged in my pocket and held up a shiny new door key.

"I don't need that now", she said.

"Take it anyway, you never know you might have forgotten something."

"If I need to get anything else I'll call you and make sure you are in." She closed the door behind her, once again she had slipped through my fingers.

*****

On Thursday morning I was in the office before Brian. After about thirty minutes I heard him clump up the stairs. He emerged, red faced, carrying the biscuit tin containing the tapes and dumped it on my desk.

"This is a complete waste of time Steve. It's just giving her a chance to gloat and bang another nail in Obsidian's coffin. If it were up to me, I know where I would shove the tapes." I smiled as I thought of all the things Brian had threatened to insert into Edith's nether regions over the past few days.

The intercom buzzed on Faith's desk, she lifted the handset and listened. "There's someone at the door from Centurion Security with a delivery for Dr Stephen Rockett."

"That'll be a little something I ordered yesterday," I said. Two men struggled up the stairs with a heavy wooden crate and dropped it in the middle of the office. Brian came over bringing a large screwdriver with a puzzled expression on his face. I was enjoying the theatricality and said nothing. He levered the lid off the crate and between us we lifted out a small safe and walked it across to the corner of the room. We stood looking at it, hands on hips.

"Something about closing stable doors comes to mind," Brian said. He picked up the handbook and read out loud: "Data safe, fire proof, water proof, electromagnetically shielded, pestilence proof and surprisingly spacious," he improvised. "Well we don't need this old tin any more then do we."

He prized the top off the tin with his fingers and I hoped Chloe had been true to her word. Sitting on top of the little pile in the box was tape twenty, the missing backup from last May.

"What's this?" Brian picked it up and turned it over in his hands as if it might not be the real thing, inspecting it thoughtfully from all angles. He held it up for me to see. I should have realised how quickly his brain worked. "You knew about this Steve. That's why you've been so cool about Edith's visit." Not knowing what to say, I raised my eyebrows in what I hoped was an enigmatic expression. Brian pressed his point. "I know that tape wasn't in the box when I looked for it."

I simply shrugged my shoulders, "Well at least we have something to take the wind out of Edith's sails."

"If it's genuine." Brian still wasn't quite sure. "You haven't just taken a new tape and stuck a number on it have you? I'll have to check it."

I shook my head and began transferring the tapes from Brian's box into the safe. "Somewhere to keep the visitor's chocolate biscuits Faith?"

The safe combination was set and duly noted by the three of us. We shut the door and locked it, and checked we could open it again then, the excitement over, we each returned to our desks. But I knew the discussion about the missing tape was not over. Brian would want to know where that tape had been hiding and who had hidden it.

At ten past two, Faith returned from her lunch break. "No sign of a witch hanging around outside, Faith?" Brian was getting uptight. "She'll be wearing a pointy hat and looking for somewhere to park her broomstick." Faith ignored him. "What time did she say she was coming?"

"She didn't." I replied.

Brian screwed up a sheet of paper and lobbed it at the wastepaper bin. He missed. "I'll tell you what she'll do. I bet she'll send Sebastian. She won't dare come in person, not after sending that report."

"She won't send Sebastian, Brian. She only lives around the corner, that's why she offered to come in the first place."

"I bet you anything that..," Brian was cut off by the buzzing intercom.

Faith picked it up, listened briefly and then pressed the entry button. "Someone wants to know where to park her broomstick."

Brian buried his face in his hands. "Typical, bloody typical."

Nobody got up to greet Edith at the top of the stairs. She stood in the office doorway, her short hair streaked with grey and her face lined. Here was a woman who made no concessions to style, wearing jogging bottoms and an amorphous sweater. Edith rarely did anything for anyone else's benefit.

Brian rose up out of his chair with all the enthusiasm of someone summoned from the dentist's waiting room. "Right let's get this over with shall we?" He walked over to the corner of the office, expecting her to follow. "One fireproof, and everything else proof, safe." He fiddled with the combination and pulled the door open. "Inside you will find the Obsidian backup tapes, and here," Brian reached inside and pulled out a tape with a flourish, "Is the backup tape from last May." Brian's Scottish accent became stronger and his voice louder." It's a bit dirty of course because it's been gathering dust under my bed, but then you knew that didn't you." He stared into Edith's eyes and slammed the tape down onto his desk. "Take a look, be my guest."

Edith showed no sign of being unnerved by Brian's anger. She picked the tape up, turned it over and ran her finger thoughtfully down the label stuck on its spine.

"Well that is a surprise. The little bitch."

"Who?" Brian sat on the edge of his desk.

"Miss Defrey," Edith said brightly. "I assume she told you everything. Not that she knows much and she's far too stupid to work it out. But you boys, Brian and Stephen, you're the clever ones aren't you." She pulled over a chair, sat down and folded her arms. "You've probably got it all sorted out."

Brian looked over at me. "Am I going mad here? What's she going on about Steve?"

"Chloe moved the tape, that's what she came around to tell me on Tuesday evening. It was always in your flat, she just moved it so it looked like you had lost it. Then she put it back in the tin under the bed again."

"I don't believe a bloody word of it, why would she do that? Why did she tell you and not me?"

I didn't say anything. In spite of his protest I knew he believed me. But Brian couldn't admit to being taken in by anyone, he prided himself on his ability to judge a personality. I stood looking at him while it sunk in, blow by blow, like a nail hammered into hard wood.

Edith remained seated, she had more to say. "You ask why she did it? Because she's a greedy little bitch, that's why." She figuratively dismissed Chloe with a wave rubbing her thumb and forefinger together.

Brian towered over Edith and for a moment I thought he might even hit her. His face was red and the corners of his mouth flecked with spit. "OK Doctor Summers, you've tried to destroy our

210

livelihoods and you've verbally assaulted Chloe, so let me tell you how it's going to be. You sit here and tell me what is going on or I drive over to Axiom this afternoon and create merry hell."

I glanced over at Faith who had given up all pretence of working. "Look, let's ask Faith to go and make a pot of tea and we can sit down and…"

"No Steve, This nonsense stops right now, I want to know what's going on, and why has she come round here to check the tape anyway? It's water under the bloody bridge now isn't it. Obsidian is already down the river, around the corner and out of sight."

Edith opened her hands out. "You can storm over to Axiom if you like and I can guarantee you won't get past the gate house. Not after I've made a phone call. But I'll happily tell you what is going on and save you the trouble. Then we can perhaps start to work together and not against each other."

She pulled a small cloth out of her trouser pocket, took off her spectacles and began to polish them with slow circular movements, holding each lens up to the light in turn to inspect it. She made us wait.

"The report which you are probably getting so worked up about has not gone any further than the three of us. You can think of it as a little insurance policy. And by the way, frankly it doesn't matter whether you can produce the backup tape or not, it was Sebastian's idea and he's gone. The plain fact is, Brian, that you and your precious Obsidian are of very little significance, and what you know, or think you know, is unimportant and lacks credibility to say nothing of evidence. When it comes to either listening to one of their longest serving and most respected scientists or taking notice of Obsidian which has been shown to be negligent in so many ways, you only have to look at the report so see that, then I think I know who Axiom will choose, don't you?"

I decided to pre-empt her revelation, addressing Brian. "Chloe told me some of it last night. She came to me for help because she didn't want to upset you and she didn't know how you would react when she told you she had moved the tape. As it happened, you and Paul interrupted us and I haven't had a chance to discuss it any further with her. Don't jump off the deep end just yet, I was going to tell you once I knew the whole story from Chloe."

Brian sat back down on the edge of his desk, his large frame still looming over the seated, stick-limbed Edith. I continued, "Dr Summers here, has her own little company which offers diagnostic services, reporting on batches of microscope slides from drug trials. In her capacity as group leader at Axiom she sub-contracts this work to her own company, thereby having a steady stream of very profitable business from the Sigma project."

Edith sat impassive, sucking her lower lip. "But to squeeze a little more profit out of the process, she doesn't employ qualified microbiologists or histologists to do the work. She gets in a couple of temps like Chloe and trains them to use a microscope and what to look for on the slides. She pays them the minimum wage," Edith shook her head, "wrong." I carried on. "And she pockets the healthy fee that Axiom pays, to what they think is an independent diagnostic consultancy."

I paused and Edith jumped in, raising a finger. "First point; I pay well above the minimum wage, it's not a Victorian sweat shop. And secondly, you can train pretty much anyone to read a slide in a few hours. In some ways the less intelligent they are the better, they follow the rules and don't think too much about it. Temps are ideal."

Brian paced up and down. "But they're not bloody qualified woman", he shouted at her. "They could be writing anything down on the score sheets. Do you really think you can substitute three year of post-graduate training in microbiology with a couple of hours of show and tell? It's pure exploitation."

"Look don't come the 'poor innocent victims' to me, Chloe knew exactly what she was doing and was very happy to take the money. Even to obligingly lose the back-up tape when I asked her. Anyway, as I said Dr Calder, it doesn't really matter what you think does it, because you're discredited. As far as I, and anyone

212

else, is concerned, I have done nothing wrong. Axiom get the results they need and the temps get the work they need." And you get a nice restored farmhouse in France, I thought to myself. I wondered how long she had to go before she retired to the Dordogne.

Edith braced her hands on the arms of the chair, about to push up out of it. "But hang on a minute." Brian put his index finger in his mouth and nibbled the nail whilst looking into the distance. "The new blockbuster drug for Parkinson's, Sigma, it's going down the tubes isn't it. Merlin dug something up from the latest trial data that casts a big shadow over it." Edith slumped back into her chair and shook her head. Brian continued, "So if Sigma fails then your stream of income dries up, no more subcontracting of the diagnostic work. That's the end of your little scam. So the question is, how did you know about the problems, which we only discovered with the aid of Merlin?" Brian looked across to me. I was following his argument.

"The microscope slides." I turned to Brian. "It would have been clear from the analysis of the tissue sections on the microscope slides. And what a perfect position she was in to be able to cover up that little bit of information. All she had to do was falsify the scores for the slides which showed a problem and then throw the glass slides out with the rubbish."

Edith sat back and folded her arms with a smile on her face as if congratulating primary school children. "Well aren't you two the clever boys then."

Edith got up out of her chair. "Take it any way you like, the point is it's a zero sum game, we can't both be right, and I hold all of the trump cards."

"Unless those microscope slides turn up," I said. And then, for the first time, I saw a hint of doubt in Edith's eyes. "Quite," she said, "but that's not going to happen, they have been destroyed. Meeting over I think." Edith pushed the door open, then paused and looked back.

"By the way, you can call off your little Indian girl. I know what she's been up to."

Edith let the door slam behind her and was gone down the stairs. I looked at Faith who reached into her desk drawer and pulled out a crumpled packet. "Three chocolate biscuits left. I wasn't going to give her one."

I didn't have a good feeling. Clearly Edith had something to hide and she had gone to great lengths to discredit Obsidian in case we found out what it was. If she circulated that report to our other clients it may well be the end for us. But the risk she was taking was high. Would she put her career and reputation on the line simply for money? The chance to make a few quid from the lab in her basement? A farmhouse in the Dordogne? She would already be well paid by Axiom as a group leader and with only herself to look after she could still retire on a very good pension. There had to be more to it. There had to be more at stake.

Chapter 22

Later that evening I pushed my way through the heavy doors into the Victorian interior of the Nag's Head. It was already heaving with people, three-deep at the bar. Dil was setting up his drums on the low stage in the corner, the Brondesbury Jazz Quintet now had a spot once a week. Judging by the crowds, they were proving to be quite a draw. Kris had called me earlier asking if we could meet up that evening to discuss her findings at Axiom. I scanned the room and saw Brian's raised arm at the bar, he was standing next to Kris who was sat primly on a bar stool with a straight back as if balancing on something much smaller. I made my way over to them, edging through the crowd sideways with an outstretched dividing arm. Brian cupped his hands and spoke into my ear.

"This is hopeless. I thought it would be quiet on a Thursday."

I smiled at Kris who hunched her shoulders. "We'll have to go somewhere else, It's far too noisy." I looked from Brian to Kris, they nodded. "Drink up. If we go now, we can still be back in time to listen to the band."

Brian finished his pint in one great gulp and wiped his mouth on his sleeve. We weaved our way back to the door and out into a yellowy light diffused by drizzling rain. Kris shivered and carefully buttoned her coat up to the neck. This was an old part of London; cobbled mews' and narrow streets. I imagined a Dickensian scene, the hiss of gas lights, the clatter of horse's hooves and the rumble of drays with metal rimmed wheels delivering barrels of beer. "Follow me." I headed off. A few doors down a bright light shone out across the pavement. The sign above the shop read, 'The New Ankara", and in smaller letters underneath, 'Eat In or Take Out.'

I stopped outside and posed like an usher, grinning. Brian could be a bit of a fussy foodie at times, I knew he would hate it. I had no such worries about Kris.

Brian was shaking his head. "No Steve," he appealed to Kris for support and got none. I don't want to be throwing up all night."

"Don't be ridiculous," I said. "I've had a takeaway from here dozens of times. It's famous."

"It's empty," he countered.

"Which is why it's the perfect place to have a chat. Places like this don't get going until after ten." We ordered two large kebabs to share between the three of us and sat on fixed metal benches running down each side of a spotless white folded metal table. Brian watched fascinated as the meat was sliced off the rotisserie and dropped into pitta bread pouches. It was as if he had never eaten a kebab in his life. The lad behind the counter put the kebabs and a sprinkling of salad in polystyrene boxes and placed them on the counter. Brian added a few cans of fizzy drink, picked up some plastic cutlery, and ferried it all to our table.

Kris picked at the salad while we shovelled food into our mouths. "You asked me to have a dig around in Axiom to see if we can find out what's going on. That's not an easy thing to do these days, you can't go anywhere without having a swipe card, and even then it will only permit entry into specific areas, however," Kris allowed herself a quick smile. "After a few phone calls, I managed to get an appointment with you know who."

"Ray?" My voice was muffled by a mouth full of kebab.

Kris nodded. "It's amazing how a couple of free mugs can open doors."

It's not the mugs, I thought to myself, it's you Kris. How on earth are we going to replace you.

We all knew Ray Glover, he turned up at every exhibition and seminar, collecting freebies and chatting to anyone who would listen to his opinions. He was a lab manager close to retirement. His duties were to look after the lab facilities that various research groups used. In spite of complaining how boring he was behind his back, people from 'the trade' would always listen to him because he usually had a budget to spend and because he kept his ear close to the ground. If you wanted to pick up on any gossip or simply book a car parking space, Ray was your man. I pictured his florid face and yellowing teeth, stooping slightly, glasses sliding down his nose, attentive to Kris as if she was a favourite niece.

Kris continued in her 'well spoken' home counties accent, no trace of her Asian roots. You could read the news on the BBC, I fantasised. You could be an eloquent lawyer arguing a case, beguiling the jury.

"First you have to listen to Ray's moans and groans. How Axiom isn't the company it used to be, how they get reorganised every six months and now that Axiom is in trouble, how he could have told them this would happen if only they had listened."

I interjected. "Is Axiom in trouble?"

Kris inclined her head from side to side. "Not really, there is talk of closing one of their labs in the States but their shares are still holding up. I think their drug pipeline is a bit thin but they will probably buy a couple of little start-ups to kick off some new projects. They're big enough to ride out the storm." Kris returned to her story. "Anyway, having let Ray get his moans off his chest I asked, in a round-about way, what he thought about Edith and I got quite a strong reaction. According to Ray she's one of the best scientists they've got."

Brian interrupted slapping a hand on the table and knocking his plastic knife and fork onto the floor. "Well we know that, no one's saying that she isn't. The question is, does she have a drop of good honest red blood in her veins or is she full of crap?" He winked at me and took a long slurp from his can of Coke.

Kris patted his hand. "Ray went on to say that she isn't popular with the people in her group. She has a tendency to fly off the handle and once you're in her bad books there's no way back. In short, she demands a lot from her staff and is ruthless if she doesn't get it; a bit of a bully. Needless to say, the upper management quite like her and her career has probably benefited from her fearsome
218

reputation. Reading between the lines, I suspect she rather enjoys the fact that people are scared of her. It's not all rosy, she does have enemies, particularly amongst the IT people who hate mavericks and some of her peers who see her as a threat"

"But there's no suggestion that she is corrupt or underhand?" I said.

"No, but I got a lot of comments about the fact that she is not in the lab much, 'Edith who?' was a common little joke. She often works at home, or has time off due to unspecified sickness. Edith does things her own way, comes and goes as she pleases. But everyone agreed that work was her lifeblood. Apart from that she does a bit of bird watching."

Brian was mopping up some sauce with a piece of pitta bread, he waved it at Kris. "She's a twitcher then. I tell you what, give me a cattle prod and I'd soon have her twitching."

I began to laugh at the image this created in my mind, Kris looked bewildered. Brian tried to maintain a serious angry face but then broke into a wide grin and began prodding his knife at the two of us across the table. "I bloody loath that woman. Tell me what you found out about that little bugger Sebastian, and then I'll tell you something interesting about him that I found out this afternoon." Brian sat back and drained a can of Coke.

"Presumably Edith wasn't in the lab when you visited?"

"She wasn't, and nobody seemed to know where she was. That was a stroke of luck, I think people spoke more freely without her breathing down their neck." Kris paused and took a deep breath, her dark chocolate eyes glistening, always happy to be the focus of attention. "I talked Ray into taking me across to IT on the pretext that I wanted to use their wi-fi while I was on site. Luckily, we bumped into James Grey who is head of IT security. When I mentioned we had had a visit from someone called Sebastian Molnar he said he had never heard of him. I told him that Sebastian was assigned to Edith's group so perhaps that was the reason but he said that was nonsense, they didn't assign IT people to specific groups."

I pitched in. "As we thought, Sebastian worked for Edith, not Axiom, and she told us he has been dismissed. She just used him to write the report on our IT infrastructure."

"Which turned out to be a pack of lies. Little bugger." Brian picked up his plastic knife again and made thrusting gestures.

"Put that knife down and tell us what you were going to say about Sebastian earlier?" Kris said.

"He only had the bloody nerve to phone me this afternoon and ask for a job." Brian leaned his chair back on its rear legs and spread his arms out in a gesture of bewilderment. "I told him I thought there was a vacancy for chief rat in the sewerage department, and that he would be ideally suited."

I tried to maintain some sort of balance, "Well don't be too hard on him, my guess is that Edith used him to create the report headings and general survey details and then altered some of the key conclusions to give it her slant. Once people trust you, like Axiom trusts Edith, then you can pass almost anything off as the truth. Nobody questions it."

Kris delicately wiped the corners of her mouth with a serviette. "What did you guys discover when Edith came around."

I summarised our meeting with Edith, including the part that Chloe played when working for her, but I decided to leave out the malarkey with the back-up tapes, that was now between Chloe and Brian. "The good news is that Brian didn't tear her limb from limb and scatter her body parts to the four winds," I concluded. "But it's not all over. Edith hasn't submitted the report to Axiom yet and we think she might try to do a deal with us if it means that she can milk the Sigma project for a little longer. It will of course eventually dawn on Axiom that they have a problem when they do further tests down the track, so I don't think we are on the verge of another Thalidomide, but by that time Edith will be pickling herself in Bordeaux reds."

Kris was frowning. "Deal. What sort of a deal?"

Brian spoke up. "It's the real world unfortunately Kris. It would look something like, we hide the problems with Sigma that

220

Merlin discovered, and she keeps the fictitious report on Obsidian close to her chest."

"Why doesn't she simply supress the data from Merlin, tell everyone it's a pack of lies?"

Brian replied. "Because she is not the only one looking at the Merlin results. The IT people are interested and their statisticians also get copies of the results. The plan is to use Merlin on all of their drug trials, not just Sigma."

Kris was incredulous. "But you won't do a deal will you?"

We piled up the left-overs and pushed them to one end of the table. I answered her indirectly. "It's stalemate, but Brian and I have been puzzling over the meeting and we think we just might have a trump card to play," I looked around the little restaurant, still empty, as if I was about to divulge a great secret. "According to Chloe, one of Edith's microscopes was equipped with a camera to take digital images. Our theory is that Edith, who is a hard-bitten scientist, couldn't bear to really throw the information on the microscopes slides away, so she decided to capture the images using the camera on the microscope and then encrypt them."

Kris butted in, "I can't see Edith doing that. According to Ray, she's great with lab technology but a complete technophobe when it comes to IT."

I continued. "She could have used Sebastian to encrypt the images. In a digital image every pixel has a number which sets its brightness and colour. All Sebastian did was to print out these numbers. Simple. So simple that Edith could understand it and recreate the images if necessary."

Kris scrunched up her nose not quite believing what I was saying.

I continued. "That would have been child's play to Sebastian. Then Edith printed out the pixel values for each image and pasted them in some notebooks. This is perfect for her; just one copy in existence, and it's sitting in the form of several black notebooks on her bookshelf."

Kris looked puzzled. "And how does any of this help?"

Brian smiled and leaned forward. He spoke quietly. "Because Kris, our good friend Steve here got hold of those notebooks. They don't exist anymore because he threw them in a skip, but we do have copes of the data because we scanned every page before Steve threw them away, and that data is sitting on the Obsidian server. We can now recreate those images from the microscope slides, and that could be our trump card." Brian tapped the side of his nose with his forefinger. He looked at his watch. "Look, I suggest we conclude the meeting now. The band will have started playing and Kris will be wanting to hear her beloved Dil. I can't wait to see the new singer Steve is clearly besotted with. We don't want to miss a moment, do we Steve? This could be your big night." He thumped me on the back and rubbed his hands together. "I think Steve and I need to have another chat with Edith over the weekend but for now, I need a pint to wash down that kebab." He stood up and belched loudly, indicating that the decision had been made.

We walked the short distance back to the Nags Head, the sound of the band getting louder as we approached, my ears straining to hear the silky voice of Madeleine. Just before he pushed the door open, Brian turned to Kris. "Thanks for your help Kris," he put his arm around her shoulders and gave a her a quick squeeze. We filed through the door which closed slowly behind us, and found ourselves in a different world.

My eyes turned straightaway to Madeleine; she cradled the microphone in both hands, eyes shut and knees bent. Bright red lips just parted enough to let the song escape.

Birds flyin high, you know how I feel
Sun in the sky, you know how I feel
Breeze driftin' on by, you know how I feel
It's a new dawn, a new day
And I'm feelin' good.

Chapter 23

Brian said that his feelings would get the better of him and it would be safer if I made the phone call. On the sixth ring she picked up, 'Summers'. Edith's pronunciation was clipped and her use of words, economical as if conveying military information. We agreed that we would meet at Park Side Café at ten o'clock on Saturday morning. Neutral territory I thought, without any good reason.

Fortunately, I hadn't told my Mum that I was planning to visit them that weekend. I put it off for another week, feeling guilty. Here I was again, putting the business first and shuffling my responsibilities to my aged parents off onto the shoulders of my good hearted sister. I called Helen who graciously said that she had been planning to visit them that weekend anyway. My Dad would have said in all seriousness, that she will get her reward in heaven, as far as I could see that was quite a gamble.

I arrived at the park with a few minutes to spare. Brian was sitting in his Mazda sports car, parked by a meter with the hood up. He opened the door and struggled awkwardly out of the low seat. It had started to drizzle, the Café was very busy. I went on ahead and peered inside, its warm damp interior offered an easy retreat from the weather, every table was taken and there was a patient queue at the counter. I stood in the doorway looking for Edith but there was no sign of her. Turning to leave I almost bumped into her, she took a couple of steps back. "No room in there," The rain began to fall heavily, Brian was still standing by his car with the hood of his waterproof coat up, he held his arms out in exasperation. Edith stood by my side, silent, brooding. Shouting for Brian, I set off at a brisk walk with Brian and Edith in tow. We trudged along the gravel path in a line towards the centre of the park, dodging the puddles. Eventually we reached the hexagonal bandstand. A couple of steps up onto the platform, and we were in the dry. Alongside the railings at one edge of the bandstand was a small pile of folded deck chairs, I picked one off the pile and unfolded it, passing it to Edith, then I unfolded two more. We swept their canvas seats with our hands and arranged the chairs around an imaginary focal point, each of us flopping into an enforced semi-reclining position.

It was a bizarre scene. Had we been in a less confrontational mood we would have been amused, but as it was we each felt awkward and vulnerable, figures of fun. The rain fell heavily, drumming on the roof, hail bounced off the path, peals of thunder growled in the distance. Darker clouds moved slowly across the sun and we sat in silence as the gloom settled, reclined in our deck chairs, listening to the rain and wondering where to start. For once Edith didn't want to take the initiative.

The rain fell in curtains around the bandstand, we couldn't even hear the sound of our own voices. Brian heaved himself out of his chair in frustration and leant against one of the pillars, looking out on the deserted park. I reached into a large map pocket in my waterproof coat and pulled out a padded envelope. I extracted several sheets of paper slowly and deliberately, taking care that Edith could see the printed images. I held them out between forefinger and thumb for her to take, she did so without saying a word. Having studied the first two carefully, she flicked briefly through the rest of them before handing them back with a careless shake of the head, as if they were of no importance. This was the opening gambit, a solitary pawn, pushed out into no-man's land.

Edith raised her voice over the sound of the rain. "Did you steal my notebooks?"

I shook my head, just once, almost imperceptibly.

She persisted. "Have you got my notebooks?"

Again I shook my head, enjoying possession of the upper hand.

The rain began to ease off and Brian slumped back into his deck chair. He spoke up in answer to Edith's question. "We did have your precious books and Steve threw them away, but not before we had scanned each page. The notebooks don't exist anymore but all the data is sitting on the Obsidian server with a backup in the data safe."

For a moment I thought Edith was about to reveal her anger. She sat up, took a deep breath and raised an accusing finger. Then, thinking better of it, she sat back in the deck chair again. "That's company property boys, you are no longer part of the Sigma project so I insist that you delete all copies of the data. If you don't, not only will you never work with Axiom again, but you will also need to find yourselves a very good lawyer because you signed a water tight non-disclosure agreement and you will be in breach of contract." She folded her arms, deep set eyes glowing, lips thin.

"I'm not aware that we have disclosed it to anyone," I separated out one of the sheets of paper and spread it out on my lap. Then I proceeded to fold it several times forming a paper dart. Holding it up high, I launched it. It glided past the pillars and out into the park, curving round and settling on the wet grass.

Edith didn't know if she should rush out and collect it or let it go. "Oh don't be so bloody stupid".

I was already folding a second sheet of paper.

"How did you get the notebooks if you didn't steal them? I got home one evening and they were gone."

I remained silent, holding my second paper dart up at eye-level, viewing it from every angle and trimming its delta wings. Bringing Evans-Peake into the picture at this stage wasn't going to help, I let Edith continue to wonder. "Let's be clear," I said. "You're making a tidy sum by milking the Sigma project, you subcontract the analysis of microscope slide to your own company and employ unskilled staff to do the work. The longer Sigma is alive the happier you are. However the analysis of the microscope slides shows that there is a problem with Sigma which may kill it, at least for the time being. You decided not to tell anyone about that and destroyed the incriminating slides, but not before you made an encrypted copy of the images." I paused, waiting for her to deny it, but she remained quiet and thoughtful, looking up over our heads.

"Unfortunately for you, along comes Brian with Merlin, they crunch through the trial data and also find the problem with Sigma. So if they tell all, Sigma will be stopped and your lucrative little game will be over. And the best way to shut Brian and Merlin up, is to destroy Obsidian's reputation so even if that little bird does start to sing, nobody will trust it. Hence the charade with Sebastian."

I screwed the paper aeroplane up into a little ball and threw it as far as I could, out of the band stand. It rolled into a water-logged gutter.

Brian was getting impatient, he struggled into an upright sitting position and spoke directly to Edith." What you do as far as Sigma and Axiom goes is up to you, our concern is Obsidian. The livelihoods of four, hard-working people depend on the business and I will not stand by and watch you destroy its reputation." He shifted in his chair, sitting precariously on the front edge. "Having discredited Merlin, you now have another problem, the microscope slides. As you can see, we broke the notebook code and now we have copies of the images from the microscope tests. We can make as many copies as we like and we can send them to anybody we like. This will be enough to halt Sigma in its tracks."

Edith's right hand shook and she clasped it with the left. I looked into her eyes, windows on her thoughts. "That's not the whole story is it? You don't have time. You don't need the money, you wouldn't go to all this trouble simply to make a few quid, not when you had a well paid job in a senior position and a generous pension. So what, if the project gets delayed, ultimately it's more money for your little operation. That's been puzzling me, it just isn't enough of a motive, it isn't life or death. I'm guessing that you face a bigger threat, if Sigma is delayed it will be too late for you. I'm guessing that if Sigma is delayed, you will be dead before it gets released."

Edith maintained her composure, stick-like legs crossed at the ankle. She looked down at the floor, considering the situation. "Well you boys really are the clever ones. I must tell Sebastian to come up with a better encryption algorithm next time. Of course it would all have come out some time, someone would have looked at the number of still births or complications in pregnancy. But not before I had had my fix. When you have been doing this for as long as I have you get a feeling that a new drug is going to be successful or not. My prediction is that Sigma is going to be spectacularly successful. If they delay bringing it to market because of some minor side effect, hundreds of people will miss their chance, including me. I won't let you take that away from me, whatever the consequences to others."

I jumped in, "That is if you regard still births as a minor side effect."

"When you two grow up and shed your puppy fat and rosy spectacles you will learn that it's a dog eat dog world out there. We are all just animals in a cage fighting to survive, at any cost."

Edith pushed down on the arms of her deck chair, about to rise. "It's going to boil down to who Axiom will trust, me or you. As far as I am concerned this meeting never took place."

She sank back into her deck chair as I fished a small digital voice recorder from my shirt pocket, it's little red light indicating that it was active. "It's that time of day isn't it." That time of day when everything goes wrong. We have the pictures and now we have the words which go with them. Krishna who you referred to as 'that little Indian girl' turns out to be very good at snooping around. She has found out that you have some enemies within Axiom. People who would be very interested to receive these." I held up the evidence.

We fell silent, dualists each having fired a pistol into the early morning mist and now we were examining ourselves to see if we had been wounded, only to discover that we were both unhurt. What should we do now? Shake hands like gentlemen and walk away without a resolution? No, we should hang on to our pistols,

228

we thought, get another shot ready in case the other side decides not to play fair. Don't trust them, wait in the fresh morning dew, feet firmly planted, this may not have been the last exchange.

Edith learnt forward, struggling. She held out an arm, eyes burning with fury. "Help me up you bastards." It was just five seconds but it seemed like eternity before Brain took her arm and pulled her up sharply, to her feet.

Edith held her shaking hands out. "What do you know, you're like a couple of children who have never been forced to grow up. Look, I can't go on like this. It's a death sentence. There are only going to be two outcomes, live or die and I choose to live. Is that so shocking. Wouldn't you?" Turning her back on the two of us, she left the bandstand, holding onto a pillar as she carefully descended the steps. We stood in silence, watching as she walked away, a lone and unhurried figure. The rain now falling heavily once again, quickly soaked her to the skin.

"Did we win that little debate?" I asked Brian.

"We'll see I suppose," he replied.

We waited until we were sure Edith had left the park and then ran, for the Café. It was still crowded with dripping customers so we bought coffees to take out and sat in Brian's cramped sports car.

I sipped my coffee, trying to find some pity and failing. Suddenly it all seemed so unimportant. We should just hand the images over to Axiom and cut our ties, it wasn't worth the time and the stress. We would survive without their business, life would go on. We had done our bit. We had discredited an old woman who was facing up to her own mortality, waving a desperate arm as she slipped under the water, and we turned our heads. Pitiless.

It wasn't an equation to be solved. It wouldn't end in a universally recognised right or wrong. I wasn't equipped to evaluate these emotional weightings, coefficients from a world of uncertainty. My thoughts turned to Lucy. I wanted to tell her everything. She would sit listening, with legs folded under, attentive, sympathetic. She would point out the obvious and then map the sensible course of action. Somehow I had lost her and I didn't know how to get her back. I could smell her perfume on the rain drops and I desperately wanted her back in my life.

Looking out through the windscreen, I expected the sun to break through the clouds, a small patch of blue should appear to re-enforce my thoughts, perhaps even a voice of blessing from heaven. Instead another burst of heavy rain drummed on the canvas hood. We sat, watching the rain drops track down the windscreen as we drank our coffee, Brian occasionally flicked the wipers across so that we could see out. Quite comfortable being silent in each other's company, we mentally filed away the events of the morning, parcelling up each thought and putting it in its place. Looking for patterns and trying to reach conclusions.

I stood the voice recorder on the dash board and pressed the play-back button. All we could hear was the drumming of the rain on the roof of the bandstand, any speech was distant and indistinct. "It turns out we were bluffing," I said. Brian nodded slowly. He finished his coffee and stood the empty cup in a cup holder. Then he started the engine and put his hand on the hand brake.

"Home?"

"Thanks but I'll walk."

"You'll get soaked."

"So what, I want to walk. I'll see you on Monday."

Brian reached behind his seat and pulled out an umbrella. I took it and got out of the car, thinking that there should be something else to say, but coming up with nothing. Stooping down, I waved at Brian as he slowly drove off down the road, turning away from the park into a side road and disappearing from view.

I stood for a few seconds, the umbrella angled into the gusty winds, in danger of turning inside out. Then I walked steadily and purposefully back into the park, tossing my empty coffee cup into a bin as I passed. The rain had eased and I listened to the scrunch of my shoes on the gravel of the radial path. I picked my way around the puddles, not looking to the right or to the left. I had another appointment to keep, another ghost to put to rest.

As I approached the bandstand I looked up and saw a dark green park keeper's barrow, abandoned, a rake and a hoe sticking out. Thunder drum-rolled in the distance, heavy rain was preparing to come around again. The deck chairs were as we had left them, arranged around an imaginary hub, two were unoccupied, the third with its back towards me, was occupied. I could see the back of his head, hair gathered in a loose pony tail pulled off the ears revealing a dangling silver cross.

I climbed the steps up to the band stand, slowly and deliberately, furling the umbrella as I went, standing it dripping against a pillar. As I lowered myself carefully into one of the unoccupied deck chairs, I felt cautious rather than frightened. My heart was racing but my head was clear. Before I had a chance to say anything, his eyelids opened and I looked into those cold vacant eyes, I took in the thin nose and loose jaw. His dark green waxed jacket was zipped up to the throat, matching waterproof trousers glistened. Draped around his shoulders was a luminous yellow high-vis jerkin. Drips fell, circumscribing a wet ring on the concrete floor around him. I reached into my pocket, pulled out the padded envelope and tossed it into his lap.

"We did it."

Evans-Peake coughed, an uncontrolled rasping and retching into a folded tissue. He took the sheets of paper out of the envelope and carefully examined each one, turning them to catch the green light as it filtered in from the park outside.

"Each page was a picture." I said. "They are pictures from a microscope. Part of a drug trial."

Evans-Peake continued to examine each sheet, pulling them out of the envelope faster and faster, now frantically. He stopped clutching a single sheet, letting the envelop fall to the ground. He held it up. Along the bottom edge of the picture was written:

Trial 14. Cohort 17. Subject No. 1712.

He tapped the subject number with his finger.

I thought back to the slip of paper which had dropped from one of the notebooks, to the confrontation in my house, to the sign he had held up when in the taxi at Marylebone. 1712 was his number, required to identify the subject but keeping the real name hidden. Evans-Peake and been a subject in the trial. Evans-Peake had been part of the experiment.

He carefully gathered the papers and inserted them back into the envelope. I took it back. "You stole the notebooks, they never were yours. You threatened me, you stalked me, you controlled me, all over some worthless notebooks which didn't even belong to you."

"I had a right to know. I am subject 1712."

"You're a petty thief. That's all you are."

For the first time Evans-Peake spoke at length. "Thief? I choose to live on the edge, in the shadows without boundaries. I borrow and I redistribute. Who owns the notebooks? The person who holds them, the person who wrote in them, the people who provided the pictures, a big multinational company which experiments on people who have no choices? Ownership isn't something I recognise. I borrow the things I need, my clothes, a saxophone or I take things which interest me, such as a pile of notebooks. When I don't need them any more I redistribute them."

"You flatter yourself, I call it criminality."

"Call it what you like, putting a name to something doesn't alter the facts. Axiom used me. I became just a number in a randomised trial, so half of us were sentenced to death and the others who got the drug might survive."

"Then why agree to be in the trial?"

"Because fifty percent is better than no percent, it was all that was on offer. When I found the notebooks, I thought I might be able to change something. I thought I might at least see which half of the trial I was in. But I needed you to decode them. You were the only one who could do it."

I held up the envelope "It turns out there is nothing in them for you." I concluded.

Evans-Peake nodded and drew his face into a tight emotionless smile. "I know, I was clutching at straws." He levered himself out of the deck chair and in a couple of quick paces he was standing right in from of me. I could smell his breath, I heard his chest bubble. He lowered his head, speaking intensely, the ends of his smile flecked with spit.

"They are playing god. Playing with our lives. They promise help but all they do is to steal from us and hoard their wealth. All the multi-national companies like Axiom, bleed the ordinary man and woman dry. God help you Dr Rockett if you ever get sick. God help you, because they only care about themselves, and their little games which they call trials, throw the dice and we will see who gets the drug and who gets the placebo."

He picked the envelope off of my lap and pulled out some of the pages. Then he began to rip them up, flinging the pieces out into the garden. They flew in front of the wind, catching on rose thorns and settling in gutters. Then Evans-Peake turned and picked up his deck chair, he lifted it above his head and smashed it against the band stand pillar, again and again he swung it until it was just a bundle of broken sticks and torn cloth. I stood up and backed away, remembering how he had flown into a rage when he had cornered me in my house. I wanted to make sure I had an escape route.

Evans-Peake wasn't finished, continuing to babble on with a confused religious sounding fervour. "And I will get justice, an eye for an eye, a tooth for a tooth, a life for a life. I will track down the people on the list and I hope they like what they are going to get." Evans-Peake dropped his voice to a whisper. He pointed out into the park. "And top of the list is Edith Summers."

Chapter 24

The knotted strands began to unravel. Kris and Brian met with Simon Bron and James Grey of Axiom in a motorway service station, anonymous figures handing over an anonymous dossier. It included the microscope images and a summary of the findings from Merlin's data analysis.

We gathered in our office when they returned. Brian was optimistic. It was clear that Merlin had performed well, better than alternative data analysis methods. Axiom would draught a new contract and buy some copies of Merlin as a good will gesture. Edith Summers hadn't been at work that week. She wasn't answering her phone or responding to e-mails, but that was nothing unusual. Simon had hinted that her career at Axiom was over.

On the surface it seemed that we had won, a triumph for the little guys. Sigma would be delayed until it was demonstrated to be safe in all circumstances. We would maintain good relationships with Axiom and hope to secure some future business. As ever, I was uneasy. I had faced my demon in the bandstand, but I needed to tie up some loose ends otherwise they would continue to haunt me. Evan-Peake's parting threat to Edith stayed with me. I was fairly sure there wasn't an immediate risk, Evan's-Peake's power was all in the threat and ensuing drama. He put on little shows, like the flaming tent in the park. Or he would suddenly appear and you wondered how long he had been following you. He was a meticulous planner, not someone who acted on the spur of the moment. I had time and, in spite of everything, I had to warn Edith.

I took a detour on my way home which took me past Edith's terraced house, situated in a tree lined suburban road. I had decided to knock on her door but that was as far as my plans went. The curtains were drawn, I peered through the small window inset in the door, post was scattered on the door mat. I knocked and waited but there was no reply. With some relief I cycled away telling myself that there was nothing more to be done. I could have left a note but it would have seemed that it was me who was threatening her. I needed to talk to her in person and tell her that it was probably all a bluff.

A couple of days later I cycled along her road again. As I approached her house I could see a removals van, other vehicles were just able to squeeze by between it and the row of parked cars. Two guys were moving furniture out of Edith's house, a third stood on the pavement, tapping on his phone. I asked for Edith Summers but got blank looks. They told me they were clearing the house under the instruction of a 'Mrs Lewis'.

I cycled on slowly, deep in thought. If the house had been sold to this 'Mrs Lewis', then Edith would be moving her belongings out and the removal men would be dealing with her. Who was Mrs Lewis? I could only think of one likely explanation. I called Chloe. She said that she hadn't been in contact with Edith for some time. She had tried to arrange a date to go around and collect a few personal items from the microscope room in the basement but had got no answer. Chloe seemed very cautious, downbeat, not her usual effusive self.

"The only explanation I can think of is that Edith is dead", I said. "The house has been passed on to her next of kin who is having it cleared out prior to selling it. Does Mrs Lewis ring any bells?"

Chloe sighed. "Jean Lewis. She's Edith's sister."

Edith had said that without the Sigma drug she was under a death sentence. Had she taken her life into her own hands? Somehow it seemed unlikely that she had just died in her sleep. Was it a sad end to a productive career or the deserved death of a monster who would happily sacrifice others to save her own skin? Was she a victim, pulled and pushed by Axiom to achieve ever shorter deadlines or do I have to look elsewhere? To the parting shot from Evan's-Peake in the bandstand, "I hope she likes what she's going to get." Evans-Peake was like stained glass, colourful and flamboyant when the sun was shining but very dark at night.

I was a lone witness, nobody was very interested in any of it now. Brian had moved on, focusing on the next release of Merlin. Soon Kris would be gone, we should have started looking for a replacement for her but it was helpful to reduce our head-count and not have to pay her salary for the time being. Faith would march on in her own little domestic bubble. I thought once more about visiting my Dad, perhaps meet up with Helen while I was down there. Now that the various strands had begun to unravel I was feeling less stressed, but a quiet weekend in Somerset would surely help my recovery.

Lucy was in the back of my mind. I called her on a pretext. "If you're not doing anything this evening could I pop round and collect those Obsidian back-up tapes I gave you for safe keeping? I think you hid them on top of your wardrobe."

"Yes, pop round any time, I'll be home at six. I'll go and find the package for you." A cheery normal response between friends.

There was an awkward silence. I tried my luck. "I could pick up a takeaway…"

Lucy interrupted. "I've made some soup, there's probably enough for two."

I heard, "Come and see me, I miss you, we could talk."

I looked at my watch, it was five-thirty, ten minutes before I needed to leave. Sitting on the sofa I waited. There was no music in my head, no puzzles, no maths. I sat, clear headed, at peace.

After five minutes my phone rang.

"Steve? You won't believe this but it's gone. The padded envelope with the tapes inside, it's not where I left it on top of the wardrobe. I've looked down the back and on the floor but it's not there. I have no idea when it went missing." She sighed in frustration. "The only people who have keys to the flat are Astrud my lodger and you. I can't think how it could have been moved or who would do it. I'll ask Astrud when she gets in but I would be very surprised if she had even been in my bedroom, let alone take a boring padded envelope."

"Do you hide a spare key?"

"Yes, but nobody would ever find it."

It seemed likely that this was the work of Evans-Peake making sure he collected up any loose ends, which now seemed to involve Lucy. I wondered how he could have known that the tapes were in her flat? Then I remembered that Chloe had been cooing in the background when Brian had asked me to look after the tapes, was there a link between her and Evans-Peake? The more I thought about it the more I realised that Chloe had often been a silent witness in the background. These thoughts ran through my head in a couple of seconds, I told Lucy not to worry, they would probably turn up and weren't important anyway. We had other copies of the data.

"Sorry Steve, I just have no idea what has happened to them." I waited and then Lucy just hung up. I looked at the phone as if it had mal-functioned. I spoke to the dial tone. "Should I still come round for soup?"

Chapter 25

Krishna's notice period was up all too soon, her last day working for Obsidian was agreed as Friday 13th December, unlucky for us. I secretly hoped that she might have a last minute change of heart, but as the days went by, hope slipped through my fingers. Deep down I knew that she would be wise to move on, Obsidian couldn't offer her the opportunities she deserved. We discussed what sort of a 'leaving do' we should organise. Brian wanted to make a big reassuring gesture and book a table in a fancy West End restaurant complete with celebrity chef. Kris persuaded him that she would far rather go down to the Nags Head for some simple food and a couple of drinks. "You probably don't remember, but that's where you interviewed me for the job," she said. "Not that it was much of an interview, I don't think you actually asked me any questions." She was right. Brian and I had been enchanted by her vibrant personality from the start, and we were sure our customers would feel the same way.

The past few months had been the most stressful of my life, these had been days which would leave their mark on me for ever, but that didn't mean they would leave me weaker. In my mind I was dividing time into 'before Evans-Peake' and 'after Evans-Peake'. I hoped I would emerge stronger and more robust, not sensitised and wounded.

On Friday morning, Faith kicked the door open and entered the office holding a cup of coffee and the post. It was gone nine thirty, she was the last to arrive. Brian and I were discussing a user's manual for Merlin and Kris stood at her desk, clearing out the drawers and filling her waste paper bin. Faith announced her presence by blowing her cheeks out and fluttering her lips. "We need to put in one of those stair lift things. It's going to kill me one of these days. I swear to god I'll have a heart attack."

Kris turned her head. "Don't worry, Brian is our designated first aider. He will give you mouth to mouth resuscitation and if you're really lucky he'll give your chest a squeeze." Brian looked up and grinned. As usual Faith's entrance had succeeded in distracting all of us from the job in hand. Her robust, well covered frame and loud voice, seasoned with a Jamaican accent, dominated the room. She put the post and coffee down on the desk and slid her shoulder bag onto the floor. Then she stood, hands on well-rounded hips and I knew we were about to receive a monologue.

"I know I'm a bit tardy this morning but Jackson usually gets a lift to school with Laura across the road. When it got to a quarter to nine I went over and I see that her place is all shut up. Probably gone away for a long weekend but she might of told me. So then I had to take him on the bus, and we had just missed one so that was another twenty minutes."

Faith paused for breath and dropped into her chair, she pressed the power button on her computer. We all kept quiet and returned to our work. But Faith picked up the post and embarked on 'act two'. "Rubbish, rubbish, magazine for Brian, office furniture catalogue for Steve, Inland Revenue for Steve, more rubbish, magazine for Kris, something here just sent to 'All at Obsidian'." Holding up a thin square envelope for all to see, Faith opened the envelope, pulled out a card and studied the picture on the front. Then she opened it up to see the message inside. "Well, well, fancy him remembering that." She leaned across her desk to pass it to Kris. Brian and I looked up, we saw brightly coloured balloons on the outside of the card. Kris read out the inscription inside.

"To Obsidian, Happy Birthday. Here's to the next two years."

"Who's it from?" I asked.

Kris passed it over. "Merry Mick."

"Well it's another reason to celebrate," said Brian. "We've survived two years and at last we've managed to get rid of Kris." Kris turned and threw a balled up sheet of paper at him.

*****

The pub was already busy when I pushed through the heavy doors, the bar staff dressed in black with long white aprons, were shuffling between the taps and the till. Faith saw me and waved. Sitting opposite her with their backs to me were Brian and, I was pleased to see, Chloe. I stopped at the bar and got a pint. As I made my way over to join them I was aware that I didn't have anyone with me; it wasn't a good feeling. Where was dependable, comforting Lucy? She would raise an eyebrow if I drank too much, or gently put a hand on my knee if I got too loud. I told myself to stop looking back and move on. Who knows what delights may be just around the corner, for example the seductive Madelaine, the new singer with the band.

I took a seat next to Faith and clinked my glass with everyone. "Here's to Obsidian." The others mumbled their assent. I turned to Faith. "And what have you done with the recalcitrant Jackson?"

"He's gone for a sleep-over with one of his friends from school. Not that they ever get any sleep, we should call it a 'stay-awake-all-night over'. I'll go and get him tomorrow morning and he'll be all grumpy because he's tired. Don't have any kids Steve, that's my advice." She laughed and clapped her hands together.

Time marches on, if I want to have any kids and be young enough to enjoy them I need to get cracking. Unbelievably I hadn't ever discussed it with Lucy, it was just understood that one day we would settle down and have a family. Not anymore, now I had to start all over again.

"Where are the happy couple?" I asked nobody in particular. Brian was looking at the laminated menu card, Chloe tried to read it over his shoulder as if cheating at an exam, he made no attempt to share it with her. I looked across to the door just as it opened and in walked Dil and Kris. Such was their elegant appearance, that I expected everyone to turn and look. Kris was dressed in a deep red sari wound tightly around her figure all the way to the floor. The colour of her lips matched her dress, her eyes were shadowed in

240

black and a red tikka had been dabbed on her forehead. Dil was dressed in beige chinos and a loose fitting white shirt open at the neck with a tan leather jacket slung casually over his shoulder. His black hair flopped down over his forehead. They paused at the door, Dil with one hand holding his jacket and the other in a trouser pocket. Kris' arm was threaded through his, as if awaiting their turn at the start of a fashion show cat-walk.

Brian looked up from the menu as they approached, his gaze settled on Kris and he expressed what we all felt. "Bloody hell Kris, you look absolutely gorgeous. I feel distinctly under-dressed." He stood up and kissed her on both cheeks, then he shook Dil's hand. "You're a very lucky man." Brian went off to the bar to get more drinks, happy in the role of beneficent host. Kris and Dil sat down at opposite ends of the table. "Full marks for being the best dressed couple in the pub," I said. Chloe sat opposite me, she looked grey and tired as she silently nodded her head in agreement. The usual vibrant spark of liveliness having deserted her.

Kris, vivacious, snatched up the menu. "Enough of that, you'll have me crying. I'm starving, what's on the menu? Dil tells me the food is much improved since they got a new chef."

"There was definitely room for improvement," I said "Usually it's a toss-up between here and the kebab shop down the road. On the other hand, I hope the Nag's Head isn't going to turn into some sort of gastro pub. We don't want the food to get too good, I still want to be able to go into my local boozer and order a pint without also having to have a side order of pitta bread and humus."

"It's not that good," Dil nodded his head from side to side.

Brian returned with drinks. The menu was passed around and we all made our choices. Faith wrote them down on a scrap of paper and went over to the bar to place the order. Service was a little slow but, when the food came, it was excellent. Dil declared that his beef wellington was the best he had ever eaten. I asked Chloe how her chicken and leek pie was. She nodded and swallowed hard. "Good thanks". Then smiling at me briefly, she dropped her eyes in seeming embarrassment.

The dirty plates were cleared away. We ordered a couple of desserts to share and got another round of drinks in. Then the reminiscing started; stories from the past two years. Eventually the conversation around the table split into two. Faith was animated, telling a story about her ex-husband, Stanley, to Dil and Chloe. Dil sat back as she leaned forward, waving her hands. Chloe, dislocated, looked on only half listening. I turned to Kris. "Has it been fun? Because if it's not fun, what's point?"

She pursed her lips and nodded slowly. "There have been a few frustrating days but you get that with any job. We've had a few ups and downs haven't we." She looked at me and Brian. "I know I can be a bit fiery at times, so thanks for putting up with me."

"I think we need a bit of fire in the office from time to time," said Brian. "Steve and I can be a bit cold. We're going to miss you Kris." I nodded in agreement. She had brought a lot of colour into our lives. We continued to reminisce about good times, carefully avoiding recent difficulties.

I was now on my fourth pint, loosening up and getting a bit loud. I clapped my hands a few times for silence. "Come on Kris, time for a speech." She looked at Dil who nodded vigorously. Brian banged his glass on the table in support. "Speech".

Kris sipped her lime and soda, taking time to assemble her thoughts whilst we looked on expectantly. She put her glass down and received an enthusiastic round of applause from Brian and me. "Well you've been a great bunch of colleagues and I've enjoyed working with you. You took me on when I was very green and gave me a chance to prove myself." I stood up and held my glass out in salute. Faith pulled me down, "Give her a chance Steve". Kris continued. "But I also count you as my friends and I hope we can keep in touch. I'm going to try commuting to Surrey University for a bit, I will be out and about visiting customers anyway, and that means that Dil can continue to play with the Brondesbury Quartet."

Dil drummed his hands on the table in a flourish. "Quintet. Don't forget the gorgeous Madeleine."

242

Kris acknowledged the correction. "Here's to Obsidian, and Merlin". She held up her glass and we all clinked ours with hers. "And also to the gorgeous Madeleine," I added. "Time for another round. Same again?" Faith and Kris who were on soft drinks nodded, Dil and Brian held up near empty beer glasses, Chloe put her hand on top of her glass. She whispered something in Brian's hear. When I came back from the bar with a tray full of drinks, she had gone.

"Where's Chloe?" I asked Brian. "She's gone home," He answered. "Not feeling too good".

I looked at him and frowned but he shook his head. My phone vibrated in my trouser pocket, I ignored it, listening to Kris telling a story about Merry Mick. My phone vibrated again. This time I pulled it out of my pocket and struggled to find the buttons to unlock it. It was Helen calling, she gave up before I could answer. I fumbled it back into my pocket. "Bloody sis' on the phone," I shouted at everyone.

I caught a glimpse of a tall girl in a red dress heading for the toilets. Turning to Dil I asked. "When are you going to introduce me to Madeleine then? Why didn't you invite her tonight?"

"She's probably out with Martin" he replied.

"Martin?"

"Martin from the band. They're an item."

"Martin?" I repeated aghast. "That lecherous old…." I waved my hands not able to find words.

"Well she must see something in him. Perhaps he speaks French." Dil smiled, looking a bit glassy eyed.

I put my arm around his shoulder. "I think I'm in love with Madeleine," I slurred.

"Well you're too late mate, she's taken," he said.

"I'm playing the long game," I looked at him sincerely. "Le jeu longue."

Chapter 26

Saturday morning. I woke, leather mouthed, pulsing behind my eyes and an empty nausea in my stomach. I fumbled for the glass of water on my bedside table and knocked it over. I snatched my phone before it got wet, swearing under my breath. Then I reached down to the floor for a discarded T shirt and mopped up the little pool of water. I slumped back in my bed, the world spinning, trying to piece the events of the previous evening together.

I had made a fool of myself, I was pretty sure of that. Hopefully I hadn't spoiled it for everyone. I remembered Kris and Dil, looking so elegant and comfortable, full of self-confidence and in control of their lives. Then I thought of Brian and myself. Shapeless fleeces over T shirts with facile slogans printed on them. Stained worn jeans and dirty trainers. This was freedom, this was living life on our terms, this was our true character, unashamed for all to see. We both had PhDs from Imperial College in London, one of the top-rated universities in the world, but what did we really know? Did we deserve to be the happy ones? Shouldn't we be the ones full of confidence in a bright future, like Kris and Dil?

Out of habit I looked at my phone and saw that I had missed three calls from Helen. I levered myself out of bed and pulled on a fleece and boxer shorts, then I made my way slowly down to the kitchen, wincing as my head throbbed with every movement.

I switched the radio on while waiting for the kettle to boil and the toast to pop-up. My fingers inspected the crack in the plastic body of the radio, we were both survivors of that morning when Evans-Peake had cornered us, both suffered but both unbowed. Whilst I may have been strengthened by the experience, the radio certainly hadn't been.

I sat down at the dining table with a mug of strong coffee and bit into a thick slice of toast generously spread with butter and my Mum's home-made marmalade. Turning the radio down I picked up my phone. Helen answered on the second ring.

I tried to sound bright and breezy. "Hi sis, sorry I missed your call. We had a leaving do for Kris last night, it was her last day. Can't remember all of it but I think I had a couple too many and made a bit of a fool of myself. We were in the Nags Head and I didn't hear the phone above the noise." I lied. "Anyway it's the end of an era for Obsidian."

I paused, aware that I was rattling on and Helen hadn't said anything. I heard her sniff twice in quick succession. "What's up?" I asked.

"It's Dad." She said, pausing to let those two game-changing words to sink in. I was suddenly very wide awake.

"Oh Christ, not another stroke? Is he....?"

"No, he's still alive as far as we know, but he's disappeared. We don't know where he is," she reiterated, perhaps in case I was thinking of the invisible man. A tumble of words came out, "Oh Steve, why didn't you go down this weekend like you said you would. If you had been there..." She started to weep, little choking sounds followed by sniffs. Then barely audible, "You said you would go and now nobody knows where he is. You should have been there."

This wasn't time for excuses, deep down I knew she was right. I looked at my watch, it was nearly ten o'clock.

"Where are you now?" I asked.

"I'm on the train and everyone's looking at me." She was struggling to keep her emotions under control. "I'll be there in about thirty minutes. Mum's going to meet me at the station."

She must have been on a very early train. "When did he go missing?"

"Yesterday, after lunch he told Mum he was going to visit a friend around the corner, you know the one who's into stamp collecting. Dad hadn't returned and it was getting dark so Mum phoned this chap up and he said he hadn't seen Dad. Mum panics, thinking he's fallen over, and she goes out looking for him. Then when she can't find him she calls the police." The details came tumbling out. "They sent a policeman and a police woman around who asked her a load of insensitive questions which upset her even more." I could hear in Helen's voice that she was about to break down again.

"Alright, try not to worry. I'm on my way," I'll give you a call when I'm on the train." Quite what I could do, I wasn't sure.

I took my half-drunk cup of coffee upstairs and got dressed, shoving a couple of T shirts and underpants into a rucksack. If I left now I might just make the eleven-fifteen train from Paddington. I ran to the local tube station, arriving breathless and feeling sick. Hearing a rumble from the depths of the station I ran down the escalator and just managed to slip between the carriage doors as they slid shut.

I collapsed into one of the many empty seats, head spinning. Trying to formulate a plan made my head ache all the more, I couldn't think clearly, running on auto-pilot. What was I going to do that hadn't been done? He must be lying dead in a ditch somewhere, what other explanation could there be? People of his age didn't run away from home, he probably had another stroke. His decomposing body would be found in a few days under a hedge by someone walking an inquisitive dog. And all of the time I was thinking that if I had been there he wouldn't have gone out. If I had been there he would still be alive and not lying dead in the gutter. Please God, let him be alive, I still have things to say, I still have things to ask.

I stumbled off the tube train and walked up the escalator. Looking at my watch, there was just time to buy a bottle of water from the newsagent to wash down some more pain killers and try to re-hydrate myself. I should still make the eleven-fifteen. I pushed through the barrier at the top of the escalator, out of the underground network into the large intercity station concourse, my eyes immediately went to the departures board, searching for the train to St David's Exeter which would stop at Templecombe. There should be a fast train at eleven-fifteen but I couldn't see it on the board. There were trains to the midlands and to Aylesbury but nothing to the West Country; Exeter, Plymouth or Truro. I stared at the board unable to comprehend what I was seeing. Was there a problem with the lines to the South West, had all of the trains been cancelled? I watched as the information screen was continually updated with platform numbers and departure times. A soul lost in a dream, I stood bewildered. Looking around at familiar surroundings, I read 'Marylebone Station' several times before I realised my mistake.

Sinking down onto a red metal bench, I felt foolish and angry at my own incompetence, various thoughts crowded in. I was at the wrong station and had no chance of getting the eleven-fifteen train from Paddington, there wouldn't be another for two hours. Once again I had let everyone down. I couldn't even be trusted to get on a train. Somehow, in my head, I had confused Lucy's home with my home. In a hung-over fog, I had followed the well-trodden path in my haste and ended up in the wrong station. I sat, not knowing what to do next.

An incoming train from Birmingham ran up to the terminal buffers. Families and young couples chattering happily as they made their way out of the station, eager to see the sights of London. My mind went back to the last time I had been here. The time Lucy left me. I was sitting on the same bench. Looking down the length of the platform I watched the last few stragglers making their way to the automatic ticket barrier. Straining to see, I rose up from the bench. To my relief, Evans-Peake was not among them. I sat for some time with my arms on my thighs looking down at the concrete floor, occasionally taking a long swig from the bottle of water.

The leafy hills and lanes of rural Buckinghamshire were only forty minutes train ride away. I noticed for the first time that the weather was fine, bright sunlight streamed through the glass roof forming sharp shadows. Lucy would be there, her mother had

247

broken her hip, Lucy would be helping her convalescing Mother cope with her healing hip, taking the strain off her Dad for the weekend. I pictured them, mid-morning, sharing coffee and discussing lunch, a pair of crutches propped against the edge of the kitchen table. Laurence would have been out on his regular walk, buying a paper on the way to give it purpose.

I pictured my own Father, frowning at me. 'You see Stephen, that's where excessive drink gets you, you suffer afterwards and you don't live up to your responsibilities. You've let me down Stephen. Just when I needed you, you weren't there. Have you forsaken the straight and narrow way?' The 'straight and narrow way' sounded as meaningless now as it had done when I was a teenager. But I should have been there.

I looked again at the departures board and then at the two-carriage sprinter train at platform three. It was about to leave for Aylesbury, stopping at Amersham. Make the decision. Without thinking further, I got up from the bench and headed for the platform, swiping my Oyster card over the barrier as I went. As soon as I had taken a seat on the near empty train, the doors closed and it started to move. My phone rang, it was Helen. I let it go through to voice mail, hoping she would think there was no phone signal. She left a voice message asking if I was on my way. I didn't call back, how could I explain what I was doing? It made no sense. Yet it was the right thing to do. I was responding to an unseen hand and an inaudible voice.

Once we were out of central London I called Lucy, praying that she would pick up the phone. She answered on the fourth ring.

"Hi Steve", she yawned sounding relaxed. "Haven't heard from you for a while. How are things at Obsidian?"

I ignored her question. "Are you visiting your parents?"

"Yes." She spoke cautiously.

"Lucy, I need your help. I'm on the train from London. Can you meet me with a car at Amersham station in about twenty minutes? If you leave soon you can make it."

"Why?" She wanted to establish that she wasn't automatically available at my beck and call.

"It's my Dad, I can't explain now. I really need your help. I could get a taxi but…" I paused, not sure what to say. "I need you Lucy. Please."

I felt tears welling up in my eyes and was grateful when she said in a matter of fact voice, "See you in twenty minutes then."

I got off the train at Amersham and ran across the footbridge, squeezing past the other passengers with mumbled apologies. Lucy was waiting outside in her Mum's little Fiat, I jumped in and pushed my bag through onto the back seat. Then I put my hand on her shoulder and kissed her cheek, enjoying the familiar contours and smell. She didn't respond. "Thanks for coming", I said.

Lucy put her spectacles on. "If you're coming for lunch we need to stop off at the co-op." She looked behind and drove out into the stream of traffic, automatically heading for home. "Where are we going then or is it a magical mystery tour?" Lucy gripped the steering wheel tightly, competent but not at ease.

"Lee Common." I knew I needed to say more than that but I couldn't organise my thoughts. "I'm sorry Lucy, I thought I would be able to explain, but I can't."

We sat in silence, I was breathing heavily, opening my mouth to get more air in, occasionally swallowing hard. My hands were clasped as if in fervent prayer, knuckles white. Lucy snatched a worried glance at me and briefly put her hand on my knee.

"What's wrong Stevie?"

I didn't answer and was grateful that she didn't pursue it. I just didn't know what to say. We drove through South Heath, past the road which Lucy's parents lived in, and in a mile or so we reached the little hamlet of Lee Common. The green in the middle of the village was edged with mud where cars had parked. A handful of people sat outside The Bell, with coats zipped up, enjoying the weak warmth of the winter sun. A stream of Lycra clad cyclists slid past in ones and twos, wearing shiny aerodynamic helmets, not belonging in this world. The scene hadn't substantially changed for a century or more. It hadn't changed at all since Lucy and I were children, running around together, making up games. Across the common, brooding protectively over it all, was the Church, set in a neatly mown grave yard. Somewhere inside was a board listing the names of all of the incumbent vicars going back hundreds of years, my Dad's name, Hugh Rockett, would be near the bottom. Alongside the church was the large brick and flint-built rectory, now sold off by the church to a retired businessman, surplus to requirements since three parishes had been merged into one about ten years ago.

Lucy parked the car and we got out. The freshness of the grass and wind-blown trees filled my nostrils. I felt I could breathe freely at last. I stretched tall, holding my arms out and letting them fall at my side. Lucy stood by me. "Remember the village fete every year? Your Dad having to judge the vegetable competitions, and the boy scouts running the barbecue. And my Dad in the stocks having wet sponges thrown at him. Remember the cricket team dressed in white, filing into The Bell for afternoon tea of home-made cakes and scones, served by plump motherly women. Remember learning to ride bikes together and falling off on the grass, you were always faster than me. Remember floating the little boats that you and your Dad had made in the pond, and when your boat got stuck in the middle, your Dad put on his wellington boots and waded in to get it."

I took her hand and held it tightly, it felt small and delicate. I did remember all of those times. Memories encrusted by layers of education and apparent sophistication. Memories shared it seemed then, with Lucy, and nobody else. "We were the birthday twins," I spoke quietly with a smile.

I led her around the common to the Church. We walked into the great stone porch and I lifted the latch and pushed on the big heavy doors. They were unlocked. I opened one door just enough for us to squeeze through into the gloomy nave. Despite the bright sunny day, little light filtered through the stained-glass windows. We stood at the back while our eyes adjusted to the gloom. The cruciform interior was very familiar, from the nave we looked down the aisle to the choir stalls and plain altar table at the end of the chancel, in the arms of the cross, to the left and right, were additional pews. That left a large space in the middle of the church directly below the tower. Hanging there, motionless, was a single thick bell rope with an ornate knotted loop at the end.

I took it all in at a glance. Nothing had changed since I was a choir boy, robed in deep blue with a crisp white surplus, following a golden cross held high, slowly processing down the aisle, my Dad bringing up the rear. I gripped Lucy's hand tighter as I saw a lone figure sitting, head bowed, in a pew close to the front. We walked down the aisle and I edged into the pew, he shuffled along to make room. Lucy followed me, feeling for my hand and we sat, the three of us, in a row. His lips moved in a whisper as he read from a pew bible, absorbed in the words he read quickly, as if there was no time to lose, turning each page with licked finger and a quick flick. There was a gentle thud from behind as the wind blew the heavy door closed. A blanket of silence fell, blocking out the sound of the occasional car outside and the shouts of the children on the common. We sat for a while each absorbed in our shared memories, good and bad. At some point I was aware that Lucy had let go of my hand and had quietly left.

I looked into the space in front of me. "Everyone's looking for you Dad," I said. "I've come to find you. I've come to take you home."

He stopped reading and chuckled, almost giggled. I could smell his breath, musty and familiar. "They didn't know where to look, did they Stephen? But you knew where to find me didn't you." He put his hand to his mouth and coughed, chest wheezing. "Take me home you say? It's too late for that I'm afraid, far too late for that. You still have time but perhaps not the will. Time to make things new."

We sat side by side and I listened, straining to hear the words, as he read eternal words from Psalm 100:

Enter into his gates with thanksgiving and into his courts with praise, be thankful unto him and bless his name. For the Lord is good; his mercy is everlasting; and his truth endureth to all generations.

When he had finished reading he shut the bible. I stood up, edging my way out of the pew and walked a few steps to the space at the centre of the Church. Gripping the bell rope, I pulled it as I had done when I was a teenager. I pulled rhythmically setting the bell rocking higher and higher until it sounded, deep and resonant. With each pull, it sounded throughout the Church, it sounded throughout the village, at that moment I thought it must sound throughout eternity.

Outside Lucy sat on a bench overlooking the common, swinging her legs. I joined her, sitting close. A mother held tightly to a toddler's mitten-clad hand as they peered into the pond, pointing. A group of boys kicked a ball. The little post van was parked, engine still running, while the postman went from house to house like a feeding bee. An old red sports car throbbed by, the hood down and the driver wearing a brown cloth cap, his elbow resting on the top of the door.

My phone vibrated and I pulled it out of my pocket reluctantly, shading it from the sunlight with a cupped hand. It was Helen. Hesitating with hanging finger I pressed the 'reject call' button, knowing she would be calling to say they had found our Dad. I would call her back, there would be tears, there would be guilt, there would be fear, there would be arrangements to be made and papers to be signed, but this was where the good memories were. For the time being I didn't want to let go my grasp on the living and have to face mourning the dead.

Lucy and I sat together in silence, the Birthday Twins. I felt very tired but now relaxed and unhurried. The sun, at its zenith, warmed us as I lifted my head up and squinted. I listened to Lucy breathing, soft like distant waves, barely audible. We had mixed our colours, hoping to make gold, but only ended up with yellow. My heart said it could never work, my head said it just might.

252

Epilogue

A heavy car door clicked shut and the powerful engine surged as it pulled away, effortlessly gathering speed. Evans-Peake made his entrance into the park, taking short quick steps, his feet carefully placed as if on an imaginary tight rope. He made his way into the interior of the park, stopping by a chosen bench, but not sitting down. His chest expanded and his shoulders rose and fell as he waited. Apprehensive but excited. His left hand held a thin black case kept shut by two gold clasps, it was about as long as a man's forearm but thinner. Hung on his right shoulder was a black leather satchel, fastened by two buckles.

Passers-by; mothers with toddlers, joggers in loose fitting clothes, old men with newspapers, cast glances with interest but only children stopped to stare at this living statue. Evans-Peake was dressed for dinner. A short brocaded black jacket over a ruffled white shirt, closed at the collar with a black bow tie. The silver-grey cummerbund, wrapped around his waist, hid the junction between the shirt and his perfectly creased, grey pin-striped trousers. His sleek-contoured black Italian shoes reflected the light, shoes made for standing, not walking. Polarising, not mirrored, sun glasses sat uncomfortably on the bridge of his sharp nose, protected his smoke-grey eyes. Thin faced, you could see every contour and the way his jaw was loosely attached.

Evans-Peake looked at his watch, then continued to stand. It was not yet time. Skate boarding teenagers and sniffing dogs came by, but Evans-Peake remained unmoved. Although he would have liked to sit on the bench, this was not a time for sitting down, he had to fight the growing weariness in his legs and stiffness in his back. These days, Evans-Peake generally sat down if he could.

At the self-appointed time he looked from left to right, as if preparing to cross a busy road, then marched purposefully to the bandstand at the centre of the park. He climbed the two steps and crouched, setting the case and satchel down on the smooth concrete floor. Out of the satchel he brought two small battery powered loud speakers and a tiny MP3 music player. Evans-Peake unwound the wires and plugged them together, then set the speakers carefully on the floor, about six feet apart. Then he produced a black folded music stand from the satchel. He stood, facing out to the park, unfolding and adjusting it for height, moving slowly and deliberately, as if making a demonstration. Then he stooped down again and pulled some sheets of paper from the satchel, which he set on the stand. Finally, having checked everything else was ready, he crouched down again and flicked the catches simultaneously, one in each hand, opening the thin hinged case. Inside, resting on blue silk as if asleep, was a slender white baton. Evans-Peake picked it up and held it delicately between forefinger and thumb, trying it for balance. He pressed a button on the MP3 player and then rose, standing before the music stand, at the edge of the bandstand, facing out into the park. He took off his sun glasses, folding them and slipping them into his trouser pocket. Evans-Peake blinked a few times, tapped the music stand, then raised the baton with a flourish and waited, legs together, feet slightly turned out and head held high. The opening chords of Beethoven's fifth symphony burst out of the tiny speakers, sounding loud in the quietness of the surroundings. Evans-Peake beat out the first few dramatic bars with the baton, then bending at the knee he brought his other hand into play, raising it up to a crescendo, then furiously describing the strident fortissimo with his baton and a fierce shake of his head.

People stopped to stare at this foolishness. Some sitting down on benches, amused. A little crowd formed, children pushed their way through a forest of legs to get to the front.

The first movement over, Evans-Peake pulled a white handkerchief out of his pocket and wiped imaginary sweat from his forehead. The music started up again, but this time Evans-Peake pointed at a little girl and imitated a trumpet with one hand held up, moving his fingers up and down in time with the music. She copied him, measuring up to the responsibility of being the chosen one. Then he pointed at a boy and imitated banging a drum, frowning and nodding his head in time as he did so. More children began to join in and before long Evans-Peake had an orchestra of violins, trumpets, flutes and drums. He continued to conduct, encouraging the crowd to join in, some of the less self-conscious adults joined in with their children. At the end of the movement there was a hesitant ripple of applause. Evans-Peake bowed deeply and swept his hand from left to right in acknowledgement of his musicians.

He bent down and pressed a button on the MP3 player. The music started again. This time it was a Viennese waltz. Evans-Peake described an ornate triangle with his baton as he beat out three in a bar. The music swelled to a warm climax of soaring strings and Evans-Peake, carried away, began to sway from side to side. He turned full circle, and set free from the lectern and the sheets of manuscript, Evans-Peake began to dance. He waltzed around the bandstand, circling and skipping on his toes, embracing an imaginary partner with outstretched bent arms. Little children began to jump up and down and spin around in their excitement, and a few less inhibited adult couples turned to each other and joined in. The music in their ears seemed impossibly loud as they swayed and danced in the winter sunshine.

Such a sight had never been seen on the bandstand in the park. Nor would it be likely to be seen ever again.

Lightning Source UK Ltd.
Milton Keynes UK
UKHW021154080319
338738UK00005B/638/P

9 780244 983017